ΠAVARRO'S PROMISE

LORA LEIGH

BERKLEY SENSATION, NEW YORK

THE BERKLEY PUBLISHING GROUP
Published by the Penguin Group
Penguin Group (USA) Inc.
375 Hudson Street, New York, New York 10014, USA
Penguin Group (Canada), 90 Eglinton Avenue East, Suite 700, Toronto, Ontario M4P 2Y3, Canada
(a division of Pearson Penguin Canada Inc.)
Penguin Books Ltd., 80 Strand, London WC2R 0RL, England
Penguin Group Ireland, 25 St. Stephen's Green, Dublin 2, Ireland (a division of Penguin Books Ltd.)
Penguin Group (Australia), 250 Camberwell Road, Camberwell, Victoria 3124, Australia
(a division of Pearson Australia Group Pty. Ltd.)
Penguin Books India Pvt. Ltd., 11 Community Centre, Panchsheel Park, New Delhi—110 017, India
Penguin Group (NZ), 67 Apollo Drive, Rosedale, North Shore 0632, New Zealand
(a division of Pearson New Zealand Ltd.)
Penguin Books (South Africa) (Pty.) Ltd., 24 Sturdee Avenue, Rosebank, Johannesburg 2196,
South Africa

Penguin Books Ltd., Registered Offices: 80 Strand, London WC2R 0RL, England

This is a work of fiction. Names, characters, places, and incidents either are the product of the author's
imagination or are used fictitiously, and any resemblance to actual persons, living or dead, business
establishments, events, or locales is entirely coincidental. The publisher does not have any control over
and does not assume any responsibility for author or third-party websites or their content.

NAVARRO'S PROMISE

A Berkley Sensation Book / published by arrangement with the author

PRINTING HISTORY
Berkley Sensation mass-market edition / April 2011

Copyright © 2011 by Christina Simmons.
Cover art by S. Miroque.
Cover design by Rita Frangie.

ISBN: 978-0-425-23978-0

BERKLEY® SENSATION
Berkley Sensation Books are published by The Berkley Publishing Group,
a division of Penguin Group (USA) Inc.,
375 Hudson Street, New York, New York 10014.
BERKLEY® SENSATION and the "B" design are trademarks of Penguin Group (USA) Inc.

PRINTED IN THE UNITED STATES OF AMERICA

10 9 8 7 6 5 4 3 2 1

continued . . .

Mercury's War

"Erotic and suspenseful . . . Readers will laugh, readers will blush and readers will cry."　　　　　　　—*Romance Junkies*

"With two great twists, fans of the Breed saga will relish [*Mercury's War*]."　　　　　　　—*Midwest Book Review*

"Intriguingly powerful with plenty of action to keep the pages turning. I am completely addicted! A great read!"
　　　　　　　—*Fresh Fiction*

Dawn's Awakening

"Leigh consistently does an excellent job building characters and weaving intricate plot threads through her stories. Her latest offering in the Breeds series is no exception."
　　　　　　　—*Romantic Times* (4½ stars; Top Pick)

"Held me captivated."　　　　　　　—*Romance Junkies*

"Heart-wrenching."　　　　　　　—*Fallen Angel Reviews*

"Erotic, fast paced, funny and hard-hitting, this series delivers maximum entertainment to the reader."
　　　　　　　—*Fresh Fiction*

Tanner's Scheme

"The incredible Leigh pushes the traditional envelope with her scorching sex scenes by including voyeurism. Intrigue and passion ignite! . . . Scorcher!"
　　　　　　　—*Romantic Times* (4½ stars)

"Sinfully sensual . . . [This series] is well worth checking out."　　　　　　　—*Fresh Fiction*

Harmony's Way

"Leigh's engrossing alternate reality combines spicy sensuality, romantic passion and deadly danger. Hot stuff indeed."
— *Romantic Times*

"I stand in awe of Ms. Leigh's ability to bring to life these wonderful characters as they slowly weave their way into my mind and heart. When it comes to this genre, Lora Leigh is the queen."
— *Romance Junkies*

Megan's Mark

"A riveting tale full of love, intrigue and every woman's fantasy, *Megan's Mark* is a wonderful contribution to Lora Leigh's Breeds series . . . As always, Lora Leigh delivers on all counts; *Megan's Mark* will certainly not disappoint her many fans!"
— *Romance Reviews Today*

"Hot, hot, hot—the sex and the setting . . . You can practically see the steam rising off the pages."
— *Fresh Fiction*

"This entertaining romantic science fiction suspense will remind the audience of *Kitty and the Midnight Hour* by Carrie Vaughn and MaryJanice Davidson's *Derik's Bane* as this futuristic world filled with 'Breeds' seems 'normal' . . . [A] delightful thriller."
— *The Best Reviews*

"The dialogue is quick, the action is fast and the sex is oh so hot . . . Don't miss out on this one."
— *A Romance Review*

"Leigh's action-packed Breeds series makes a refreshing change . . . Rapid-fire plot development and sex steamy enough to peel wallpaper."
— *Monsters and Critics*

"An exceedingly sexy and sizzling new series to enjoy. Hot sex, snappy dialogue and kick-butt action add up to outstanding entertainment."
— *Romantic Times*

*To my son, Bret, who breaks my heart daily with the
sheer, unavoidable fact that he's growing up, becoming
a man, and making me realize what an incredible job
he's done in maturing. I can't take the credit for the
wonderful young man he's becoming; that success is his
alone to claim. And it's one he's improving upon daily.*

*And to Roo Roo. Yeah, you know who you are. I
couldn't have been who I am, do what I do, or live as
I live without those first years that you befriended me.
There are no words to describe . . . There are no ways
to express . . . You saved me with the gift you gave me in
faith, in belief, and in love.*

To both of you, you bless me daily.

Throughout the ages man has struck against man with merciless strength through prejudice, ignorance or fear.

Humanity, in all its often courageous, intuitive and compassionate acts, is still capable of great evil against one another.

Blood has been spilled.

Power has been sought, fought for, betrayed for, and souls destroyed in the quest for.

And those who spilled the blood; started the wars; betrayed their countries, their friends and their children for power; sold their souls for it, have still had their moments of kindness, their moments of compassion.

But have we really learned from the past?

Have we taken to heart the mistakes our forefathers made and begun the quest to ensure they're never made again?

This is the "What If . . ." behind the Breeds.

Have we learned from our past?

Have we learned from the prejudices, the acts of mercilessness, and the unthinking search for power our forefathers sought?

Or is man, in all his, or her, humanity, only waiting for the chance . . .

· P R O L O G U E ·

He fascinated her.

Tall. Male power was an intricate part of his perfectly proportioned frame, which only increased the appeal of height, muscle and lean deadly grace. He would be perfectly suited for the cover of *GQ*, in a boardroom or standing, weapon drawn, teeth bared and facing any enemy.

Or better yet, naked, aroused and more than ready to possess and conquer a lover too inexperienced to see beneath the surface to the male animal that awaited.

He made her only too aware that she was a woman. He made her fantasize about being that lover, of finding the experience to tease and to satisfy a man in his arms.

She was walking on dangerous ground, and Mica Toler knew it, but no matter how hard she tried, she couldn't seem to resist the intense draw the Wolf Breed Navarro Blaine had on her.

Her father would have a coronary if he knew. Her mother would probably attempt to ground her. It had been years since

Serena Toler had attempted to threaten her daughter with anything, let alone a grounding. But Mica could see it happening this time. Her mother definitely wouldn't be pleased to know her daughter had taken one of the most dangerous, most in-danger, men that she could choose.

The truth was, even if her mother had had such power, Mica admitted it wouldn't have mattered. She couldn't seem to keep her mind, or her hormones, off of the elegantly arrogant Wolf Breed, no matter how hard she tried.

And she knew well exactly how dangerous that could be.

Mica wasn't best friends with Cassandra Sinclair for nothing. There were few people, human or Breed, that the younger woman trusted, and Mica was one of those that Cassie did trust. And Cassie talked to her. Mica had information that she knew was considered highly confidential. Information that could get Cassie and her parents into a hell of a lot of trouble with both the Breed Ruling Cabinet and the individual Wolf/Coyote Breed Ruling Cabinet.

Mica was perhaps the one of the very few people, human or Breed, that Cassie confided in. Like Mica, she had issues with trust, and those issues kept her more isolated than being a part of the Breed community did.

More to the point, now that Styx, the only other friend Cassie had allowed herself, had found his mate, Storme Montague, Cassie had no one else she confided in period, except Mica.

Mica knew about mating. It was a secret that wasn't nearly as closely guarded as the Breeds would like it to be. It was a secret that she knew they feared would destroy the Breed communities.

The thought of that was almost amusing. The world was so fascinated with Breeds that it was insane. Those who loved them defended and protected them fanatically.

Those who hated them hated them with a passion usually reserved for the greatest evil. It seemed there was no in-between when it came to either the dedication or the hatred aimed at the Breeds.

The truth of mating heat would only make those who loved them love them more. And it really wasn't possible for those who hated them to hate them more, but it would definitely intensify the fear from that group, as well as the violence.

It could cause the Breeds problems, she admitted, but she didn't believe it had the power to destroy them.

"Have the files come in from the EU yet?" Cassie Sinclair's slightly distracted tone drew Mica from her scrutiny of the Breed in question and had her turning away from the window of the office of Haven public relations.

"Not yet, but my sources assure me there's nothing in them that could harm the Breeds." Mica forced her attention back to the electronic news spread that scrolled across the holographic display on the far wall.

From all over the world, news stories concerning Breeds were streamed into the holo-spread, many well in advance of the hard-copy papers and website uploads they would later appear on.

The United World Internet Laws allowed the Central News Monitoring organization time to review what could be the most seditious posts before they were uploaded. Those laws allowed the Breeds to monitor any inflammatory or potentially dangerous stories that could possibly cause violence against Haven or Sanctuary. They had little prep time, though, between the stories coming in and the actual live feeds as they posted to the Internet. Less than twelve hours in some cases.

"I see Tanner is once again wowing the crowds," Mica

drawled as the Bengal Breed appeared briefly on the spread, his infamous smile charming the world.

And damn if he wasn't fine-looking. All that rich, midnight black hair tipped with the finest gold and that deep, sun-darkened skin. A body worth panting for. He was almost as fine-looking as Navarro.

"Tanner's good at it," Cassie murmured as she flipped between news stories. "He's the face of the Breeds."

Cassie had always said that, even as a child.

"Germany's articles are late coming in." Once again Cassie's tone grew worried.

"Are you expecting something, Cassie?" Mica finally asked, mystified by the other woman's demeanor.

Cassie seemed unaccountably anxious as she mumbled a "No" and gave a quick shake of her head.

Cassie's deep blue eyes were narrowed on the e-pad once again as she scanned information coming through before her gaze went back to the halo-vision screens.

"Germany is always late, Cassie," Mica reminded her as she glanced at the clock. "We still have an hour or so before we can consider them really late."

Cassie's lips thinned before she went back to work on whatever file she had pulled up.

"It would help if they were on time." She sighed, shifting in her seat and causing the mass of blue black curls that fell around her shoulders and down her back to ripple in a wave of midnight color.

How the hell she managed to hold her head up with all that hair, Mica didn't know.

"Why don't you tell me what has you so nervous?" Mica suggested. "You know it doesn't help to keep these things in, Cassie, they just make you crazy."

It was no less than the truth. Cassie was unique in more

ways than one. She was completely unusual and, sometimes, damned frightening.

There were "gifts" she possessed, friends she walked with that others couldn't see. There was one friend in particular that Cassie seemed to be losing touch with though, and Mica knew it worried her.

"Have you seen her?" Mica asked matter-of-factly after several seconds of watching her frown at the holo-vision.

Cassie stilled. The sudden stiffness was telling, and worrying.

Cassie had "friends" that others only dreamed of having. Her imaginary friends weren't imaginary though. They were very real to her, and Mica had learned over the years that however Cassie knew what she knew, she was tortured by information she had more than once stated she wished she didn't know.

The other girl shook her head slowly after a moment. "No." Her voice was small, soft. "I haven't seen her."

The "her" was the one Cassie had called a fairy as a child. The young woman was beautiful, Cassie had once told Mica. Fragile and frail, with such an air of wisdom, warmth and grace that she had possessed the power to calm Cassie even during the most horrible events of her young life.

The "fairy" had recently begun disappearing though. At first for only a few days, then longer and longer, until lately it seemed that the woman only Cassie could see hadn't reappeared at all.

"I don't understand it," Cassie finally said, the fear in her voice rocking Mica to her toes. "She warned me of the future, Mica, then she just disappeared. As though it was too horrible for her to have to stay and witness."

Mica's friend turned from the screens. Deep blue eyes

were damp and welling with moisture, thick black lashes spiking with it as she obviously fought to hold the moisture back. There was the slightest tremble of her lips before she could contain it.

Cassie was obviously becoming more distressed by the day with the disappearance of the woman that had been a part of her life since she was a very young child.

"She's done this before, Cassie," Mica reminded her.

"But not for this long," Cassie whispered, the cool calm she had adopted as a young adult disappearing to reveal a frightened young woman. "And not after such a warning."

What could Mica say? She was never comfortable discussing the "fairy," the ghosts that had come later or the other visions that sometimes visited Cassie.

"Give it time, Cassie, she'll come. She's always come back just when you thought she wouldn't."

"I don't understand it." Cassie moved quickly from her chair, those long loose curls waving around her in a manner that had Mica totally envious. "She's never been gone this long before, Mica."

Mica struggled to come up with something that would comfort Cassie. That was part of her job as Cassie's part-time personal assistant. A damned fine-paying job, as she well knew. Whenever Dash Sinclair realized his daughter was becoming anxious or overloaded with work, then Mica was excused from her job as an accountant for a major news firm and flown to Sanctuary for however long Cassie needed her. Mica helped Cassie in the PR office, sometimes did minor accounting for the office and generally did all she could to take as much pressure as possible off Cassie's shoulders.

If Mica felt bad about the fact that she was being paid

to help her friend, then she tried to put it behind her. She forced herself to remember that without the Breed's willingness to pay her, then Mica could never have afforded to help Cassie as she did. And the fact that Cassie needed someone to talk to, to confide in, had never been more apparent than it was now.

"And like you've said before," Mica reminded her, "sometimes, she does things to make you work it out yourself. Maybe that's why she's absent longer this time. Sort of like a mother leaving a child with a babysitter so her baby doesn't rely so heavily on her. You know?"

"Perhaps." Cassie shrugged as she shoved her hands in the back pockets of her designer jeans.

That was a classic Cassie move. She was worried and fighting to make sense of whatever she was worrying over.

She turned to Mica again, her delicate, pretty face pulled into a confused expression. "Do you ever feel as though the world is simply spiraling out of your control?"

There was a hint of fear in her friend's voice now, a haunted quality to her gaze that worried Mica. But, despite the worry, Mica couldn't help but see the irony in her friend's question.

Mica's brows arched at the question. "Cassie, *you* are my best friend," she stated with knowing emphasis. "I'm normally completely surrounded by Breeds and their hectic, dangerous lives. I'm at your beck and call at any time, whenever you need me, and often harassed by reporters anytime I'm in public. Do you think my world ever feels as though it's already spiraled, crashed, burned and drifted into the far corners of the earth?"

It was the truth, though Mica often found it more amusing than anything else. She'd learned early to take the

Breeds, their arrogance and often calculating, manipulative personalities, with a grain of salt. She was stuck with them, plain and simple, so she may as well make the best of it.

The journalists were harder to deal with, and she thanked God daily that she had found a job with the *National Journal*, owned by the family of Merinus Tyler Lyons, the mate of the Feline pride leader, Callan Lyons.

The *National Journal* was one of the few papers left still in hard copy, as well as on e-feed and satellite upload. It was also one of the few that didn't attempt to "reveal" gossip against the Breeds as truth. Instead the paper reported and reminded the world of the hell the Breeds had endured.

Finally, Cassie's lips twitched as Mica continued to stare back at her archly.

Then, she cleared her throat delicately. "Perhaps I'm asking the wrong person?" Thankfully, a hint of amusement gleamed in her unusual eyes.

"I'd guess you are." Mica rolled her eyes, silently thankful that the tears had disappeared from Cassie's gaze.

She couldn't stand to see her friend cry. It rarely happened, but when it did, it destroyed those who loved her. And Mica did love her. Cassie was her best friend, her sister, her confidante and, sometimes, her partner in crime. Those crimes were few and far between these days.

They'd become women together, and Mica couldn't think of anyone she'd rather have as a friend. She also couldn't think of anyone she'd rather have watching her back than Cassie. The other girl was small, delicate, but the Breeds had taught her, and Mica also, some of the most advanced forms of martial arts.

They had met when Cassie's stepfather, Dash Sinclair, had returned home from war to search for the little girl who had been his pen pal and her mother, both of whom supposedly had been killed in an apartment explosion.

Cassie and her mother, Elizabeth, had not been dead though. They had been running, fighting to survive and to escape the drug kingpin who had bought Cassie from her father. The father who had conspired with a Council scientist for money and had allowed his wife's eggs to be used to create a unique, highly specialized Breed. A Wolf-Coyote mix. The scientist had hoped the hybrid genetics would create the killer the Genetics Council sought and hadn't yet been able to reliably produce. And he'd wanted to further the experiment by having that child raised rather than trained, to see how reliable those killer genes would be.

Instead, Cassie had been born.

An inquisitive, precocious child who loved, not killed.

And one whose father feared her and her ability to betray him for the monster he was the first time she had to see a doctor after the scientist that created her disappeared.

He'd known he was about to be found out, and without the money the scientist had been providing, his gambling debts had been mounting.

So he'd sold her to the criminal he owed the money to. Fortunately, Elizabeth had been smart enough not to trust her husband after they split up. She'd rescued her daughter and gone on the run with her until Dash had found them and brought them to the Toler ranch until he could contact Sanctuary, which was at that time the only Breed community, and arrange protected status for her.

During the time Cassie had spent at the ranch Mica had become attached to her despite the few years difference in their ages. Cassie had needed a sister, and Mica had seen in the little girl a desperate hunger to be loved despite whatever haunted her.

Hands still shoved in her back pockets, Cassie paced over to Mica's desk, breaking into her thoughts, sighed and let her gaze move to the reports scrolling over the e-pad.

"There's the Germany reports," she murmured.

Mica glanced at the screen. They were indeed there.

"Play file mark seven point six three," Mica ordered the computer.

"File seven point six three," the computerized voice authorized a second before the file flashed on the holo-screen on the other side of the room: "File seven point six three, Berlin, Germany. Breeds suspected in rescue of Prime Minister's daughter kidnapped from her home; Feline Breed pride leader, Callan Lyons, to visit Luxembourg; suspected Genetics Council lab discovered by teens while hiking." No mention of mating, hormones, phenomena, or blood irregu-larities. Each article title was read and a report given after each, as Mica and Cassie watched intently the words scroll-ing across the holographic screen.

Dozens of articles flashed through the automated pro-gram set to search specific words, phrases and information listings. Each came back with a negative response.

Mica watched the screen intently, her gaze taking in many of the headings dealing with the Wolf Breed Haven and Feline Breed Sanctuary. The compounds were treated like mysteries. Reporters fought to get permission to visit, camped at the outer gates and had tried to fly as close as possible for pictures before the areas were designated no-fly zones.

"It looks as though it's all clear," Mica stated as the last file winked out. "Another day, another reprieve."

"Another reprieve," Cassie repeated softly. "Isn't that how it feels sometimes?"

Mica had to admit that was exactly what it often felt

like. Each time she was drawn here to help Cassie with
the PR office, she was once again reminded how in-depth
Breed awareness had to be. They had to keep their eyes on
every new article, every reporter and reporter wannabe, as
well as those who simply wanted to make up the stories
and stir the flames that were often licking at the Breeds'
heels.

It was irritating, aggravating, but Mica knew there were
times when Cassie thrived on the work.

Turning her gaze back to the window, Mica was once
again greeted by the sight of the Breed she knew in the end
was going to completely mess her life up.

Yep, this fascination was much too strong, and no matter what the Wolf Breed scientist Nikki Armani said, Mica
knew the potential for mating heat had to be there.

The tests for the mating hormone in the blood had
advanced over the years. The Breed scientists were now
able to pinpoint the smallest abnormalities that could
make a human female a viable candidate for being a Breed
male's mate. And Nikki had assured Mica more than once,
after several tests, that there was no chance in hell Navarro
was her mate, or had the potential to mate her.

The fact was that Mica's tests had shown a mating via-
bility, though there was still no way to tell exactly who that
mate could be. All they could do at this point was tell who
the mate wasn't, and supposedly, Navarro wasn't viable as
her mate.

It was hard to believe that potential wasn't there.

Watching him now as he stood in the communal courtyard that sat in the center of the large block of cabins and
small houses, talking to another Wolf Breed, Stygian, the
Coyote Cavalier and the Coyote second in command, Brim
Stone, Mica feared the doctor had to be wrong. She could

feel her skin prickling, a sense of arousal and anticipation flaring inside her, and an overwhelming curiosity she couldn't seem to fight.

Navarro stood confidently, his arms crossed over his chest, his expression thoughtful as he leaned against the heavy trunk of a large oak and nodded back at the other men.

Dressed in silk slacks and a white Egyptian shirt, his perfectly styled black hair in a moderate length brushed back from his face, he was the epitome of a successful, strong male. A human male was his cover. His recessed genetics allowed him to move around the world as the Blaine media empire's reigning heir rather than the Breed Enforcer created and trained to trick and deceive.

She knew the fierce canines most Breeds displayed proudly at the sides of their mouths were absent in Navarro's case because of his recessed genetics. She didn't know if he had body hair, or if like other Breeds his was absent as well, but she would have loved to have found out.

What she did know was that despite the fact he was indeed a Breed, there wasn't a test on Earth that could prove it. He was what they called "recessed," his Breed genetics buried so deeply on the cellular level as to be almost impossible to find.

That didn't make him less of a Breed though. She knew he could snarl just as brutally and fight just as mercilessly as any other Breed.

"He's hot, isn't he?" Cassie's smooth drawl had Mica jerking around, guilt flashing through her at her friend's knowing look.

The guilt turned quickly to amusement. "Yeah, he is," she agreed, sneaking another look outside as Navarro straightened from the tree, his gaze wandering from the other men before coming to the window Mica and Cassie were sitting in front of.

Mica nearly winced as Cassie waved enthusiastically.

Navarro's gaze narrowed, and, a slight, wary nod was given in return.

Cassie's light laugh was affectionate and much too interested. "He's so reserved. It makes you wonder what he's like with a lover."

Mica's teeth clenched. Hell no, she didn't wonder what he would be like with a lover. Unless that lover was her.

"Wow, Mica . . ." Cassie's tone was shocked, amazed, causing Mica to barely bite back her curse.

Damn, she knew to watch her reactions, to make certain she didn't let herself feel strongly, or react with anything more than mild interest. She knew the dangers of it more than anyone else could possibly know.

And now, she had just fucked up in the worse possible way, around the one person Mica knew better than to mess up around.

"You're jealous," Cassie said, releasing a breath, amazement widening her eyes now. "What have you been hiding from me, Mica?"

"Nothing." A lie, oh God, a lie. She had to steel herself. She knew better than to outright lie to Cassie.

Cassie stepped back slowly, the pure amazement in her face strengthening as she stared at Mica, shock overriding the amazement an instant later.

"Mica, you just lied to me," she said in wonder, as though she'd just received a gift she had never expected.

"Cassie, stop this," Mica warned her, feeling a sense of panic welling inside her now. "Let it go."

Things were going from bad to worse here, and she couldn't seem to stop the spiraling results from crashing through her. There were some things Cassie just didn't need to know. If that damned "fairy" that liked to tell everyone's secrets hadn't told her, then Mica felt it was best her friend didn't have to worry about it.

"You're keeping secrets from me?" Cassie's voice lowered as an edge of hurt entered her tone.

No. No. "Cassie, don't do this to me," she groaned. "Nothing happened. There are no secrets."

That pesky damned lie thing. She swore there were times she could almost smell a lie herself, Cassie had told her so many times what one smelled like. And she swore she could smell that hint of acrid sulfur now, like hell considering a visit.

Mica wanted to groan in defeat but knew better than to allow Cassie to even suspect such a weakness.

Cassie stepped closer, bent, her nostrils flaring as she breathed in deeply, and Mica could do nothing but stare back at her friend in resignation.

Cassie blinked and jerked back. For a second, for just a second, a curious expression came over her face before her gaze became shuttered, her expression stilling to that calm, serene look that hid every thought and emotion she could be feeling.

Mica hated that expression. There was simply no way to convince the other girl to tell her anything when she adopted that look.

"Well, how interesting," Cassie stated, her tone just as bland as her expression now.

This, Mica hadn't expected. Her gaze narrowed. "What's interesting?" There was that panic thing again. It was making her heart race, making that sense of impending doom rise inside her. "There's nothing interesting, Cassie. Do you hear me? There's nothing interesting, nothing period. Tell me there isn't."

What was Cassie seeing, or what had she seen as she

leaned closer and drew in whatever scent Mica couldn't smell herself?

That was the worst part about Breeds. Sometimes they could sense more about a person than that person knew about him- or herself.

"Of course there isn't." Cassie cleared her throat and blinked back at her.

Mica came slowly to her feet. "Don't make me strangle you, Cassie," she warned her, her voice low. "And I can do it. You know I can do it."

Cassie grimaced, her bow lips pouting as amusement began to sparkle in her gaze. "Dad made a mistake when he had you trained alongside me. He should have foreseen all these threats you would make against me."

"Don't try to distract me, Cassie." Mica breathed out roughly. "What did you see?"

The secretive little smile that twitched at Cassie's lips was terrifying. It was horrifying. Mica knew she would have nightmares for weeks if Cassie didn't tell her what was going on, simply because of that smile. Too knowing, yet with a hint of concern, of uncertainty.

"I didn't *see* anything." Cassie waved a hand as though it were nothing to be concerned about.

Anytime Cassie had a vision, a visit or whatever the hell it was, it was never, ever, nothing to be concerned about.

"Cassie, don't you play games with me."

"It was a scent." Cassie shrugged. "A feeling." A frown flitted between her brows as she glanced at the window, then back to Mica. "Mica, I don't think I know what I smelled."

Mica doubted that. She came slowly to her feet. "I may not have your nose, but I know you," she warned her friend. "Don't lie to me, Cassie."

"I would never lie to you, Mica." Her eyes widened as though she were innocent. And Mica knew better. She knew that expression. It was anything but innocence.

"Cassie," she bit out between her teeth, irritation beginning to surge through her. "Don't do this to me."

Cassie's brow arched. "Don't do what, Mica? What am I doing?"

"Hiding the truth from me," Mica accused her. "Tell me what you saw."

Cassie's brow arched. "I didn't see it, I smelled it," she repeated. "But it's not a scent you carry now, Mica. It's one you could carry later."

There was the panic again. It was making her sick. Her stomach felt weak, shaky.

"And it will be what?" Clenched teeth, frustration. She hated it when Cassie played with her like this.

"Contentment," Cassie finally answered. "You know, Mica, as much as you may hate the thought of it, I smelled contentment."

◆   ◆   ◆

Cassie watched her friend, fighting to hold her expression, fighting to convince Mica everything was fine, to hold back the worry and the concern. She wasn't lying to Mica, the "future" scent was one of contentment, but it was a potential contentment. A maybe thing. One of the many paths Mica could take. And beside that path was deceit and rage, to the other side was agony and heartache.

The path would depend on too many things.

It would depend on Mica and on a Breed . . .

And the Breed it would depend on wasn't Navarro Blaine.

And that was the scary part. Because the other scent

she detected was so slight, so subtle, that Cassie doubted it would even show on tests. That other scent was Navarro's, and a hint of mating heat.

Mica was Navarro's mate, but her friend's happiness would lie in another Breed's hands. A Breed other than her mate.

· C H A P T E R I ·

Thunder crashed, lightning blazed and sheets of rain poured from the sky as though rage itself were given a physical presence. It slashed through the windswept streets and tore through the back alleys as most inhabitants of the city watched from indoors. There were few brave enough to venture into the streets and face the wrath of the storm pounding furiously outside their windows, but they were very few and very far between.

The streets were all but deserted at four in the morning. New York might never sleep, but it definitely rested for a while, especially during the furious, driving rains that descended on the city that night.

Pouring moisture that saturated hair and clothing, washing it into Mica's eyes, mixing with the tears and washing away the blood that had eased from her scalp after the initial attack that had come earlier. An attack she couldn't have expected, that she'd had no warning was coming.

She stumbled through the alley, breath shuddering,

chills wracking her body as she fought to find a haven, a business, an opened door, a cabdriver.

Anything. Anyone.

And there was nothing. There was no one. She was alone in a city that was sleeping when it wasn't supposed to, amid a storm she should have been safe from, comfortable and warm in her own bed.

She wanted to be in her bed.

She wanted to pull the blankets over her head and dream those hot, erotic dreams she'd been having lately of a Breed she shouldn't dream about.

She didn't want to be here.

A sob tore from her chest, ripping through her ribs in agony as terror had tears mixing with the cold rivulets of rain pouring down her face.

She wanted to be home.

She should have never left her apartment, she should have never trusted that bastard little mouse of a waiter who claimed to be in trouble. After leaving the office, she should have just gone home and ignored the message on her phone that he had important information for her.

She was just an accountant; she wasn't a reporter. But she often ate at the little café where he worked, and he called her, he said, because he didn't know who else to call.

Bullshit.

He had drawn her right from the restaurant bar and into the grip of a damned Coyote.

The son of a bitch had tried to knock her out.

She touched the side of the head, biting her lip at the tenderness there.

With her arm wrapped around her ribs, she leaned against the brick wall of a tightly closed restaurant and fought to catch her breath.

She'd been kicked after she was thrown in a van. She remembered the feel of a steel-toed boot ramming into her ribs before she could protect them.

Assholes. She hated Coyotes.

Except Brim Stone. And Del-Rey.

Well, she didn't hate Ashley, Emma or Sharone.

She hated Council Coyotes. Every damned fucking one of them, and now she was hiding in a dirty alley as she tried to escape them.

She didn't dare venture out to the street to hopefully flag down one of the few cabs trolling for the few passengers that could be found. Cabs weren't the only ones out there.

There was more than one black SUV. There were men with communication ear sets, and there was a Breed. Sharp-toothed, eyes black and spitting evil as he'd leaned over, a twisted smile contorting his scarred face just before she'd slammed her heavy hiking boots into the ugly, sneering expression of Marx Whitman, the Coyote that had already betrayed the Breeds once.

The vision was one that nightmares were made of.

Shuddering, shivering, she forced herself from the wall and eased to the shadowed entrance of the alley she'd ducked into. Keeping low, staying close to the dark, sodden walls of the buildings, she rushed down the sidewalk, quickly making her way through the streets and fighting to keep an eye on the vehicles moving slowly behind her.

There was no way to hide from a Breed. There was no way to still suspicion if the men in the SUVs caught sight of a lone figure moving down the sidewalk.

Ducking into the next alley, she moved quickly through the sinister shadows, her stomach heaving with fear as lightning flared overhead and thunder rattled the very air around her.

A scream erupted from her throat as she stumbled against a garbage can, causing it to crash to the ground as a shadow erupted from her side.

Like an emerging, vengeful beast, it came at her. A sound like a demented growl, a whip of cold air, arms outstretched . . . Mica screamed again, falling backward as the shadow followed, whipping against her, knocking her to the ground despite her attempts to stay upright.

"Dammit, Mica!" Harsh, animalistic. She should know that voice, but hysteria was tearing through her, pain a blazing sensation of agony in her ribs as she fought to get free.

The stench of urine, the feel of filth on the alley beneath her palms, and a nightmare of sensations she couldn't process. Instinct had her rolling, finding her feet, slipping, then finally gaining traction to force herself into a run.

The sound behind her too closely resembled a curse. Demonic, sending a flash of terror racing through her as a sob left her throat and she rounded the corner of the alley into a side street.

"Mica." Rough, a fierce rumble, and it didn't sound in the least friendly.

As she caught herself against the corner of the wall, lightning split the skies, illuminating a tall, broad form, eyes like hammered gold, a face savage, too fierce and unknown.

In the next breath Mica turned, running in the opposite direction, only to face another shadow, taller, darker. Throwing herself to the side, low, nearly skidding along the street, she went beneath an outstretched hand, skidding, only to have her back pushed against a brick wall as hard male arms surrounded her.

"Dammit, Mica, stop fighting me before I have to knock your ass out!"

Her gaze flew up, breath suspending in her lungs, relief and weakness shuddering through her all at once.

He was the animal whose voice had sent her running once again. Black eyes glittered with rage as lightning lit up the world around them.

The scene seemed surreal. The lightning, the rain sheeting around them. His exotic, fierce expression framed by heavy, ribbon-straight black silken hair that fell around his face and wet from the rivulets of rain running over it.

Eyes wide, shuddering, she could only stare up at him as his hand lifted, palm cupping her cheek, the intense warmth of his touch rushing through her as his thumb stroked softly over her lips.

"Amaya." He spoke so softly she barely heard, the dark, Asian flavor of his tone shocking her as he whispered the nickname he had given her years ago. "Are you ready to get out of the rain now?"

"Navarro." His name was a harsh gasp, relief pouring through her, weakening her as the warmth of his hard body began to seep through the saturated clothing between them.

"Navarro, we have to move." Harsh, a male Feline growl rumbled in the night.

Mica tried to swing around, her heart dropping to her stomach as fear suddenly tore through her again.

"Can you run?" The harsh question was a grating, furious sound that seemed suddenly to rumble in Navarro's powerful chest.

For a Breed it was said didn't growl as others did, that came awful close to a growl.

A quick nod as he caught her hand, turned and began pulling her through the rain-lashed night.

Shadows reached out from the buildings around them,

twisting fingers of darkness colliding with the rain-dimmed glow of sparse streetlights interspersed with the shadows through the alleys.

Mica was aware of the figure moving behind them, though she'd only managed to catch a quick glimpse of a dark figure. Features were impossible to see or to recognize through the sheets of moisture.

She could feel the presence at her back, a prickling awareness that kept her nerves on edge.

"We're almost there," Navarro assured her, as though he could sense, could somehow feel, the fear that continued to rise inside her.

Damp weather was supposed to affect a Breed's sense of smell. If he could still smell her fear, then there was the chance the Coyote that had attacked her, or any working with him, could catch her scent as well.

Forcing herself to tamp down the emotion, to bury it in that same dark, hidden corner of her mind where she tried to hide things from Cassie, wasn't easy. Terror was like an oily, vicious specter shadowing her, one that seemed to refuse to allow her to escape.

She was with Navarro now though. She wasn't alone. That was the lifeline she held on to, the fragile thread of awareness that kept her centered as she began to push the fear to that enclosed place where it couldn't be detected.

He was the one Breed she should be wary of personally, but she'd always known, from the first day their eyes had met, that he would never allow anyone to hurt her.

I'll protect you, Mica. I swear, as long as I breathe, I'll keep you from harm.

That promise made, as explosions ripped through Haven's central courtyard on a night meant to be celebrated, echoed through her mind.

He had sworn to protect her. Covering her body with his own as Breed traitors attempted to kidnap Storme Montague, one of the newly mated women within Haven, and Cassie, he had sheltered her from the danger.

How many times had she replayed that night in her nightmares? Each time though, the terror turned to something else, to something softer, hotter. To something that only frightened her more, on a deep, intensely personal level.

He made her want him. Nightmares turned to erotic fantasy whenever she dreamed of that night. To the sensation of his lips caressing her ear, then her cheek. To the feel of his lips at first only brushing against hers, then taking the curves with a hungry, primal passion she couldn't seem to deny.

"Fuck!" The furious curse had Mica jerking her head around, desperate to see what had caused the exclamation.

She had only a second to catch a glimpse of lights turning into the alley before Navarro pulled her quickly into a deep, sheltered recess between two buildings, before pressing her into the brick wall.

"Sons of bitches couldn't have picked a warm night for this bullshit, could they?" he growled at her ear as Mica felt his arms sheltering her, the long leather coat he wore wrapping around her as he tucked her head against his chest.

Beneath the coat, he was heavily armed, an arsenal strapped into the lining of the leather covering and holstered beneath his arm, at his waist and thigh.

She could feel the cold metal of the automatic submachine gun holstered at his side by a leather harness. An automatic handgun was holstered at his lean hips, while he carried one of the lightweight, powerful laser-powered defense weapons holstered at his left side.

A knife was strapped to each thigh, and God only knew what else he was armed with.

"Cougar, do you have visual?" she heard him murmur, no doubt speaking into one of the small, secured ear sets the Breeds used for communication.

"I have him. Just what the hell we needed, Farce's little brother, Loki, on our asses," he grunted a second later.

Farce, a Coyote that had been working for the remaining members of the Genetics Council, had ended up dead weeks before, when he had gone against another Wolf Breed. His little brother, Loki, who carried the mythical name with pride and did his best to live up to it, was rumored to have sworn vengeance for his brother's death.

"Coyote's night out," she said, trying for weak humor as a shudder raced through her.

She could often trap the emotions inside, but that didn't mean they didn't still affect her.

"You have no clue, baby," Navarro sighed as she felt his hand stroke up her back.

That motion, such a small, almost insignificant caress, had Mica dropping her head fully against his chest and breathing in roughly as he continued to talk quietly to whatever Cougar was on the other end of the comm link.

Several times lights passed by the entrance to the narrow lane they were hidden in. They stopped long enough to have Navarro lowering his hand from her, shifting her just enough to the side that he could get to the laser-powered sub-shot burst, a laser version of the compact submachine gun, strapped to his side. Finally, after tense moments, the vehicle eased forward once again, moving slowly, obviously searching intently for something.

For them.

"They've stopped a few feet from the entrance," he whispered in her ear as thunder crashed overhead and the rain seemed to fall faster, harder. "Cougar's watching them from his point outside. He has a vehicle and he's ready to roll as soon as they're out of line of sight."

She nodded against his chest, her fingers curling into the shirt she was pressed against as she breathed in his scent and concentrated on keeping her emotions locked away.

"Cassie said you were good at holding back your scent." His hand stroked down her hair. A large, warm hand that spread a sensation of warmth along her neck. "I can barely smell you at all, sweetheart. You've been around nosy Breeds too long, huh?" There was an edge of amusement in his whispered observation.

"You learn," she breathed out with an edge. "Especially around Cassie."

Cassie could make her crazy. Self-defense had created whatever gift Mica had adopted to keep her emotions so carefully contained that even animal senses couldn't pick them up.

"Cassie could make a saint curse," he agreed, then his hand stroked to her hip and tightened there. "Get ready. The SUV has pulled out. Cougar will be easing in within seconds."

"I am so ready to get out of the rain." She held back the hard shivers that threatened to shake through her as she turned her head and watched the entrance.

There were no lights. She wouldn't have known a vehicle had pulled up if she hadn't been watching carefully and seen the dim lights in the alley glittering on the black sheen of paint.

"Move." He was right there, his arm going around her waist and pulling her against him as he began to race for the vehicle.

The passenger door was thrown open as they neared,

a dim flare of light revealing the hard, scarred face of the Breed in the driver's seat.

She had to bite her lip to cut off an agonized cry as Navarro lifted her and all but threw her into the backseat before following behind her. The vehicle was moving before the door slammed behind them, Navarro coming over her as the SUV began moving through the alley.

"Stay down," he warned her when she would have tried to push against him and straighten. "They obviously suspected we were in the lane; they could be watching the alley in case you tried to run at some point."

She couldn't breathe.

The pain in her ribs was like fire, biting at her senses with jagged teeth as she fought to hold back the weakness.

It was habit. She'd been practically raised among the Breeds after Cassie and her family had come into their lives. She'd learned early never to show a weakness, to never let them suspect she wasn't as tough as she pretended to be. And she could pretend to be damned tough.

But with Navarro lying over her, the heat of him seeping through her cold flesh, she couldn't contain the pain building in her ribs.

"Please," she finally gasped, unable to lie against her side much longer, or to bear the pressure on her tender ribs.

He stiffened, easing back just a moment as a growl sounded from the front seat.

"They're behind us, man. Sensors are showing heat-seeking radar. If you so much as shift the wrong way, they're going to get a lock on body heat. Stay put."

She tried to breathe.

Each indrawn breath was agony, tearing at her chest, sending waves of pain surging through her system.

She didn't know if she could bear it. Her ribs weren't

broken, she doubted they were cracked, but the bruising would be extensive. She could feel it, spreading across her side, around her back, into her chest.

"Get a safe distance from them," Navarro snarled. "She's in pain. She won't be able to hold this position for long."

"Look, the bastards are damned suspicious," the other Breed argued. "They've been on my ass since we pulled out. We need to troll nice and easy to the hotel. We'll take the underground parking garage. Without a pass, they can't follow us."

"Navarro, just a little bit." She couldn't hold back the plea any longer. "Please, it hurts."

"Move so much as an inch and they're going to have us before we're close enough to the hotel to be safe," the driver bit out furiously. "Just a few more blocks, Navarro. You don't have a fucking inch to spare. You're already all but crawling into the front seat here."

Navarro could feel the impulses raging inside him, tearing at his senses as he fought to hold his place. Another part, a more primal, intent part of his mind demanded he move, that he ease the pain he could more than feel. He could smell it. A thick, rich scent of heat, like wood burning. In Mica, it was stronger than that of an ember, but not yet a blaze.

Scents were odd; different emotions, different levels of sensation or feelings could inspire the body to radiate far different scents.

With Mica, a woman he knew could bear, and hide, a certain amount of discomfort, the fact that he could scent the heat of the pain so clearly was telling. She was hurting, and the longer he lay there, the pressure of his body against hers, the more the pain increased.

He could sense it. The knowledge of it had his muscles

tensing, had him fighting to keep his weight from her as much as possible.

"We're almost there," he assured her as he turned his head to catch a glimpse of the buildings they were passing. From between the front seats he could glimpse the towers, watching as each passed by and counting off the streets left to go. "There's a nice warm room awaiting us, Mica. A hot meal, a hot shower, then I'll check your ribs and see the damage those bastards managed to do. I'll care for you. Haven't I always cared for you whenever you needed?"

"Yes." The tightly worded response destroyed him.

He'd never wanted anyone's trust, especially a woman's, but he wanted hers.

She made him wish, when he'd learned years before not to wish. She made him hunger, she made him want to learn how to dream.

The contradictions were often disconcerting because he couldn't ignore them, and emotions were something he'd learned to ignore as a child.

With Mica, he found it impossible to ignore anything she forced him to feel. Especially the arousal.

"I remember the first time I saw you," he whispered against her ear as he felt her trembling beneath him, the scent of pain growing stronger as it wafted from her. "Do you remember, Amaya?" Night rain. She reminded him of the dark peace, the gentle touch of a summer rain at night.

"I was fifteen." Stress filled her voice, pain tightened it. "They were calling Cassie names."

Some of the younger Breeds, those who had been rescued from the labs while still in their teens. They had dared to stand before Cassie and call her a freak when they detected the slightest hint of her Coyote genetics.

They had made Cassie cry before they even realized who

she was. They'd known only the scent of her, Wolf and Coyote mixed. And at that time, Coyote had been a hated scent.

"You pushed in front of her and blacked Josiah's eye."
He closed his eyes tight as he fought against a wild, impul-
sive need to tell the men following them to go to hell and
lift his weight from her immediately.

"Josiah deserved it." Her voice was tighter, a hint of a
sob, the scent of tears ripping at him.

"Josiah deserved it," he agreed before turning his head.
"Cougar, dammit, tell me we're in safe territory."

"They're still on our fucking asses and that body heat
sensor is still active," Cougar snarled back. "Five more
minutes, Nav. She's not dying, it just fucking hurts."

The scent of her pain was affecting Cougar as well. The
other Breed was hard-core, cold to the pit of his soul where
males, human or Breed, were concerned. But he hadn't
quite learned that women were just as strong, and a hell of
a lot more dangerous in some cases than any man could
ever hope to be.

Women were Cougar's weakness. Mica was Navarro's.
And it made no sense. She wasn't his mate. He'd pushed
that limit, tested her response to him; he'd kissed her, and
still, the mating hormone hadn't risen inside him.

"Navarro please . . ." she whispered again, her breathing shallow, the scent of her tears destroying him. "I can't
breathe."

The soft heat of an ember that indicated her pain was
now beginning to glow brighter, threatening to blossom to
a full flame.

"Three more minutes," Cougar assured him, his voice
tighter. "Bastards are still on our asses."

"I'm going to kill them," Navarro promised. "Find out
who it is, Cougar. They're dead."

Mica whimpered beneath him.

Son of a bitch, he hated hurting her.

"We're coming up on the hotel," Cougar stated. "Once we turn in, we should be home free."

"Just hurry the fuck up!" It was Mica's voice, vibrating with pain now, thick with tears but heavy with anger.

"I thought you said she was sweet and shy, Nav," Cougar snorted then. "She sounds like a brat to me."

"I see a black eye in his future too." Clenched teeth, feminine ire and that damned pain.

"I know how to duck," Cougar assured her. "I always was better at that than Josiah was."

"But Josiah also knows how to keep his mouth shut now. A lesson you need to learn," Navarro stated warningly, a flare of jealousy he couldn't have expected rising inside him at the flirtatiousness in Cougar's voice.

He shot a glare toward the other Breed and found himself biting off a growl.

"If he doesn't hurry, I'm going to kick his ass," Mica promised painfully.

Navarro wanted to grin at the irritation in her voice, and he would have, if he hadn't known it was caused by pain.

She didn't make idle threats. He'd seen her go nose to nose with Breeds before, and they didn't always back down simply because she was protected by Dash Sinclair.

"Here we go," Cougar murmured.

As he made the turn, Navarro was suddenly thankful Mica was on her stomach, not on her back. If she had been on her back, staring up at him, he wondered if he could have withstood the temptation of her kiss, despite her pain.

She made him hot. She made his dick damned hard, and she made him feel, whether he wanted to or not. He couldn't help it. No matter how he fought it, she made him as hungry as a damned rabid Wolf and as off balance as a human teenager after his first love.

"We're clear." The relief in Cougar's voice had Navarro realizing the tension that had been tightening inside him.

Navarro shifted back quickly, his hands moving to her back, one easing against her side to check for injury.

Her clothes were sodden, chilled against her flesh, but he could feel the heat of her beneath the clothing, indicating a deep, painful bruise.

There was no scent of broken bones, of blood or internal bleeding. Just her pain, and the wounding of the flesh clear to the bone. The knowledge of the pain she must be feeling had an effect on him that he couldn't have anticipated. Regret that seared him, and a fury toward her attacker that assured his death if Navarro ever learned his identity.

"The elevator goes straight to the penthouse suite," Cougar informed them as Navarro clenched his jaw and helped Mica sit up in the seat.

Gripping her ribs, she eased up with his help, her golden green eyes almost the color of a Breed's. Almost. That gold was sparse, like small flakes of glitter that peeked in and out of the soft green.

"Let's go." The moment the SUV pulled up to the underground elevator, Navarro was out of the vehicle, moving around quickly to throw Mica's door open and help her from the seat.

"I can walk. I'm just not in the mood to have your heavy ass laying all over me." She almost slapped at his hands as she glared up at him while moving gingerly from the backseat.

He almost winced at the biting tone. He'd learned young, though, to never back down, no matter the strength of his adversary.

Ignoring her glare, he gripped her arm and steered her quickly to the elevator as he pulled the electronic key card from the inner pocket of his coat.

Sliding it into the security strip, Navarro glanced around quickly, his gaze narrowed, his senses on high alert as the door slid open.

"He man," she muttered as he pushed her gently inside the small cubicle.

"Brat." Affection rose inside him as he chose the penthouse suite from the digital menu.

"Jonas went all out, I see." A delicate, feminine sound of ire was sniffed from her delicate little nose. "And all for little ole me."

Glancing down at her from the corner of his eyes, he wondered exactly how to diffuse the temper he could feel brewing. He hadn't been trained in this particular combat situation. The war of the sexes wasn't exactly on the list of training assignments the Genetics Council scientists and military advisors had approved.

"All for you," he finally agreed. "Once we realized a team had been sent to capture you, your team was ordered to bring you in. Unfortunately, they had already been identified by the men sent for you. They took your team out before the Coyote tried to grab you. Cougar and I were here on another assignment when the distress signal went out and we came to help."

They had been there to meet with someone Jonas had been searching high and low for. Years of investigative work had gone into locating this particular scientist. The moment Navarro had caught the call on the comm link that Mica's team had been hit, he'd left the assignment immediately.

He could still hear Jonas screaming through the link

and Lawe and Rule's amused laughter as he and Cougar
sped away to the heart of the city.

"I had a team?" She sounded faintly surprised.

"Of course you had a team," he informed her as the elevator slid to a smooth, soundless stop. "You've always had one,
Mica. Since the day Cassie declared you were her best friend
and informed her father that her 'fairy' said she needed you,
you've had a team covering you."

He felt her stiffen, as though that information had somehow surprised her, or upset her. The faintest scent of anger,
a heat more like a volcano preparing to erupt than the
embers of pain, drifted to him.

"That long?" Her voice was faint, disappointed.

Without waiting for the doors to fully open, she stepped
into the penthouse, obviously ignoring every rule of entry
she had ever been taught.

Shaking his head, Navarro stepped in front of her with
a sharp growl, his gaze slicing back at her in warning and,
thankfully, bringing her to a stop as he moved ahead of her.

"Anger is no excuse for ignoring the rules," he snapped.

The thing about Mica? A man had to take control immediately. Begin as he intended to go on. She could push right
over anyone who thought she should be spoiled or treated
gently.

"Being male is no excuse for arrogance, but I've noticed
Breed males have it in abundance," she retorted without an
ounce of the sweetness displayed in her voice.

She would make any man a hell of a woman, mate or
wife. She wasn't weak, but neither was she a shrew. She
could be gentle, she could soft, or she could be an explosive, as unstable as hell in the wrong hands.

She would be a handful, Navarro had always known
that, but there was a part of him that looked forward to the

challenge. A part of him that was glad she wasn't his mate, while another part mourned it.

Thankfully, so far, as he seemed to be safe of the dangers of mating; he refused to marry, and he wouldn't allow himself the convenience of a mistress or a steady lover.

He was created for deception, created to deceive and to lie, and trusting a man, or a Breed, created and trained for such things, wouldn't be easy for any woman. But even more, he was one of only a few such creations, and his gifts, or his curse, was needed for the survival of the Breeds at large. Mating would change that. It would change him. And Navarro wasn't certain if he was ready for that.

He knew well what he couldn't have, no matter the desires that haunted him in the darkest hours of the night. And this woman, sharp and so very prickly on the outside, heated and warm on the inside, was the very thing he couldn't allow himself.

He ignored the arrogance comment and opted instead to draw the sub-shot burst from beneath his jacket before checking the suite carefully.

Cougar would be back soon with the equipment to ensure there were no electronic or video bugs, while Navarro knew Jonas was currently working on a plan to get Mica out of the city as secretly as possible.

The team they had bypassed earlier wasn't the only one sent for her, scouring the city to locate her even now.

Hell no.

At last count, there were twelve teams searching high and low for Mica. Twenty-four men determined to take her. There were surface-to-air, handheld missiles in the city, and plans to waylay anyone who tried to drive her out or any heli-jet that dared to fly her out. If they could catch sight of it.

Find a hole and stay put, Jonas had warned them, until he found a way to get her back to Sanctuary or to Haven. Keep her under wraps. Keep her safe. *And do it all while trying like hell to stay out of her pants* had been Navarro's warning to himself.

Unfortunately, the last part was the very order he was truly afraid would never be obeyed.

Getting in Mica's pants was one of the first things on his list of things to do while Jonas and Stygian searched for an escape route out of the city. He didn't have to change to fuck her.

He almost winced. No, he could never fuck her. A woman like Mica, a man, no matter his species, could only make love to such a woman, whether he allowed himself to love her or not.

And this would be his only chance to have her; it might well be his last chance to know exactly what he was leaving behind. It was time for him to go before nature caught up with him and gave him a mate. It was time to return to the life of lies and illusion he'd been a part of before taking the mission to search for Jonas's scientist.

Besides, Mica was a weakness that could get them both killed.

✦ CHAPTER 2 ✦

Standing beneath the steaming hot spray of the penthouse shower and allowing it to wash away the bone-deep chill that had seeped inside her, Mica finally felt she might live rather than die from the cold.

She hated the cold. She hated winter. She hated having to feel the chill of it or to look out the window and see the snow swirling. That had made the night worse than it would have been otherwise, that bone-deep cold. She'd been terrified she would never be warm again.

With the warmth came a determination to ignore the danger she knew was also swirling outside the doors of the hotel. She closed her eyes and forced herself to slip into the darkness there, to create that wall between her and the reality of the memories that threatened to take hold.

That whole head-in-the-sand attitude never failed to make Cassie crazy when they were together.

Mica loved ignoring the fact that she didn't have a real life. That she was always surrounded by danger, Breeds, and the realization that at any time the Breeds' enemies could strike out at her instead of her friends.

They finally had.

A hard, rough breath shuddered through her as she pushed back the knowledge again. It was harder this time. Of course, she hadn't faced another night quite like tonight either.

Yep, she was an ostrich. Feathers, plume, head in the sand, whole nine yards.

Well, except those long bird legs. She still had the short legs. But the rest of it. Yes indeed, just list her name with the feathered genera of the world, because she wasn't about to open her eyes and accept reality anytime soon.

She'd just put that little thing on her to-do list for next year, maybe.

"Are you okay in there?"

Mica jumped, startled to hear his voice so close, just outside the frosted glass of the shower door.

"I'm fine. Go away."

She needed just a few more minutes to assure herself, to convince herself she wasn't here standing beneath the pouring hot water because she had just spent hours in the driving rain running from Breed enemies. After all, she wasn't a Breed, right? She was as human as they came, and no one could say any different.

"Go away? Mica, my feelings might be hurt. Are you certain you don't need your back washed? Or perhaps your front?" He was clearly amused, the exotic edge of his voice stroking over her senses.

God, she loved that little hint of an accent. Just a hint, one was never certain it was really there, but the sound of it just stroked across her senses like an erotic caress.

"You'd have to have feelings first, Navarro. And I'm able to wash my back, and my front, perfectly on my own."

A feminine sniff of disdain met his suggestion, though she could feel her heart trying to race in excitement.

This wasn't the first time Navarro had made such a comment, but they never failed to steal her breath.

She couldn't help it. Unlike many other Breeds, there was simply something about Navarro that she couldn't force herself to ignore.

Or perhaps she didn't want to ignore it. The excitement, the sense of wonder, the surge of aroused adrenaline were a pleasure in and of themselves that she seemed to be becoming addicted to.

"You're wounding my heart, Amaya," he drawled. "I believe I may have to come up with some punishment in retaliation."

One of these days, she was going to ask him exactly what that word meant. She knew it was Japanese, but she hadn't yet forced herself to learn the meaning of it. If she learned it simply meant friendship, or some kind of child, her ego might be irreparably stripped.

"As long as that punishment doesn't include invading my shower or anything cold," she assured him, though she could feel every cell in her body threatening to send out a scent that would attest otherwise.

"Mica, I want to see your ribs." His voice hardened imperceptibly.

Mica's nipples hardened.

Just that fast, the thought of him touching her ribs, so close to the swollen mounds of her breasts, and she was becoming flushed with an arousal she couldn't hide.

Would the water cover the scent?

Heat flushed her face at the thought of being unable to hide the telling scent of an arousal so strong that even now she could feel the betraying slickness gathering between her thighs.

"I'm just sore," she tried to assure him as her fingers glanced over the area. "Nothing's broken, just bruised."

She stroked the curve of her own breast, her fingertips eliciting a wave of pleasure that swept through her entire system.

She would love to have him touch her. To feel his fingers stroking over her flesh gently, his lips touching her, not just kissing her, but stroking against her flesh, covering her nipple, suckling it, licking it.

"I would rather see that for myself. We're going to be leaving soon. I need to know the true condition of any injuries in order to know how to proceed should we run into trouble."

Of course he did. Breeds believed in always being completely prepared, often to a level that bordered on the ridiculous. Even her father, an army Special Forces soldier, wasn't as detailed as Breeds were without even thinking about it.

"It's fine, Navarro." She closed her eyes, fighting the need to have him touch her.

"I would like to see for myself that it's simply a bruise," he stated firmly. "When you've finished, I'll be waiting for you in the bedroom."

Opening her eyes and turning her head, she watched as he left the bathroom, the shadow of his tall, leanly muscled physique easing from the doorway.

Pushing her face beneath the pouring water, she debated running cold water rather than hot, but the memory of that icy chill was still too sharp.

As aroused as he had her, still the thought of anything

but warmth washing over her sent a wave of fear crashing through her mind. She was afraid the thought of icy rain would only be a fearful thing in the future now, rather than simply something to avoid as it had been before tonight.

Pushing the thought and the memory of that chill to the back of her mind, Mica finished her shower before shutting off the water and wrapping a towel around her sodden hair. Drying quickly, she pulled on a thick, ultra-soft white hotel robe and belted it loosely.

She hoped he had thought to get her more clothes; otherwise, her stay here was going to be pretty awkward, she thought, as she quickly towel dried her hair.

Running her fingers through the heavy, straight strands, she quickly used the blow-dryer to knock most of the dampness out of them. She didn't want to feel anything cold against her flesh for a long time.

When she moved from the large, luxurious bathroom to the bedroom, she came to a slow, hesitant stop as she saw Navarro sitting on the bed, his gaze directed to the e-pad he was scrolling through as he waited on her.

His head lifted.

Eyes as dark as the black of night stared back at her silently, unblinkingly.

Mica cleared her throat as a wave of nervousness washed through her.

He'd changed clothes. Sodden black mission pants and the lightweight black shirt were gone. In their place perfectly creased, obviously pricey black jeans and a white long-sleeved cotton shirt tucked snugly into the band. A black leather belt cinched his hard waist, and on his feet he wore obviously expensive leather boots.

Never let it be said that Navarro Blaine didn't know how to dress, and how to dress well.

His hair was pushed back from his face, falling to his nape, and the thick, heavy strands invited her fingers to explore and play.

It was as straight as her own, though thicker, heavier, the midnight color such a rich, glistening sheen it looked blue in a certain light.

"Are you finally warm?" He laid the pad aside as he rose to his feet, the primal, animal male grace he displayed nearly stealing her breath.

"Warm enough." Tucking her hair nervously behind her ear, she tried to fight back an attraction she had no hope of defeating.

"You'll need to take off the robe." His gaze flickered with something, some almost hidden heat that had her heart suddenly racing between her breasts.

"I don't think so." There wasn't a chance in hell she was pushing her libido that far.

Rather than removing the robe, she untied it and carefully eased it from one arm while holding the abundant remaining material over her breasts. Revealing her side, she knew why his eyes suddenly narrowed and his lips thinned.

The dark bruise, a vulgar, spreading stain from the impact of the Coyote Breed's boot against her side, from the area beneath her arm to just below her breast. It encompassed her rib area and had already turned a vivid, ugly black, an assurance the bruising went clear to the bone.

"I can see the bruise much better if you remove the robe," he assured her, playfulness entering his voice.

"That and much more." She stared straight ahead and simply concentrated on trying to control the betraying dampness of her juices gathering between her thighs.

His fingertips brushed against her flesh.

"Why do I have a feeling you're lying to me?" he murmured as he glanced back at her teasingly.

Mica rolled her eyes mockingly. "Let me guess, you smell it?"

He actually chuckled, a dark, deep sound that played across her senses with a stroke of pleasure. "You're actually rather good at hiding it, but my sense of smell isn't the same as other Breeds. I imagine it has something to do with the recessed genetics."

Her brows arched. "You can't smell things as the other Breeds do?"

"Your fear was rather sharp tonight, as was your pain . . ."

"No kidding. I should have guessed. Cassie's dad's sense of smell wasn't very good either because of his recessed genetics." There was a sense of relief so sudden she barely held it in.

She hadn't expected recessed senses as well, though she knew she should have. Cassie's father, Dash, had had recessed senses until he mated Cassie's mother, Elizabeth. His sense of sight, hearing and smell had been better than normal, but they hadn't been at Breed level.

With that knowledge came another, relieving thought.

Perhaps Navarro couldn't sense her arousal.

He couldn't smell the liquid heat gathering between her thighs.

This was good. This was actually much better, she thought. If he couldn't smell it or sense it, then perhaps she could pretend it didn't exist.

Yep, that was her, the ostrich.

"I don't think it makes you any less effective though." A sense of hope cheered her a little. At least she wouldn't have to worry about every emotion, every want or need revealed to him as easily as Cassie seemed to pick it up. "And really, you don't have to be able to smell a person's emotions. I think it's highly unfair that Breeds have those senses anyway."

Perhaps, just maybe, because of that, she could defend herself against this attraction, this fascination rapidly spiraling out of control.

◆　◆　◆

Navarro knew he should feel at least a shade of remorse for not completing his sentence and assuring her his sense of smell was actually more advanced, despite his recessed genetics, than most Breeds. After all, she couldn't smell his lie as he could hers. She couldn't smell his hunger for her, as he could smell hers. And she hungered. She was lightning hot, flaring with peaks of arousal and making him insane each time she flared.

His genetics were recessed; therefore, most humans and Breeds alike assumed his senses weren't as heightened as other Breeds'. The opposite was actually the truth. His senses were stronger, sharper, more advanced than 90 percent of the Breeds created.

Recessed genetics, in his case, did not mean recessed senses.

They simply meant his animal genetics hadn't yet showed up on a scan. They hadn't found a variable yet that would pinpoint whatever slight anomaly had to be in the genetic string to identify the recessed DNA.

For now he was safe.

Other Breeds could smell nothing but his human genetics, and humans could find nothing but normal Asian-American

DNA. He couldn't hide his scent, but he could alter his scent easily. So far, he hadn't mated a female, but he'd learned young exactly how to please them.

Still, the race to run this woman to ground and have her admit that desire seemed to be the only battle he couldn't find a positive weapon for.

"Does it make you uncomfortable, being different among the Breeds?" she asked as her head tilted inquisitively to the side, the scent of her arousal suddenly peaking with a strength that had him clenching his back teeth. Damn her, had any woman ever grown so hot, so quickly for him?

Watching her with a bit of a crooked smile, Navarro debated for a second telling her the truth. Damn, the decision was one he simply couldn't make.

"Doesn't it make all of us uncomfortable sometimes? When we're different from those around us?" he asked her. And that wasn't a lie. He was different, far different than other Breeds, or humans.

"You're not answering my questions, you're just asking more," she pointed out. "Why do you do that?"

So he wouldn't have to lie to her.

Brushing his fingers over the bruise, his touch light as air, he probed the flesh, feeling the delicacy of it, the internal temperature of the bruise and the mottled feel of the blood beneath the skin.

It went to the bone. No doubt, the bone itself was bruised as well, but nothing was broken, merely excruciatingly tender, and with very little additional pressure, something would break in a second.

"He did a good job on you," Navarro growled, the sound that rumbled in his throat surprising him. "Was it Loki?"

Farce's younger brother was a hothead, despite his

exceptional training in the genetics labs. Still, as Navarro heard it, Loki hadn't been happy that his brother had been killed, and he blamed the Wolf Breeds for the death.

Mica shook her head as she slowly drew the robe back on and held it together rather than belting it. "I haven't seen Loki. No, it was Marx. And he wasn't happy."

Navarro nodded shortly, when he wanted nothing more than to snarl in rage. He would kill Marx himself for that bruise, and the scent of pain mixed with the scent of wounded flesh, once he got his hands on him. Truth be told though, there were a lot of Breeds eager to get their hands on the Coyote Breed.

Hatred was an emotion he tried to never feel. Strong emotion denoted even stronger trouble. What he was beginning to feel for this woman would have been worrisome if it weren't for the fact that he had shown none of the signs of mating heat after kissing her weeks before.

She paced, or rather walked gingerly, to the other side of the room before turning to face him once again. "Is there another bed?" She gestured to the bed he stood beside.

"Sorry, baby, this is it." He grinned back at her. "But don't worry, we shouldn't be here long. Jonas and Stygian are working on a route out of the city straight to Sanctuary. There, we'll have a heli-jet arriving to take us to Haven."

"The heli-jet can't come after us now?"

"They're all on a mission, including Jonas," he answered in an unconcerned voice. "Don't worry, Mica, you'll be protected. Didn't I promise you I'd keep you from harm?"

Mica felt her heart crash in her chest. A quick, hard bounce of emotion that flooded her body with sensitivity and tightened her throat with the strength of it.

"You promised." It was all she could do to whisper the words as the memory of that night washed over her.

Staring back at him, her lips parted, the memory of that kiss sent a wash of furious need shuddering through her.

"You remember that kiss." His voice dropped to a rough rasp, the black of his eyes growing impossibly darker. "You've distanced yourself from it. Why?"

Mica inhaled sharply. "You don't mince words, do you?"

To retreat as he paced closer would have been the same as admitting fear. She'd learned in the years she had been raised around Breeds to never show fear.

It wasn't fear, though. Trepidation maybe.

He stepped closer, his broad chest nearly touching her breasts where the robe covered them. It made her want to breathe deeper, to draw in enough oxygen to clear her senses, enough to make the material covering her breasts press against the hard, muscular contours of his chest as his hand cupped her cheek, his thumb finding the curves of her lips.

Mica froze. Standing still beneath his touch, she felt the rasp of the calloused pad of his thumb against her sensitive lips.

"Silk or satin?" His voice was a hard, graveled tone. "There wasn't enough time to determine before."

"There was enough time for you to shove your tongue in my mouth." She wanted to cap her hand over her mouth, to hold back the words that had already slipped past.

She could feel a flush of embarrassment, a sense of mortification rolling through her. But not enough to pull back or to break his touch.

"Ah now, that sweet tongue is another story. Definitely velvet and silk. Just enough rasp to tempt a man's imagination." His voice dropped as a wash of sexual intent seemed to spread over his expression. "Or a Breed's libido."

Weakness flooded her limbs, a sensual, highly sexual

weakness that threatened to steal even her ability to breathe. The heated flood of her juices spilled along the inner walls of her sex, lubricating her, preparing her for him.

For a Wolf Breed. A man whose humanity was so closely related to the animal whose genetics he shared that one day, one woman would become more than his soul.

One day, he would find his mate.

And nature had proven she wasn't his mate.

She tried to remind herself there was no future here, with this man, this Breed. As his thumb pressed against her lips, parting them, the memory of that fact seemed hazier by the second.

Pleasure swirled through her system, heating her, drawing her deeper into a chaotic world of sensations.

"Please, Navarro." Finding the strength to deny what she sensed awaited her was harder than she had ever imagined it would be. "I know what you are. I know what mating heat is. I know what I will never be to you, and it isn't fair to tempt me to care for you."

She wasn't going to love him. She couldn't allow herself to love him, but she knew it wouldn't take much, it would take very little to cause her to lose every part of her woman's soul to him.

"The world was exploding around us and all I could do was taste you," he growled, his voice rough. "My pack leader could have been in danger, only my mate's safety can supersede his. I never gave him a thought. All I could focus on was your kiss. My genetics are recessed, Mica. Perhaps so recessed that I'll never know what mating is. But I'll be damned if I can walk away from the pleasure I know awaits in your kiss."

Mica stared back at him in shock. A Breed was judged by his loyalty to his mate first. With no mate, he was then judged by his loyalty to his pack, and/or his pack leader, as the two were considered interwoven.

To know he had ignored that basic rule, one that seemed almost genetically coded into the Breeds, for a single kiss, was almost more than she could believe. It was considered worse than a crime in the Breed world, a taboo he had committed for a woman that was not a mate.

He hadn't raced to his pack leader's side to ensure his safety as well as the safety of the leader's mate, the one person whose death would destroy his pack leader and thereby possibly weaken the pack as a whole. And he had done this for a woman he wasn't mated to.

Lips parted, her breathing shallow, Mica stared up at him as he dragged his thumb back from her lips and lowered his head.

It was coming. She could feel it beginning to burn the air around her. She knew what his kiss felt like. What it tasted like. Just that little hint of honey.

His lips brushed against her. A heated rasp of sensation, a precursor to an exquisite pleasure that she knew would capture all her senses.

She felt snagged, bound, unable to fight the pleasure as his lips brushed against hers.

It was insane. She could feel the cautious, wary part of her mind screaming in denial. She should be fighting. She should be pushing away from him. It wasn't as though it could go anywhere, despite his excuses to the contrary where a lack of mating heat was concerned.

She wasn't his mate.

But she could be his lover.

She could experience what she knew for a fact no other female at Haven had experienced. She could be the woman to share his bed. If only for tonight.

His tongue brushed against her lips, probing, easing against the narrow part as he sipped at them, easing her slowly into the exquisite sensations building between them. That subtle hint of honey teased at her senses as he slipped past, his tongue licking against hers.

Mating heat was often described as a taste of cinnamon, or spice. Sometimes it had been referred to as the taste of a summer storm. She'd never heard it described as anything more, even among the Feline Breeds.

This wasn't cinnamon, spice, or a warm rain. It was all male, dark and filled with pleasure. It didn't taste any different than any other kiss she'd ever had, except for that tease of sweetness.

And it was drawing her in.

Her hands flattened against his chest, above the silk of his shirt, before pushing slowly upward, easing around his neck before pushing into the heavy strands of silken hair and holding on tight.

She needed.

She'd ached for him in the past weeks until she'd felt as though she would go insane from the need.

Fantasies kept her distracted. Sleeplessness plagued her. For this.

A low, throttled moan escaped her throat, where she'd hoped to keep it trapped.

As she arched closer, his arm eased around her un-bruised side as his lips and tongue tasted and teased her with unbridled hunger.

The reserve he kept wrapped around himself was easing, breaking away as the fingers of his other hand moved to the front tie of the robe she wore and loosened it easily.

The edges of the thick, soft cloth fell apart, allowing a wash of cool air to ease across her overheated flesh.

A whimpering cry of pleasure filled the air around them as his hand flatted against her belly and with exquisite gentleness began to caress up her torso, until it curved beneath the swollen mound of her breast.

The kiss intensified, growing in heat and in pleasure as the pad of his thumb stroked over the tight, hard bud of her nipple.

Mica jerked her head back, desperate to breathe now, to think, just for a moment.

But he had no intentions of allowing her to find her common sense once again.

Navarro took the opportunity to lower his head to her breast, to swipe his tongue over the painfully sensitive bud.

She hadn't noticed the rough rasp of his tongue as he kissed her. Not this time, not the time before. But as he licked her nipple like a favored treat, she felt it.

Not as rough as a cat's tongue, just a hint of an unusual raspiness over the painfully hard tip that had the hunger for more suddenly tearing through her.

"Navarro. Again." She wanted that lick. She wanted the feel of that roughness against her nipple one more time.

He licked again. Slow, easy, his tongue rubbing against the nerve-laden flesh as the muscles in her stomach tightened and her clit began to throb furiously.

As she arched against his mouth, the press of the steel-hard contour of his thigh inserting itself caused her teeth to clench.

To hold back the pleas.

She wanted to beg him to suck her nipple.

God, would begging help? Would he just do it then? Just part his lips and suck her inside . . .

"Oh yes." The hiss should have shocked her. She was

certain it would later, once the cold light of day and reality intruded upon her once again.

For now, there was only the most exquisite pleasure in the world.

Looking down, she watched. She couldn't help but watch. His black eyes stared up at her, narrowed and glittering with sexual heat as his lips parted and covered the small bud.

A shudder rippled through her body as her fingers clenched in his hair tighter, holding him to her as his tongue swiped over the tip and he began to suck.

"Navarro. Oh God. Yes. Suck me. Suck me harder."

Where had those desperate words come from? The plea, filled with desperation, couldn't have been more shocking. But still, it wasn't shocking enough to pull her out of the heated maelstrom she was being drawn into. A vortex of incredible rapture she was loath to lose.

She couldn't lose it. She wanted more and more.

The feel of his tongue stroking over her nipple with quick little licks had sharp flares of sensation shooting to her womb. His thigh pressed harder against the swollen flesh of her pussy, the hard muscle clenching, the tiny flex against her clit spiking the pleasure rushing through her.

More. She just wanted more.

A throttled groan rasped in his chest as she felt his hand stroking from the curve of her breast to her hip. Sucking her nipple deeper, harder, lighting flares of explosive through each nerve ending, he let his fingers caress from her hip to her thigh.

Mica froze. She could feel it. The threat of a growing, out-of-control rush of sensations began to build inside her.

She could feel it. It was an unending crash and surge

of pleasure so intense there was no hope of escaping. No hope of wanting to escape.

Hell no, she wanted more.

"No. Don't stop." She jerked in his arms as his head lifted, his expression so sexually tight now that she wondered why she wasn't feeling fear.

She should be damned scared. She should be fighting tooth and nail to make herself jerk out of his embrace.

She didn't want a broken heart.

She didn't need a broken heart.

"Navarro." She moaned his name again as she felt his hand stroke to her thigh, his fingertips, calloused and heated, caressing over her sensitive flesh as his hand drew closer to the saturated folds of her pussy.

Oh God, she was so wet. She could feel the slick wetness beginning to spread to her inner thighs.

Slick. Hot.

And if he didn't touch her soon, if he didn't do something, anything to ease the ache, then she just might not be able to survive it.

· CHAPTER 3 ·

"I'm not about to stop." The dark, rich male sex in his voice had her trembling with arousal as the stroke of his fingertips against her thighs had her hips shifting forward, desperate for his touch between her legs.

"No," she whispered again as his fingers eased back.

In the same second his head lowered, that slight rasp on his tongue rubbing against her other nipple, making her realize how neglected it had been, as he began to ease back toward the bed.

"Navarro . . ." She didn't know if she was protesting or begging for more as she stepped with him.

Was she really ready for this? She was dying for it, but could she handle the aftermath?

His gaze lifted as he delivered as gentle, sensation-rich kiss to her nipple and turned her slowly, easing her knees back against the bed.

"I'm not . . ." She couldn't force the words out as he stared back at her.

She wasn't sure of this. She didn't know if this was the right time. If she was ready for it.

She didn't know if she could bear it if he stopped touching her.

Her eyes met his, the conflict raging in her, shaking through her body as she fought to decide which she could bear the least—letting him go or facing the morning if she didn't.

"It's okay, Amaya." The endearment rolled off his lips, a soft, dark drawl that stroked over the indecision tearing her apart. "Just tell me when to stop, when to go slow, whichever you need. It's all for you. Just this." His head lowered, his lips stroking against hers gently. "Just for you."

Her lips parted.

His tongue eased inside, and she welcomed it with a low, breathless moan as she submitted once more to the incredible veil of sensuality he'd wrapped around her.

His lips worked over hers as his fingers returned to her thigh. Petting, stroking, his fingertips rubbed against her flesh as though he knew instinctively that her juices were rushing from her pussy, easing to her thighs, eager to meet him.

Her body was no longer her own. She felt as though it had been overtaken, possessed, her senses now controlled by the slightest touch of his body against her.

His lips moved to her neck, sensual, destructive little flicks of his tongue, his fingertips moving steadily closer to the slick, hot essence of her juices where they collected on the sensitive lips of her pussy.

Weakening, submissive arousal continued to grow inside her. She couldn't make sense of so many sensations or the fact that she couldn't fight them.

His teeth raked against the side of her neck, drawing

a startled, surprised cry of pleasure from her. One hand stroked her back, trailed along her spine, then moved to the back of her thigh, to mere inches from the clenched rise of her ass.

The hand at her thigh moved steadily closer to its ultimate goal as she felt the heated moisture moving lower.

"Navarro, it feels too good," she gasped as her own body betrayed her further.

Her hips jerked forward, the hollow ache clenching the muscles of her sex as her clit throbbed in eager anticipation of his touch.

The ache centered between her thighs was becoming tortured. Her clit was so swollen the ache was painful, the need for touch dragging muted, needy whimpers from her lips that she knew would have her flushing in shame once morning came.

"Can it feel too good, babe?" His tongue licked over her nipple again before he sucked it quickly into his mouth, the immediate, hard suction and firm rasp of his tongue across the nerve-laden bundle causing her nails to bite into his shoulders as she jerked against him.

Oh no, it couldn't feel too good. The pleasure was destroying her though.

Where his touch had been slow and gentle before, the leashed quality of each caress apparent in the tension tightening his body, it was now as though a measure of that restraint had escaped.

Closely clipped, blunt nails scoured a sensually heated trail along her thighs before moving back. Hesitancy was replaced by male hunger, and when his fingers met the thick, slick essence of the juices spreading along the folds of her pussy, Mica lost what little restraint had been holding her back as well.

His thumb raked around the swollen bud of her clit as his head lifted. Black eyes narrowed, his lips appearing swollen, he stared down at her, his expression tight with hunger.

"Say no," he growled. "When you want it to stop, Mica. If you become afraid. If you change your mind at any point, you've only to tell me."

Her lips trembled. She couldn't change her mind. She didn't have the strength.

"I can't. Help me, Navarro." Because she knew this was a mistake, she could feel it, that edge of warning burning in the back of her senses.

His lips tightened as a growl suddenly rumbled hard and deep in his chest.

"Your choice. Not mine."

His fingers slid through the saturated slit of her pussy, the roughened caress further exciting the sensitive nerve endings that lay beneath the swollen folds as he went to his knees in front of her.

She couldn't stand.

As though his kneeling before her, hard hands gripping her hips, his lips brushing against her lower belly, were too much, Mica felt the strength leave her legs.

She eased back, at first only sitting on the bed, her fingers moving to his head, playing with the long, dark strands of his hair as his tongue ran over the swollen mounds of her breasts once again.

"Lie back for me, Mica." His head lifting, his hands gripping her hips to pull her to the edge of the bed, Navarro eased back slowly. "I just want to taste you, sweetheart."

A punch of sensation, hard and vibrant hot, slammed into her womb at the huskily spoken words.

Just taste her?

She eased back, feeling his lips stroke across her

abdomen as his hands pressed against her inner thighs in a silent prompt to part them.

Staring down her body, Mica watched. The way his long hair framed his face, his black eyes, onyx bright as he parted the curl-soaked folds with his hands before his head lowered. Then, with a low, desperate moan, she watched as his head lowered and he delivered a firm, suckling kiss to the tortured, silky wet bud of her clitoris.

A sizzling, erotic firestorm seemed to whip through her, jerking her hips upward, her knees lifting to grip his hips as she arched, desperate to drive her pussy closer to the suckling heat of his mouth.

Burying her hands in his hair as though she could hold him to her, force him to end the torturous pleasure raging through her.

It wasn't supposed to be like this without mating heat, was it?

"Like melted sugar," he spoke against the ultra-sensitive, throbbing bundle of nerves he'd held captive. "I knew your pussy would taste this sweet, Mica."

She tasted sweet? Was that a good thing? Did she really care? Did anything matter but easing the burning need raging through her?

His gaze lifted, the jewel-bright black glittering in his bronze face.

As she watched, her eyes locked with his, his head lowered once again, and then Navarro got serious about the pleasure. Wicked, confident and experienced, his tongue raked in an erotic circular motion around her clit as one hand lifted, the thumb tucking between the soaked folds of flesh to find the entrance to her clenched vagina.

He pressed against the fragile opening, rotated his thumb and his lips covered her clit.

Mica jerked, completely unbalanced by the sensation whipping through her and the tension building inside her. There was no way to stop it, no way to catch her breath or her control.

Her hips arched; the need to get closer, for more, to find the end to the delicious pressure building behind her clit drove her.

Hunger was like a fever raging inside her. She couldn't get enough of him. Enough of his touch, enough of the pressure barely pressing into her pussy, enough of his tongue flickering in ever tightening circles against her clit.

The building, pulsating waves began to burn, to flame, her stomach tightening, her womb clenching as her breath caught.

She could feel the edge, so close, pulling her over, looming like a specter of ecstasy, when suddenly, it was gone.

In a single breath Navarro was off her, the comforter flipping over her even as he jerked her from the bed to the floor.

She wasn't stupid. She'd learned, trained with the Breeds in how to protect herself and how to help any Breed body-guard in her protection.

Without being ordered to do so, Mica rolled to the side of the wall, flipped the comforter back from her face, and stared at the scene before her in shock.

Mica crouched, the large, laser-powered handgun clenched in his hand as the bedroom door flew open.

Cougar stood in the doorway, his gaze narrowed on the room, obviously taking in the fact that she and Navarro had been doing a hell of a lot more than discussing the weather.

"We have company," he growled. "We have a vehicle

waiting for us outside the fire entrance, but we have only seconds to get there before our friends show up. Let's roll."

Before she could move to extricate herself from the comforter, Navarro was jerking it from around her, even as he shoved the thick robe into her hands and grabbed the packs of weapons and supplies he'd thrown to the floor earlier.

Having jerked the robe on, Mica was tying it quickly as Navarro grabbed her hand and began pulling her through the door that opened from the bedroom portion of the suite into the empty hallway.

"Jonas has feelers out in the city," Cougar stated, voice hard as they pushed through the stairwell. "Word came through minutes ago that they'd located us, the name of the hotel and the suite you were in."

"And how the fuck did they find us?" Danger thickened Navarro's voice.

"He hasn't learned anything further." Cougar pushed communications headsets into both their hands as they moved quickly down the stairs.

Mica had trained with them, but she wasn't as good as even the lowest, youngest Breed. She couldn't put that damned headset on and activate it as they rushed down the stairs.

She was aware of Navarro doing it, his hard voice rumbling as he requested Jonas.

The night wasn't over, she thought. It was going to be wet out. Wet and cold, and she didn't have shoes or clothes. She had no defenses, nothing but Navarro to protect her.

And it looked as though whoever was after her was damned serious. They were going against Breeds to take her.

✦   ✦   ✦

"Get her out of town. We'll cover the hotel once you leave and attempt to neutralize them, but we're working blind. We have no idea where they are, what they know, or who they are," Jonas stated as Navarro pulled Mica behind him down the stairwell to the vehicle waiting outside the doors.

"Stygian will follow you until you pass the tunnel, after that you'll be on your own. Get to base two, that's the closest point of safety for her. As soon as we can, we'll have a heli-jet out to you."

Base two being Sanctuary. As Jonas stated, it was the closest, safest point.

"Navarro out." He cut the transmission as they hit the final floor and Cougar moved carefully to the exit door.

Pulling Mica against the wall, Navarro waited, his weapon ready as the door was eased open.

"Clear." A dark, low snarl in the dark.

A Breed's anger was typified by a snarl, a growl, or a rumble of danger. For a Cougar Breed, though, to show any of the three meant the situation had already passed the point of pissing him off.

The door was open just enough to allow them to pass through, and a second later Mica was pushed into the back of the dark SUV, lying full length along the back while Navarro sat imperiously in the upright seat beside her.

"This is ridiculous," she stated as the vehicle pulled away from the hotel in a sedate, unhurried manner. "It would look much better if a couple were sitting up front."

How the hell she had become stuck lying down while he sat like the reigning Breed prince, she hadn't quite figured out.

Navarro snorted at the statement. "The impression is

one of wealth," he informed her. "A driver and his employer in the back. The impression is less suspicious than a couple, especially when they're looking for a woman."

Her lips thinned. "Is Jonas still on link?" She hadn't bothered to pull the communications set on or activate it.

Navarro gave a quick shake of his head. "We're on communication blackout until we reach Sanctuary, except for emergency. Bitching about the riding conditions doesn't constitute an emergency."

She rolled to her side and stared back at him. For all appearances, he wasn't the same Breed that had been between her thighs driving her crazy with pleasure minutes before. And she was obviously not the same woman, because she hadn't so much as ached as she strained toward him. Now her ribs were simply giving her hell. As were the questions that had raged through her mind earlier.

"Why?" she suddenly asked. "Why would they want me so bad they'd risk going against Breeds to capture me?"

CHAPTER 4

It wasn't her they wanted.

Navarro glanced down at her. Her pale face, the soft green of her eyes, the dark blond hair splayed around her, disheveled and falling around her like thousands of tiny ribbons, straight and tempting with their silken sheen.

As beautiful as she was, as intelligent, it wasn't necessarily Mica they wanted. It was Phillip Brandenmore. Somehow, the bastard had managed to escape Sanctuary's secured cells, and for over twelve hours he had been free. Long enough to contact the men he had been working with, long enough to tell them he wasn't dead and where he had been. Long enough that before he was recaptured, he'd managed to create a mess Jonas still hadn't been able to clean up.

That was why they wanted Mica. She was the only weak link within the main hierarchy of the Breed societies. She wasn't a Breed, but she was Cassie Sinclair's best friend and Dash Sinclair's goddaughter.

If they had Mica, then they would try to use her to secure Brandenmore's release, as well as the research he was demanding from the Breeds. Research they didn't have.

In Brandenmore's crazed state, he refused to believe that research didn't exist.

"No answer?" The edge of fear in her voice, the scent of her still-simmering arousal mixed with that fear, had his fingers clenching on the hilt of the weapon he held at the side of his leg.

"It's not a question I can answer," he corrected her. "Jonas doesn't share the details with his enforcers, Mica. Sometimes, he just gives the orders."

That wasn't necessarily the truth. Jonas hadn't told him why, but he hadn't needed to. Navarro had known Mica would be at risk. That was the reason he'd made certain his comm link was tuned to Wyatt's. If it happened, he wanted to know.

"Sometimes he just fucks lives up too," she retorted, anger flashing across her expression now and filling her scent.

God knew he preferred her anger over her fear. For some reason the scent of her fear seemed an affront that threatened to send him into a rage.

He, who had been created and trained to have no emotions period. And for the better part of his life, he'd assumed his creation and his training had been successful.

Until he had laid eyes on her, ten years before, no more than a child herself, facing off against irate young Breed males with nothing more than bravado and fury.

He heard the heavy sigh she tried to hide, and fought to keep from comforting her. Hell, he wanted to pull her into his arms, warm her, ease her, and it simply wasn't possible.

He couldn't risk her being seen. He could risk no suspicion whatsoever that she was in the vehicle, heading for Sanctuary.

"I should have stayed at Haven," she finally said softly.

"Why didn't you?" She would have been safe there. There would have been no way in hell the group searching for her could have reached her inside the main compound protected by the majority of the Wolf Breeds in existence.

Looking down at her, he saw the flash of vulnerability in her gaze, the aching need, the feminine awareness of an attraction she couldn't fight.

"You were there," she said softly.

Navarro turned his head forward, his jaw clenching. He understood what she wasn't saying. It was the same reason he rarely stayed long in Haven when he knew she was there. Because the temptation was simply too great.

The communication link at his ear beeped, signaling an incoming communiqué from Jonas. Lifting his hand, he pretended to adjust the earpiece as he pressed twice, indicating he was listening but would only answer if necessary. Mica hadn't donned the link, and if he could keep her from being more frightened, then he would do just that.

"I take it Mica's in the dark?" Jonas drawled, waited and then continued. "Stygian and Rule are in the vehicle ahead of you, Lawe, myself, Mordecai and Cavalier are coming in behind you. There are reports all roads to Sanctuary are being watched. Enforcers are mobilizing along the way and will be pulling in with us. This is a well-organized, determined group and they're pulling out the stops."

Navarro clenched his teeth and fought back a curse.

"Do we know how many?" he asked. There was no hiding this from her.

Beside him, she was pulling on the earpiece, and the sound of activation clicked across the line.

"Ms. Toler," Jonas said, greeting her presence. "How are you?"

"Cold, hungry and pissed off," she retorted sweetly.

Jonas chuckled. "And none of us can blame you for that. I'll see what I can do to fix the first two; the last, I'm sorry to say, I can do nothing to fix at the moment."

"Unless you're at fault, then it's not your place to fix it," she responded. "It's not your fault, is it, Mr. Wyatt?"

There was more than one sound of amusement across the shared, secured line.

"Not this time," he assured her. "Though I'll see what I can do about the next adventure you're forced to make."

"What's our status?" Navarro cut into the byplay as he reached behind the seat and pulled free the pack he had thrown there earlier.

"Up shit creek," Jonas grunted. "Thankfully, we do have a few paddles. We have teams mobilizing and due to begin meeting us on the other side of the tunnel. By the time we reach the state line, we'll have a fucking convoy moving to Sanctuary, with more waiting ahead of us. We should have over three hundred enforcers, Feline, Wolf and Coyote, on the drive to Buffalo Gap. I rather doubt our friends will attack that."

"Or they could use the opportunity to strike and take out the majority of your first responding enforcers," Mica stated.

"A situation we've considered," Jonas agreed. "Thankfully, we also have two planes in the air, satellite backup, and several other contingency plans at our disposal. Until we have one of the heli-jets available, safe transport is something we can't depend upon. We have you covered though. You'll be safe and sound within hours."

"Who's behind it?" she bit out, the anger, the fear in her voice raw now.

"A subject we'll need to discuss at a later date," Jonas informed her. "Until then, stay low and out of sight. I'll update you if other reports come through."

"With all the security, what's the point in staying low?" she asked, her voice tight.

"That way they're not certain which vehicle to target on the off chance they'll decide to attempt to kill you rather than kidnap you." That was Jonas. Mating sure as hell hadn't taught him to soften the blow, it seemed.

Navarro watched from the corner of his eye as she jerked the link from her head and tossed it across the back of the SUV. For a second, tears glittered in her eyes, before they were quickly covered.

"We'll discuss that later, Jonas," Navarro promised him softly.

"No doubt we will," Jonas sighed. "Look, Wolf, I don't have time for tender feelings here. We're both well aware of the stakes. If we lose her, then we chance losing Cassie for the simple fact the guilt will destroy her. Our enemies know that as well as we do. If they take the girl, then they're effectively kidnapping both women. I think we agree that's not the best scenario for the Breeds at the moment."

Because Jonas would be forced to give up the prize he had stolen months before when he'd captured Phillip Brandenmore and had him secured in Sanctuary's underground cells.

If he had to make a choice between Brandenmore and the pair of Mica and Cassie, then Cassie would win hands down. Her importance ensured Mica's for the simple fact that the two young women were so close.

"We'll have a few things slipped into the vehicle at first opportunity to make her more comfortable," Jonas promised when Navarro refused to comment further. "We'll discuss this more at Sanctuary."

"Bet on it," Navarro stated coolly before disconnecting the link and turning back to Mica.

She was staring at the ceiling of the SUV blankly, obviously distancing herself as much as possible from the entire situation.

She had that habit. He'd watched her do it plenty of times when she'd been forced to Sanctuary or Haven for the sake of Cassie's safety over the years.

"I have to say, he's still an asshole," she sighed, continuing to stare at the ceiling. "I'd rather go to Haven as soon as possible."

"As soon as possible," he agreed. "I'll make the arrangements as soon as one of the heli-jets is back from mission status."

"They need more heli-jets."

And wasn't that the truth.

The fact was, at the moment, there wasn't a damn thing he could do about it though. There were no more heli-jets, and they were stuck on land, driving through the night in an attempt to get her to safety.

As they passed beneath the Hudson River, through the Lincoln Tunnel and into New Jersey, the heavens opened up again with their liquid fury pounding down in driving sheets around the SUV.

Cougar, thankfully, was in his element. The SUV never lost speed, but continued on at a smooth, hard pace as the other Breed sped them toward Sanctuary.

It was the Feline Breed home base, but it was shared with Wolves and Coyotes who were in need. All Breeds inhabited both bases, though they had originally been designated one Feline, the other Wolf.

Mica was as at home in Sanctuary as she was in Haven, though it was Haven she spent the most time in, due to its proximity to her father's home in Colorado.

She wasn't at home in the middle of a rainstorm, racing across an interstate at eighty miles per hour while lying in the back of an SUV, at the mercy of a Wolf Breed and a stubborn Feline with an attitude problem.

And she was staring up at the Wolf as though she had all the trust in the world in him.

That look in her eyes made him want to crawl in the back with her and show her exactly why she shouldn't trust him. There was nothing in the world he wanted more right now than to sink his cock as deep inside her as possible.

Fucking her had become an obsession. It wasn't a heat, thank God, but it was a hell of a lot more than a want. It was a driving need that made his dick so fucking hard it was ready to burst straight from his jeans.

"Cassie warned me not to come home," she sighed into the uneasy silence that had descended in the vehicle. "She said I was going to end up running through the rain." A soft laugh feathered around his senses as he glanced down at her, watching as she stared up at the ceiling of the SUV. "I told her I didn't melt."

He could just imagine that conversation. Cassie rarely understood the many visions she had now that she was maturing. As though her mind no longer wanted to accept the paranormal world that existed around her and often dragged her into its sphere.

"She's not going to be happy with me," she sighed again when he remained quiet.

"She rarely is when you leave." Most Breeds who knew Cassie well knew she was rarely pleased whenever Mica returned to live the life she was trying to build for herself.

It was a life Breeds were often messing with just enough to keep it from growing, or to keep her from drawing away from them.

Navarro wondered if even Mica understood her friend, or whatever needs drove her. Sometimes, Navarro was certain no one had a chance at fully understanding the Wolf/Coyote hybrid Breed or the friend she was so close to. Definitely, there was no Breed capable of it.

But Navarro had found himself considering the second job. There was something about Mica, a mystery he needed to figure out, and it pulled at his training, at the genetics that had gone into his creation.

He was created as a man of many faces. A Breed made to fit any situation, any personality or temperament needed for any mission.

He was a liar. A traitor. A Breed that could never be trusted because he was created to be the ultimate deceiver. He wondered what Mica would think if she knew the genetics that had gone into creating him.

"You're not talking to me," she stated irritably. "I'm not exactly feeling safe and secure here, Navarro. That makes me a little nervous, you know?"

He glanced down at her again, his jaw clenching as he fought against the need to growl.

It was emotion. Emotion was such an unfamiliar sensation that many Breeds could only react to it instinctively. A growl, a snarl, a sound of danger that they had little control over.

"Do you know many Breeds who do talk much?" he asked her quietly, aware of Cougar in the front, well able to sense and scent the emotions swirling behind him.

"Cassie?" There was a note of laughter in her soft voice.

Navarro allowed his lips to quirk. "She does have her moments, doesn't she?"

"There are times you can't shut her up," Mica agreed. "Then times you can't get her to talk if your life depends upon it."

"In other words, a woman?" His brow arched as he looked down at her again, tempting the arousal that pounded between his thighs.

"That isn't nice." She peeked back at him through the veil of her lashes. "At least we talk. Have you tried to get a Breed to talk lately when they wanted to be silent? Talk about mule stubborn. Some of you would put the mule to shame."

"The pot calling the kettle black?" he questioned, holding back the smile he wasn't certain what to do with.

"I'm not in the least stubborn," she said in denial.

She was terrified. He could smell it wrapping around his senses, and the need to alleviate it had his fingers forming fists as he fought against it.

"You are the most stubborn woman I've met," he argued, fighting back the anger.

In the seat ahead of him Cougar made a rumbling Feline sound of displeasure. It was too low for Mica to hear, but Navarro had no problem hearing it. The fear reaching the Feline Breed's senses was abhorrent to him. Women were simply his weakness, and their fear was guaranteed to piss him off.

Perhaps that was what made most Breed males so very different from their human counterparts. They responded to a female's pain and fear, even a female that was not a

Breed. Especially perhaps a female that was not a Breed, because she was even weaker, even less capable of defending herself against predators. That fear and pain seemed to dig into an unnamed animal instinct the Breed males found almost impossible to ignore. Those found to be able to ignore that instinct were rare. Even those Coyotes who still gave their loyalty to their Genetic Council masters were affected by it.

"Oh, wait, you do know Cassie Sinclair, right?" she pointed out.

The false amusement in her voice would have fooled most humans, perhaps even a Breed whose senses truly were recessed.

His weren't recessed though, despite what he'd led her to believe.

"I know Cassie," he answered ruefully, though he didn't grin, he couldn't smile back. It would take far more inner strength than he possessed at the moment to find something to even fake a smile for.

The pain and fear were too much. He wanted nothing more than to pull her to him, to hold her, to remind her that he would give his last breath before he would allow her to be harmed, just as he had promised.

Reaching out, almost without thought, Navarro let his fingertips stroke down her arm with a gentleness he hadn't thought himself capable of.

Her head jerked back from her study of the top of the SUV, widening as she stared back at him.

"I promised to keep you safe." He couldn't pull her into his arms, but he could tell her again and hope that it would help.

"I remember." She nodded slowly.

"I keep my promises."

She licked her lips with a hint of nervousness.

"I know." He could see her breasts rising and falling faster, her gaze darkening with an awareness he hadn't expected.

Then, something dimmed the fear and pain, even the pain that radiated from her very bruised ribs. An emotion he didn't want to scent, one he didn't want to sense swirling around him as it reached out to him, as though begging to be allowed in.

It wasn't love, not yet. It was that tender, exploratory emotion that leads to it, that reaches out so very tentatively to a man from a woman, stroking against the wall that blocked his own emotions.

Psychic tendrils. He could sense them just as any animal could. He could identify it and make the choice to accept or to reject it.

Only humans were unaware of their own extrasensory gifts. They closed their eyes to them once they learned that their adult counterparts refused to accept the gifts.

Animals didn't block them, they didn't deny them. In many ways they communicated with them, letting their senses do for them what man allowed his lips to do. To speak of emotion.

"Don't, Amaya," he whispered, blocking the fragile threads of emotion determined to reach inside him.

"Don't what?" The whisper of emotion paused, as though even subconsciously she knew exactly what he was warning her against.

"I didn't promise I wouldn't break your tender heart, Mica. Protect it from me. Don't let me touch that part of you. Don't let me destroy both of us that way."

It was a warning, and the only one he would give her.

Her lips trembled, and though he expected her to pull

back emotionally, expected the heated warmth of that emotion to recede, still it lingered.

"What do I do, Navarro, if it's already too late for the warning?"

❖   ❖   ❖

Sanctuary was one of the most beautiful prisons in the world, Mica thought the next morning as she stood at the window of her bedroom and stared out into the pristine landscape that surrounded the main house of the Feline pride leader and his prima.

Callan and Merinus Lyons were the reason the world knew about the Breeds. The reason they had been rescued, the reason they were now fighting to hide mating heat and a variety of other secrets that the world would never understand.

Secrets that even Mica didn't know. Genetic experimentation and breakthroughs in such incredible gifts, given to the creatures that weren't wholly human or wholly animal, but were that mysterious in-between that was nothing short of terrifying, fascinating and completely supernatural.

She remembered she'd felt that fascination the moment she'd watched her first television documentary on the rescues. In school, they were taught that the Breeds were humans too, that they were no different than another race or another nationality. But Mica had known otherwise, long before she'd heard the first teacher give the first lecture.

"Mica." A soft knock at the door had her turning from the window to rub at the chill in her arms as the door cracked open.

"I'm awake," Mica called out as Merinus paused outside the door.

"Excellent." Filled with gentleness and an innate compassion that could calm even the most fierce of the Breed personalities, Merinus stepped into the bedroom, stood aside and with a smile allowed a young Breed female to step in with a small serving cart loaded with coffee, two cups and Mica's favorite breakfast.

Her brows lifted. "This is a nice surprise." She smiled back at Merinus gratefully. "Breakfast almost in bed. I've been up for a while."

"That will be all, Janey." Merinus smiled back at the quiet, somber girl.

She wasn't a Lion Breed, nor was she a Wolf; Mica could normally identify them.

Janey gave a barely imperceptible nod before turning and leaving the room.

"I've had to find a way to drag her out of the hole she created for herself in the communal housing," Merinus said softly as Janey left the room. "She loves cooking though, so I've managed to drag her up here and convince her to cook for us."

Merinus was good at that, convincing those around her to do what she wanted them to do. It helped that she always had their best interests at heart.

"She's very shy," Mica agreed.

Merinus glanced back at the door almost thoughtfully. "Yes," she finally said softly. "Janey is very shy."

"She's not a Lion Breed, is she?" Mica asked Merinus as the other woman pushed the cart the short distance to the small table and two chairs that sat next to the window Mica had been standing in front of.

"No, she isn't," Merinus agreed, but then busied herself setting the coffee and breakfast on the table.

"She's not a Wolf or Coyote Breed either," Mica said, probing more deeply as she waited until Merinus finished.

"No, she isn't." Merinus stepped back before taking the seat closest to her and motioning to the other. "Have a seat, Mica."

Mica wanted to roll her eyes, but her respect for Merinus simply wouldn't allow it.

"Is it a secret?" Mica sat down gingerly as Merinus poured their coffee. "A Breed species no one is aware of yet?"

Merinus gave a brief shake of her head. "No, she's no secret, simply rare. Janey's a Bengal, and still very damaged. The Breed location group found her about three years ago in a lab they would have never found if it hadn't been for a tribal hunter in the area that heard the screams one night. He contacted one of the hunters who had been through before and led the group to the area."

"There are still more out there, aren't there?" Mica asked as she sugared and creamed her coffee.

"Unfortunately," Merinus agreed. "Now, let's talk about something else as you eat breakfast. I refuse to allow anyone in the house to discuss anything depressing before I've eaten."

Mica almost grinned. "How are the children doing then?" she asked.

"David's growing up too fast and Erin has her father and every Breed on the place wrapped around her finger," Merinus laughed. "Including her big brother who's convinced she's going to get into trouble the moment she begins walking."

"Knowing her parents, there's no doubt," Mica agreed. "David should have a few years before he really has to worry though."

"Let's hope so." The prima sighed. "Otherwise, Callan may start actually growing gray hair."

They should both have at least a few gray hairs by now,

Mica thought, still astounded by the fact that with their mating, their natural aging was far different than that of humans.

Merinus was nearing forty years old, and she barely looked the twenty-five she had been when she first met Callan.

And Callan, who had already celebrated his fortieth birthday years before, still looked as fit, muscular and in his prime as he had when he first stood in front of a television camera and made his incredible claim of being a Breed.

It was no different than Cassie Sinclair's parents, Dash and Elizabeth, or the other mated couples who were often at Sanctuary and at Haven for long periods of time, if they didn't make their homes there.

Most mates moved immediately to one or the other Breed communities for safety. The world still wasn't a safe place for them, not entirely, especially for mates. There were Council scientists who were well aware of mating heat, as well as the unscrupulous members of the pure blood societies who were becoming desperate to prove to the world that the Breeds were a danger to them.

"Surely there's something we can talk about that isn't completely depressing." Merinus laughed after sipping her coffee. "Callan said Navarro Blaine brought you in last night with Cougar. What do you think of Cougar?" Merinus leaned close, her gaze both curious and amused.

It was that curiosity that had Mica stifling a light laugh. "Matching doesn't work with Breeds," she reminded her. "It's all hormonal, remember?"

Merinus sat back, a look of patently false innocence on her face.

"Mica, I would never attempt to matchmake," she said, lying outrageously.

"I might not be able to smell a lie like your mate can, but

I know you," Mica laughed back at her. "And I know good and damned well you're more than capable of attempting it, and failing quite often."

Merinus hadn't yet seemed to have a success when she attempted to pair either Breeds with each other or human and Breed pairings. It still never worked out, because it wasn't the emotions that mattered.

"Eat your breakfast," Merinus said, chiding her, barely able to hold back her own laughter.

Mica followed her advice as Merinus began to catch her up on everything that had occurred since Mica's last visit to the Feline Breed stronghold the year before. Especially where Jonas, his daughter, mate and sister-in-law were concerned.

"Diane is making his life hell, you can tell it," Merinus related with a very satisfied grin. It was no secret that Jonas often had Merinus threatening to murder him.

She'd dared him to enter into her house on more than one occasion and, whenever possible, had ensured she didn't have to be in his presence for long.

"Why would she want to do that?" Mica was listening in rapt attention. There was simply no soap opera quite so good as Breed gossip.

"Between you and me, I think she does it simply because she's a bit jealous. She had Rachel and Amber to herself whenever she was home. Their entire attention was on her whenever Rachel wasn't working. When she was, Diane had Amber all to herself when she visited. And let me tell you, that is a woman who adores her niece."

"Sounds definitely like jealousy to me," Mica agreed.

Merinus leaned forward confidentially.

"Add that to the fact that Harmony is here as well, with her husband, Lance, and we both know how well she enjoys poking at Jonas. I'm telling you, Mica, we're going to be attempting to push back the war of the Breeds any day now. Harmony and Diane would decimate Jonas."

Mica shook her head. "Rachel won't allow it." Then she thought about it and grinned; it was a fight she would love to see.

Merinus grimaced with good-natured regret. "And isn't that such a shame? I personally think she should simply stand back and allow those two to count coup and let it be done."

Mica shook her head. "Come on, Merinus, Jonas isn't that bad. He's arrogant I'll agree, but he adores all of us."

The glint in Merinus's eye assured Mica that the other woman might consider questioning her sanity.

"You and Cassie always take up for him." Merinus waved her hand dismissively after a moment. "Cassie's influence on you isn't always a good thing, Mica." Merinus shook her finger at her then.

Mica couldn't help but laugh at the admonishment.

"Nothing matters more to him than protecting us," Mica reminded her. "Besides, the pressure he's under right now has to be incredible."

They both sobered then. Merinus looked down, her expression suddenly incredible saddened. "We try to find ways to take his mind off it, I believe," she finally said softly as her gaze lifted. "And it's easy to fall back on past habits to do so. But trust me, Mica, we all know Jonas well. As soon as he's learned what that bastard did to Amber, then he'll be up to his old tricks again."

Mica could only shake her head. "I believe mating and fatherhood will make enough changes to surprise you. Besides, Jonas isn't attempting to hurt anyone. He simply wants to protect everyone."

"In the worst possible ways," Merinus complained. "He'd lock every mate and child in an impenetrable area if possible and close us completely off from the world. We're closed off enough as it is."

And that was more than the truth. For all its beauty, its pristine neatness and sense of activity, as Mica had thought earlier, Sanctuary was little more than a prison. It didn't just keep those who would harm the Breeds and their mates and children out, but it kept the rest of the world out as well. The experiences and socialization that were so important were denied the community in exchange for safety.

"At least the children can go to public school now," Mica pointed out. "That has to be an improvement."

"We have three new teachers." Merinus folded her arms on the table and stared back at Mica somberly. "But I'm beginning to wonder if we simply created more problems in forcing this issue. As far as Callan and Jonas are concerned, protection is barely adequate, though the school board often calls it outrageous, and any Breed, Breed spouse or relative of a Breed spouse is barred from running for the school board for another five years, to ensure changes that aren't beneficial to all the children can't be blocked."

"Hmm," Mica murmured. "Can't you just imagine Jonas or Callan on the school board?" she asked facetiously.

She could, and Mica was very aware of the fact that there wasn't a chance in hell she would want to go head-to-head with one of them.

Merinus winced. "I believe that might be what they were frightened of when that rule was forced upon us, if the letters from the school board were any indication."

No doubt. Mica couldn't help but laugh at that one.

Anyone who met Jonas Wyatt, let alone anyone who dared to come beneath the intent stare of those eerie silver eyes, learned quickly that he wasn't a Breed one wanted to confront.

He was quite simply spooky on a good day. Unless you had grown up getting to know him, as Cassie and Mica had done for the past fifteen or so years.

And Callan, though less terrifying, was definitely not comfortable to be around when one was disagreeing with him.

"Well, if you have no comment on Cougar, what about Navarro? Though personally, I am partial to the Lion Breeds."

No kidding. Mica only shook her head in reply to the prima's preference.

"There's not much known about Navarro," Merinus continued. "Sherra and I were checking into his lab files, and they're amazingly light on information."

That didn't surprise Mica in the least. Wolves were much less prone to allow what few files existed on them into the shared data bank. It seemed that for the most part, the Felines were less concerned about who knew what. Their attitude was that they were badasses, they knew it, and they didn't care who else knew it.

Wolf Breeds on the other hand felt it much better to keep such information in-house. Or preferably to themselves.

"And your matchmaking point is?" Mica asked in amusement.

Merinus frowned back at her. "I'm actually just completely curious. As I said, there's no information available."

"As you said, Wolves' files are amazingly light on information," Mica reminded her. "I've asked, but no one I've talked to seems to be answering."

A little moue of displeasure pouted the other woman's

lips. A charming expression of good-natured displeasure that reminded Mica why she so enjoyed this woman's company and loved her like a favorite aunt.

"So, you're stuck here for a while, as I hear it." Merinus finally stared back at her more seriously.

"Jonas said the heli-jet would be arriving this evening to fly me to Haven." But Jonas wasn't above lying if he felt he needed to.

"And it was supposed to be." Merinus nodded. "But we had a call from Russia. It was needed there immediately, and it may be a few days before they're finished with the extraction. You're safe here, while our enforcers are looking at a tight situation if transportation isn't available."

And that was the final word on it. Mica couldn't argue the need to save enforcers when she was just as protected here as she would be in Haven.

"Have my parents been notified?" She knew her mother and father would be haunting Haven, waiting for her to arrive.

"Your father is screaming because your pack leader Wolfe is refusing to allow him to travel to Sanctuary to bring you back himself. Your mother has petitioned the Lupina, Hope, for help in getting here." She smiled sympathetically. "I've talked to both your parents, as has Callan, and assured them of your safety."

That wouldn't help her father though. She was his only child, his daughter, his princess as he called her. He wouldn't trust anyone to protect her unless he was there himself.

"It's a good thing Cassie and I wear the same size clothing then," she sighed. "At least I'll have something to wear while I'm here."

"I'm sorry about this, Mica," Merinus expressed gently. "But at least you won't feel too homesick. Jonas has ordered Navarro to stay as well. It seems you've acquired a Wolf Breed bodyguard that does more than follow you at a distance. This one was told to stay as close as possible to your ass, if I heard Jonas correctly."

She'd been raised around Breeds, she knew to hold back her reactions, but Mica consoled herself with the fact that everyone slipped sometimes. If the look on Merinus's face was anything to go by as Mica's head jerked up from her coffee, then she had definitely slipped.

Merinus's brow arched. Mica felt herself flush in awareness that she'd been well and truly caught.

Then Merinus smiled. Mica had known the other woman for more than twelve years. Like Cassie, she'd spent vacations at Sanctuary, been hidden there during times of danger, and had gotten to know this family as well as she knew Wolfe and Hope Gunnar, the pack leader and lupina at Haven.

And she knew Merinus could smell interest. And that was all it took to get her matchmaking instincts shifting into overdrive.

"Well, perhaps your visit will be more exciting than we anticipated."

And that was the one thing Mica was both terrified of, as well as looking forward to.

CHAPTER 5

Breeds were trained from childhood to exist on little sleep, to take power naps, eyes open if necessary. Outside of training, they had learned how to set an internal clock while leaving their primal senses open, in order to slip into a deep, healing sleep for as long as possible.

Eight hours. It had been a long time since Navarro had found the time, the ability or the awareness of external security to actually sleep for more than three to four hours.

He was rarely at Haven long enough to lock himself into his small home and simply sleep, and the rest of the time he was either off base on a mission or tracking down the remnants of the Omega lab and the remnants of the Genetics Council now working with the pure blood societies to find a way to destroy the Breeds.

It had been fourteen years since the Breeds had revealed themselves, and still there were those who believed they had no place in the world and no right to be there. That because of their creation, because they were created rather than born, they had no rights to their freedom.

So many years since the revelation of their existence, and still they were fighting that battle.

It was a battle Navarro feared they would never win. A battle he feared would end up seeing them once again in hiding and fighting to simply survive.

Now he was showered and dressing in the fine cotton khaki pants, dress shirt and the comfortable leather boots he preferred when not on mission.

Stylish.

He brushed back the thick, straight black strands of his hair before striding from the large bathroom and through the bedroom, coming to a slow, cautious stop.

His head lifted, his nostrils flaring, as the scent of her reached him, sliding across his senses like the softest caress. Like the stroke of her fingers.

His cock hardened, and damn, just that fast he was so hard it was fucking painful.

He smothered a groan, his hands running through his hair as a hard grimace tightened his lips. This wasn't his day. It wasn't his week, that was obvious. That today—he gave his head a hard shake before quickly running his tongue over his lower teeth.

Okay, no swollen glands.

He wasn't snarling for sex, just on the verge of growling for it.

Not mating. Yet.

Gripping the back of his neck, he wondered what the hell was going on here, but he couldn't seem to stop hungering for her. His ability to take another woman had even dimmed. All interest in having any female but Mica in his bed had deserted him since the night he'd kissed her at Haven more than a month before.

She was out there. She was waiting on him.

His lips quirked, almost in a grin. And she was certain she was going to surprise him. Because she believed his recessed genetics included his sense of smell.

He almost shook his head. He was going to have to tell her the truth soon, but damn if it hadn't been nice, the moment she had relaxed, believing she could be herself with him. That she didn't have to stress out over him sensing her little exaggerations of the truth. Over her body's hot little reaction to him.

Like how hot and wet her pussy got whenever he was around.

How hot it was now.

He wasn't a Breed to ignore such need either.

Continuing his journey through the bedroom, he stepped through the doorway into the comfortable sitting room of the suite, then came to a quick stop, as though surprised.

She wasn't going to be happy when she learned the truth of that supposed recessed sense.

"Now, I'm fairly certain I locked the door." His brow arched as he stared back at her, rather impressed at how comfortable she looked as she lounged in the high-backed chair that sat across from him.

Mica smiled demurely. "I'm really quite adept at picking locks. Did Jonas forget to mention that?"

"He did," he admitted as he tilted his head slightly to the side and watched her with a curious sense of amusement and felt those tendrils of emotion reaching out to him once again.

"I hear you're the big bad bodyguard here." Her smile,

though tentative, was just charming as hell. The Cupid's bow curve of her lips and the gleam of laughter that brightened the green in her golden green eyes transformed her face from incredibly pretty to completely sensual.

"I heard I was *your* big bad bodyguard," he amended, watching her closely as she moved stiffly to her feet, his senses catching the stiffness and pain in her ribs that she refused to give in to.

"That's what I heard too." She tossed him a flirty little smile that had his balls tightening. "And I was told I had to come find you before I could leave the main house. So let's get going, bodyguard of mine."

"And where exactly would we be going?" he asked, moving behind her as he picked up the jacket she had thrown over the chair just inside the door.

Collecting the black leather overcoat he'd retrieved from the locker he maintained in Sanctuary's enforcer quarters, he followed her through the door, closed it and locked it securely as she stood back and watched him.

"Where are we going then?" he asked.

"Dr. Morrey has ordered me to the labs for a checkup," she told him, not in the least pleased by that fact. "Jonas seems to think I should have X-rays, and my parents are having conniptions because I didn't want to. To keep Mom from sobbing on the phone, I promised I'd do it immediately." She headed for the stairs.

"We could take the elevator." Reaching out, he caught her wrist before she could take the first step. "It would be easier on your ribs."

"They're sore, not broken," she informed him, that displeasure turning on him now.

"Sore enough that you willingly took the elevator when we arrived yesterday morning," he reminded her. "The only reason you didn't end up with a broken rib was sheer luck, Mica."

Her lips thinned as she tucked her hair behind her left ear and glanced at the stairs uncomfortably. "If I give in, then it's like admitting they hurt me," she muttered. "I hate that feeling."

It was a feeling he and more than a thousand Breed males could fully relate to. The Council had had enough power over them that even the thought of showing their pain could fill them with fury.

"They're not here to see it," he assured her as he drew her back from the elegant curved staircase of the historic old Southern mansion and led her to the end of the hall where the private elevator was located. "No one is here to see it but me."

He pressed the down button, then waited as the doors slid smoothly open with a soft hiss before he stepped inside. He almost grinned at the encouraging tug he had to give to her wrist.

Once they were closed within the small cubicle, he pushed the button for the medical labs, and restrained the tension that suddenly wanted to enfold him.

Even as it began to whip around him though, he felt those wisps of warmth that were already becoming much too familiar, as they seemed to reach out to him unconsciously, wrapping around him, and he swore, blocking the rising wariness he felt as the elevator began to slide far below the main floor of the house.

She was staring at the elevator doors with a frown, her expression still mutinous. As Navarro watched her through her reflection in the shiny steel of the doors in front of her, he knew those tendrils of emotion, of warmth, radiating from her had to be subconscious.

Was this the reason Dash rushed this young woman to his daughter's side whenever Cassie's life seemed to be spinning out of control? Because the empathy that seemed to be such a natural part of her reached out instinctively to those she cared for?

"I hate elevators," she sighed. "And this one has always been so slow. When is Callan going to update it to one of those nice fast little models that doesn't take all day to reach the labs?"

"I believe he may have mentioned something about hell freezing over the last time Jonas asked that question," Navarro answered ruefully. "You know Callan. He hates changing the interior of the house any more than he has to. He knows all its quirks and all its faults. Says he doesn't want to learn new tricks."

"That is just so wrong." She moved to cross her arms over her breasts, then dropped them to her sides once again with a careful sigh.

"How did they catch you?" It was a question he had avoided asking, uncertain if he really wanted to know the truth of who to begin the killing with.

"A weasel," she finally answered with an edge of self-disgust. "I was working on a story with one of the reporters at the newspaper. The contact I'd been working with left me a message to meet him, said he had some information." She looked up at him with an edge of anger. "I should have known better. They were waiting on me when I stepped into the hall that led to the back exit where I was supposed to meet him."

"Who was your contact?" he asked carefully.

A soft little puff of exasperation met his question. "You really think I'm going to answer that question, Navarro? Don't you think I've been around Breeds long enough to know exactly what happens when someone is dumb enough to cross you? You would run and tattle straight to Dash and Dad, then all hell would rain down on his wea-selly little head. Forget it."

He stared straight ahead. "I promise not to call Dash; I simply need to know who to keep tabs on if we resolve this situation."

"I'm not stupid." The elevator eased its descent, halting as she finished speaking, the doors sliding open smoothly. "You would just kill him yourself."

His jaw clenched. He wanted the name of her contact. The man wasn't a weasel, he was a fucking little mouse and Navarro was the Wolf Breed that was about to go hunting.

The sight that met his eyes as the elevator opened didn't help his mood any. The Wolf Breed assigned to lab secu-rity was one he hadn't expected.

"Mica, it's about time you got down here." Josiah Black stood just outside the elevator, his gray blue eyes narrowed on Mica as she stepped from the elevator. "Dr. Morrey has been waiting most of the morning for you. She actually expected you last night."

"Last night I was dead to the world." Stepping into the steel-lined hallway, she leaned into the gentle hug Josiah gave her, his arms wrapping around her as Navarro sensed, as well as scented, the stink of his arousal.

"It's damned good to see you again, Mica." Josiah's tone, his whole demeanor, was one of tenderness. Some-thing Breeds were not noted for.

Navarro didn't growl, but it was close before she stepped back from the other Breed's hold. He told himself he had more control than that. His fingers didn't form fists, and he didn't jerk her away from the other Breed.

It was all he could do to hold on to that part of his temper though.

Jealousy?

No, not jealousy, he told himself, simply a sense of possession. He hadn't had her yet. All he'd had was that sweet taste of her, and he wanted more. And he'd have her before Josiah had the chance to even begin a seduction.

Stepping carefully between the two of them, Navarro allowed his hand to settle possessively at the small of Mica's back before pressing her forward.

"We'll see you later, Black," Navarro stated dismissively as he ignored the tension that suddenly invaded Mica's muscles.

The fact that she wasn't pleased was impossible to miss. But he'd be damned if he cared. She had no right stepping into another Breed's arms. Hell, no man's arms period but his own.

That was a dangerous sign, and he knew it.

He checked his tongue again, damned confused over the fact that there were no swollen glands. He assured himself that was a good thing too. He was the last Breed that needed to find his mate.

He had too many secrets in his past to allow any woman to ever be comfortable with him, especially a woman such as Mica. She would demand the truth, and God help the lover that dared to lie to her.

"Mica. I'm off the next few days," Josiah told her as he followed behind them. "We could have lunch or something."

The bastard. He knew Mica was already pissed, and he was using it.

"Lunch sounds great, Josiah." Mica stopped, ignoring Navarro's hand on her back as she did so, and turned, and in that flashing instant Navarro felt and scented the pure terror that streaked through her, even as emergency alarms began blaring through the steel-lined, heavily secured underground medical labs.

Their senses, his and Josiah's, had somehow failed them. Almost in slow motion his head lifted; his reflexes, sharp and precise, were still too slow.

There was only a second to throw Mica to the side as the first blast threw Josiah forward into him.

He was aware of Mica's cry as she fell into the wall, Josiah's shock at the feel of the blast of energy that exploded into his back.

How had Brandenmore managed to get his hands on a blaster?

That thought came as Josiah was thrown into him like a ton of bricks. He felt himself going backward as they both fought to avoid the collision, to get to Mica.

And they both failed.

They both left Mica to the savage, insane mercilessness of a man that was no longer a man.

◆   ◆   ◆

Mica swirled around, the agony in her ribs reminiscent of the broken ankle she'd had when she was eighteen and Cassie had all but bullied her into coming into Haven.

That ride from her home to Haven had been so painful she'd cursed Cassie the whole time she was there. Just as she'd cursed her the time she and Cassie had been training in the gym at Haven and she had fallen and cracked the bone in her forearm.

Those earlier misadventures had taught her something though. Years' worth of accident-prone missteps, and Mica was used to having to move when it hurt. She was used to walking with a broken ankle, helping a concussed Cassie through the forest days after Mica had cracked the bone in her arm because a Coyote Breed had managed to slip into Haven to target her.

Cassie had directed her through her forest, and Mica had helped her friend walk as the world had spun around her. She'd supported her when unconsciousness had nearly taken Cassie, and she had prayed enough that she still whispered her prayers through her dreams when she remembered that time in her nightmares.

This wasn't a nightmare though. And she wasn't in the middle of a forest with plenty of room to move around and hide. She was in the middle of a steel-lined hall, floors beneath the earth, with a madman slamming her into the wall as she tried to jerk to the side to escape him.

That didn't keep a cry from escaping her though, or the agony from radiating through her. Even that was diluted, though, by the sheer terror of the creature growling at her ear, his saliva dribbling to the bare skin where her shirt slipped to the edge of her shoulder.

He was supposed to be dead.

Mica tried to dig her nails into the steel-lined wall the side of her face was pressed against, her breathing shallow, knees weak as from the corner of her eye she watched Navarro and Josiah struggle to their feet.

"I know you." The creature snarled at her ear, his fingers biting into the side of her neck, ragged nails trying to tear at her flesh. "You're not supposed to be here, whore." The fingers of his other hand tangled in her hair, jerking her head back until she could see nothing but the twisted, enraged features of a man that was supposed to be dead.

She stared into the flickering red of his brown eyes, gasping for air as spittle dripped to her cheek. As though he couldn't swallow, couldn't contain the poisonous venom in his soul any longer.

"Sorry 'bout that," she gasped. "Just give me a sec here, and I promise I'll leave." She couldn't help it. The words had just slipped out as the blaring alarms echoing through the halls suddenly stopped.

The silence her words were injected into seemed to shatter with the same discordance as the sirens.

"Whore!"

She couldn't hold back the agonizing expulsion of breath, the whimper, the pain too intense to allow enough breath to scream.

She heard a low, dangerous growl, the sound of footsteps, a curse echoing around her as the pain threatened to steal her consciousness.

"Stand down, Navarro!" Jonas's snarl was thick, dangerous, as the feel of the heavy pressure in her ribs had tears spurting from her eyes.

Brandenmore had his arm pressing tight into the tender area, putting a horrible pressure in an area where no pressure could be tolerated.

"Jonas Wyatt." The demented voice made the greeting sound more a curse. "You did this, didn't you, freak? You got her here. You found out I had plans for her."

Plans for her?

"Oh yeah," she gasped, all but writhing in agony. "Fuckup Coyote was your baby?" The bastard Coyote that had all but broken her ribs had to have been taking someone's orders.

"He'll die now," he hissed at her ear. "You got him killed."

Oh yeah, she was going to feel guilty about that one. Next year maybe.

"She's not going to help you, Phillip," Jonas warned him, and Mica wanted to just laugh.

It was the pain, it was making her crazy, and Cassie wasn't here to bitch at because of it.

"Cassie Sinclair's self-proclaimed best friend?" Phillip's snarl sounded like a Breed's. "Your little princess's favorite person, Wyatt? You'd trade your own sire for her."

"No doubt," Jonas drawled with a facade of amusement. "She likes me more."

And wasn't that the damned truth.

"Does she now?" Sardonic, manipulating, Phillip Brandenmore sounded like a monster ready to bite her head off. A chill raced up her spine as the ragged nails caressed her jugular. "Would she like you so well if she knew you'd deliberately allowed her to go home? That you'd been warned she would be targeted?"

"Too late," Mica wheezed. "Already knew."

God, she had to get his arm off her ribs before she blacked out for good. She could barely breathe. This was even worse than having Navarro lying over her in the back of the SUV.

Brandenmore laughed at the pain in her voice. "Did you know I was here, little girl?"

"Nightmares," she gasped.

Brandenmore paused. "What did you say?"

Was there a lessening of the dementia in his tone? In the pressure against her ribs. Oh God, what had she said to make him think? She would surely say it again.

"You're hurting her, Phillip, is that what you want?" Jonas asked then, his voice dropping, softening.

Those ragged nails caressed over her neck again, scraping, feeling as though they were peeling the protective layer of skin from her flesh.

"Do you have nightmares?" He was tense behind her, and so strong. His fingers were clenching in her hair, unclenching, pulling at the tender strands as her knees threatened to buckle.

His nails scraped her flesh again as she blinked against the tears.

She couldn't breathe. She couldn't inhale deeply. Her ribs felt as though a dagger were wedged between them.

"Answer me!" he roared.

Mica whimpered at the pain. She couldn't cry, she couldn't scream. There was no breath for it, the pain screaming through her body.

"Do you have nightmares?"

"Yes," she wheezed, her hands jerking from the wall to the powerful wrists of the creature holding her so effortlessly.

He was Phillip Brandenmore, yet he wasn't.

God, Kita Engalls, his niece, must live in hell knowing what her uncle had become.

"What nightmares do you have?" He seemed to pause, his nails now digging into the flesh of her neck as another little whimper slipped free.

Behind Brandenmore, she could hear Navarro growling. That low, almost unconscious growl Wolf Breeds used when pushed to their last, enraged nerve.

If Bradenmore gave him so much as a single opening, then he would be dead.

"Monsters," she answered, fighting back more tears, fighting back the fear and the panic, the knowledge that she would die if one of the Breeds didn't figure out how to get their hands, or their weapons, on the monster holding her. "Monsters find me."

It was the truth. That was her nightmare, a dream

pulled from the bleak, horrifying night she'd spent lost in the mountains around the ranch her parents had owned in Kansas, just after Cassie and her mother had been there with Dash Sinclair.

She had had a Coyote stalking her, playing with her, assuring her that her father was dead when he hadn't been.

Once again that fear was tearing through her sense.

Navarro. Why hadn't he made a move yet? Why wasn't he saving her?

"I'm the monster," he whispered at her ear, his fingers straightening until they were wrapped around her neck too snugly for comfort.

Her eyes closed for a moment, the labored breathing finally taking its toll as she felt herself weakening.

She was clawing at his fingers, but they didn't loosen.

"You're hurting her, Phillip," Jonas repeated, his voice too calm as she began to struggle, desperate to escape now.

"I want to hurt you," he snarled at her ear.

There were too many sounds. Jonas was suddenly snarling, a snap of fury behind Phillip, Callan's voice suddenly entering the fray as a sharp command. "Mica, stop fighting. If he kills you, his niece Kita will never forgive him."

Kita? Kita wasn't here. Mica had only met Brandenmore's niece once; she was the same niece he had tried to kill when he learned she had mated with a Breed last month.

Behind her, Phillip tensed again, but his hold loosened. His fingers unclenched just enough for her to take a deep breath, to prepare herself.

And then all hell seemed to break loose.

◆   ◆   ◆

Navarro struggled with the order Jonas gave to hold back, to wait. He could sense the insanity inside Phillip Brandenmore, the demented animal born of the Breed serum he'd injected himself with, clawing with feral rage as all semblance of his humanity crashed beneath the wave of fury.

The hunger for blood, for death and vengeance was a dark oil scent, putrid and abrasive to the senses. And it was focused entirely on Mica.

Her pain and fear reached out to Navarro, tendrils of them wrapping around his senses like a scream born of desperation.

Where the wisps of hunger and emotion born of evolving love had warmed and aroused him, this sensation tore across his senses and seemed to awaken the animal slumbering inside him to full, enraged consciousness.

It came to awareness with a suddenness he couldn't have predicted and damn sure hadn't expected. Clawing talons of fury raked across his senses as a furious snarl pulled his lips back from his teeth and had him crouching, preparing to spring.

He would have only one opportunity. If he failed, God forbid, if he didn't take the monster down with that first try, then Mica would pay the cost.

"Stand down!" Jonas snapped, and a distant, almost human part of Navarro recognized and fully ignored the order.

Jonas Wyatt commanded the loyalty of the man, not whatever entity was roused to full, furious life inside him now.

It was similar to what raged inside Phillip Brandenmore, except the animal snarling inside Navarro was a natural part of his genetics, of what made him who and what he was at his core.

A Wolf Breed.

Beside him, he could feel Josiah tensing as well, signaling to Jonas that he would hold Navarro back. There would be no holding him back and they both knew it. They were wasting their time in the attempt.

Josiah might try. And he might find his blood spilling for the effort to keep Navarro from the woman.

Navarro felt her weakening. The scent of her tears shredded the finely weaved bonds that had always held the animal within him in a deep, peaceful slumber.

It hadn't meant to awaken.

It gave its strength and its senses, but not its awareness. The calculated, finely honed instincts that were raging inside Navarro now were different, unusual. They were the animal awakening with a sudden, ravenous hunger for blood.

His lips drew back from his teeth. He felt it. A rumbling sound of fury, low and intense, and it was coming from him when it never had before. Rising from the pit of his stomach, building in his chest, and emitting a low-level sound of such fury that he would have been surprised if he weren't so focused on the sight of Brandenmore's fingers wrapped around Mica's throat.

"I could kill her, Jonas," Brandenmore said placidly, his tone so calm he could have been discussing the weather rather the life of an innocent woman.

The life of Navarro's woman.

That thought would have shocked him ten minutes earlier. Now there was no time for shock, there was no thought of it. There was only the imperative, overwhelming need to save her.

"I hear that animal behind us," Brandenmore chuckled at her ear. "Navarro Blaine. The liar. The deceiver. Do you know"—he caressed her neck again before wrapping his fingers around it once more—"he was created to have no Breed scent. His genetics erased to the deepest level, but for that sense of smell." His fingers tightened. "Hearing."

Further. "Sight." He hissed the words at her ear. "Created to identify and to assassinate any Breed, recessed or hiding. He thought he could outsmart me. That he could defeat me. I helped create him. He can't escape me."

Mica tensed, her breathing ragged as Josiah stepped in front of him.

Navarro was losing the last of the chains that tethered his self-control, that held back the rage rising through him with a force he could no longer control.

"Kita will never forgive you, Brandenmore. Is that what you want?" Jonas warned as though he really cared, as Navarro felt the animal rip free.

"She won't forgive me anyway—"

Brandenmore's fingers tightened, but the sound of Mica's whimper of fear and pain was overshadowed by the enraged snarl that suddenly echoed through the hall.

Josiah was thrown against the wall with a force that stole the air from his lungs and left him collapsing against the floor, wheezing with the agony tearing through his diaphragm as Jonas and Callan rushed for him. They didn't move to stop Navarro; it was too late.

In the space it had taken to make those few steps to the fallen Breed, Brandenmore was screaming in his own agony, his wrists in Navarro's grip as Navarro moved them slowly, slowly from Mica's flesh and took the man to his knees.

Brandenmore was screaming, the sound of his pain like a symphony of vengeance echoing through Navarro's ears as Breeds rushed through the hall. Lawe Justice, Lion Breed, one of two that were called Jonas's right hand, rushed for Mica as she stumbled.

"No!" The sound was primal, animalistic. Navarro threw Brandenmore, slinging him with a strength that broke the monster's wrist with a snap and a howl of agony as he crashed into Lawe and Navarro caught Mica as she went to her knees.

She was breathing.

She was weak, fear still pounding through her, reaction and shock leaving her dazed, confused as she fought to get a bearing on what had happened and the fact that she was no longer in danger.

"I will give my last breath to keep you from harm," he whispered at her ear as he cradled her against his chest and lifted her from the floor. "Did I not promise you this, Amaya?"

Holding her close against his chest, he watched as Jonas, Lawe and Rule struggled to hold the feral Phillip Brandenmore under control until the physician's assistant, Cameron Lucian, could inject him with the sedative created especially for the unique imbalance destroying the man's mind.

Once, Navarro had felt a measure of sympathy for him. Now, his gaze flickering to the woman he held in his arms, watching as she massaged the reddened, scraped flesh of her neck, he felt nothing but a killing fury.

His gaze lifted to Jonas.

"Better to let me kill him now." Hoarse, brutally dark, his voice held the promise of violence. "You'll save us both the trouble of my having to expend resources to do it later."

He didn't make promises he wouldn't give his life to keep. He would kill Brandenmore if that damned drug he injected into himself didn't kill him first.

A Breed hormonal concoction Brandenmore had created to cure the cancer killing him and to stop the aging of his decrepit body.

Instead, he'd created a serum that was slowly rotting his

mind, destroying him, and would very soon, Navarro had heard, kill him.

"Don't make that mistake, Navarro," Jonas warned him. "He's too important to allow that to happen."

A furious snarl of denial snapped through Navarro's teeth. "If the bastard were going to give you the secret to the serum he injected into your child, then he would have already," he retorted. "His mind is so gone now I doubt he remembers what he took, only what he still wants."

"Take that step, and I'll have to kill you," Jonas promised, and like Navarro, he didn't make promises he didn't intend to follow through with. "That man holds my daughter's very life in his hands." A grimace pulled at Jonas's features, then, as pain seemed to explode from him, he pulled it back. The sense of the emotions raging through Jonas sent a chill racing up Navarro's spine. "Attempt to hasten his destruction, and you will be the one that dies."

With an imperious flick of his fingers, Jonas had Brandenmore dragged, weak and incoherent now, back toward whichever cell he was being confined within.

"Let him get loose again," Navarro growled in deadly earnest, "I promise you, I'll be waiting."

Turning, he strode quickly to the turn in the hall, opposite the direction Bradenmore was being dragged, and headed toward the silent, pale Dr. Elyiana Morrey as she watched the scene.

"Take her to the examination room." Her soft, compassionate voice held an edge of weariness, and wariness. "I have to check on Phillip . . ."

"No." Navarro stepped in front of her before she could pass him and commit the ultimate sin of daring to make that bastard more comfortable as Mica fought to breathe,

the scent of her physical pain ripping across his senses. "Mica needs you more. As do I."

He couldn't put it off any longer. The mating tests she ran when Breeds mated would have to be run on his and Mica's blood now. Right now. His behavior was changing too quickly. The signs of mating heat that came with the extreme possessive moodiness were too suspicious.

The glands beneath his tongue weren't swollen. His skin wasn't hypersensitive, but his senses seemed to be remarkably stronger the moment he realized the bastard had put his hands on her.

He wouldn't allow it.

Manipulative and calculating, Brandenmore had been dangerous to the Breeds before he'd ever used them as research to create his fatal brew. If he was dying now, then it was by Navarro's own hand. Brandenmore wouldn't allow the Breeds to ever live in peace, not as long as he was living.

The only answer left was to see him dead.

CHAPTER 6

He lied to her.

Lying on the gurney of the examination room, Mica kept her eyes closed, her arm thrown over her face despite the additional pain the position caused.

Perhaps it was just that time of the month due to arrive early, or the shock and fear of the past few days. She wasn't a weepy woman, but tears were falling from her eyes like a faucet that insisted on dripping.

Except this was silent. It was a misery she couldn't contain and she didn't understand why.

It wasn't as though she hadn't been lied to by someone she loved before. Hell, Cassie was always lying to her over something, or simply not telling her. A lie of omission was no better though. Her parents had lied to her countless times over the years when they had been forced to run for Haven as though the hounds of hell were after them. Of course, that was usually exactly what *had* been after them.

But rather than telling the truth, so many times her parents had assured her they were just long overdue for a visit.

Jonas had lied to her, Wolfe and Callan had lied to her, each time Cassie had been harmed in the past. Those times, Mica had missed the calls Cassie made on a regular basis and had called the two Breed leaders.

To be told Cassie was busy, but she fine.

Studying for exams, she'll call later.

The excuses had been varied, but still they had been lies.

And now Navarro had lied to her.

People lied every day, she knew that. She wasn't a child to agonize and blame her problems on the lies she was told. It was an accepted part of life. Everyone told little white lies, black lies, and all the shades in between. She had even been guilty of it herself.

It was the specific lie that had punched her in the gut though and left her struggling for balance in more ways than the pain from Brandenmore's attack, the shock or the fear of the past two days.

That lie. The statement that his senses were as recessed as his genetics, if his genetics were even recessed, was the one tormenting her, because she had been herself around him. She had believed she didn't have to hide her emotions, her fears or her arousal, from him. She had thought she could simply be a woman in ways she hadn't been able to before.

Regular men had no place in her life; besides the fact she hadn't found one she really liked, the danger associated with her friendships was always something she worried over. After all, Breeds were stronger, tougher, and Council Breeds were merciless and vindictive. If they decided to target her, then a normal man wouldn't have a chance against them.

Just as he wouldn't have when she was attacked two nights before. Someone she cared about would have died, and where would that have left her?

Besides, no one else fascinated her as Navarro did.

And now she was crying over a mistake she should have known better than to make in the first place, and trying to hide it from him, when she knew it was impossible.

The sound of water running disrupted her thoughts for a moment. Dr. Morrey washing her hands, no doubt.

Mica had caught a glimpse of her from the gurney when Navarro first laid her on the table more than an hour earlier.

The doctor's hair was pulled up into the bun Mica remembered it always being styled in, though that mass seemed much thicker than before. Much thicker. From the appearance of it, the doctor's hair would likely fall nearly to the curve of her butt now.

Her brown gaze was more distant, her face thinner and appearing sharper than it had years ago.

She was still a beautiful woman, and still very young, but if you looked deep into her eyes, a person would swear she was much older than she actually was.

Long seconds later the water stopped and the sound of a heavy weight slapping against metal had Mica flinching.

She lowered her arm and glared up at Navarro as the doctor banged around the examination room. She knew Ely, and she knew the confrontation in the hall had upset not just her, but also Jonas, immeasurably.

"You have no idea of the depth of pain you just caused, have you?" Mica asked Navarro, keeping her voice low, but her anger no less forceful.

She hated Breed male arrogance and superiority. They were always so damned certain they were right, that they had all the answers and knew the questions before they were even asked. It was so damned irritating that there were times Mica wondered how Cassie had escaped those irritating habits.

His gaze sharpened on her. "Are you in too much pain to be challenging me at the moment?"

Mica may have been in pain, terrified out of her mind and certain she was drawing her last breath, but she had glimpsed Jonas's face when Brandenmore's death was mentioned. The memory of his expression would haunt her, and it gave her the strength now to do much more than confront Navarro.

When Phillip Brandenmore died, Jonas's hope for learning what his daughter had been injected with would die as well. That had to be hell, never knowing, always fearing from one day to the next that he could lose the child he and his wife Rachel loved so dearly, and had risked so much to save.

"That child means everything to them, Navarro," she reminded him, incensed that he could be so cool. "As long as Brandenmore is alive, then there's a chance. You can't even let them have that without trying to destroy it, can you?"

Mica could hear the doctor working in the background, but she couldn't see her. All she could see was Navarro and the blazing fury burning in his black eyes as she had never seen it before in any other Breed's.

The Breed least likely to feel more than lust, she thought in disbelief. Had she truly once believed that?

"Do you think the fact that it hurts makes it any less the truth?" Furious, rife with the promise of violence, his tone had a dangerous sharp edge of sarcasm now. "Do you think Jonas isn't well aware of that? Or that I should simply stand back and allow him to risk your life, or the lives of anyone else who gets in that bastard's path?"

"And that of course is all that should matter, isn't it?" Mica snapped back. "For God's sake, Navarro, there is such a thing as holding out for that last, great hope. And you're a fine one to let just such a high principle have your back up now, when you lied to me in the worst possible way last night."

"And don't all Breeds know the value of that last, great hope?" Heavy mockery filled his voice. "We lived it daily in those fucking labs, Mica. Tell me, did that last, great hope ever give a damn about us then?"

The pain and the cynicism in that single question had Mica's heart constricting in the knowledge of what the Breeds had suffered there. She knew it, she understood their nightmares, she'd lived with the knowledge of the horror they'd suffered. But still, that was no excuse for his actions, or his threats.

"That doesn't give you the right to ever make such a threat." Knowing that pain, and those nightmares, didn't mean he could make her understand why he had lashed out at Jonas as he had. "You and I both know you'll never lay a hand on Phillip Brandenmore unless you simply have no other choice."

"Oh, there you are wrong." He lowered his head, his palms braced on the gurney as he came over her, his lips pulling back from his teeth in a furious snarl. "Trust me, Mica, if you trust nothing else. If I see him but one more time outside the cell he's to be locked within, without a full team of Breed guards restraining him, then yes, I will kill him, before he has the chance to harm anyone else. Especially a woman. And most especially." He leaned closer. "My woman."

His woman?

"Your woman?" Mica was incensed. Livid. The sheer arrogance in the words, the dominance and utter, contemptible confidence he displayed raked over her pride like nails on a chalkboard. "Not in this lifetime, Wolf," she sneered back at him. "The last I checked, you weren't spilling a mating hormone, and I wasn't on my knees begging for your cock, and Dr. Morrey wasn't being forced to create that vile concoction of hormones for me. Three strikes, Breed. You're out of the running to ever claim me."

For a second. One dangerous, heart-stopping second, the image of Mica on her knees, lips parted and swollen, face flushed as he sank his dick inside the sweet depths of her mouth nearly shattered his control.

He almost reached for her.

His fingers curled into fists as he felt his chest tighten with another of those rumbling little growls he wasn't used to displaying.

Hard, thick, so fully engorged and throbbing in desperation, his cock ached to fuck her lips, to slide in slow and easy, filling her mouth and stretching her lips erotically.

"Navarro!" It was Ely's voice that brought him back from the brink.

The hard, cold command in her voice was pure steel. This room, for examination and testing, was her territory. It was where she ruled. The cavernous underground area was separated by partitions rather than walls, and imprinted with an indelible, invisible mark that made her demand all but impossible to ignore.

"Stand down, Wolf," she ordered firmly. "Jonas, Callan and Kane are awaiting in control room C, where your pack leader is demanding your presence on vid call immediately."

He straightened slowly. She was backing the imperious demand of right of territory with a summons by his pack leader. Again, almost impossible to ignore. But he'd ignored his responsibilities to Wolfe before for this woman lying before him; he could well do it again.

And he would have. It would have been so easy to lean into her, to steal her kiss and force her submission with the pleasure that would wrap around them both and hold them in place with bonds of sheer heated eroticism.

He could have done it so easily, if he weren't staring into her eyes. If he hadn't seen the distress that went beyond anger and physical pain in the incredible depths of her golden green eyes. Like lace, the green surrounded a ring of golden brown, weaving in and out and creating such a unique color she all but mesmerized him when he stared into her eyes.

Instead, he straightened. Slowly.

"I'll be back, Dr. Morrey," he promised her, shocking himself with the hoarseness of his tone. "When I am, you have tests to run."

Ely didn't speak.

He turned his head slowly, staring at her as she stood across the room, shoulders straight, her long dark brown hair pulled back into an intricate braided bun, defining the sharp Feline features of her face and the exotic dark brown eyes.

She was a Lioness ready to defend her charge, and he couldn't blame her. He was certain he wasn't giving the most confidence-inspiring impression at the moment.

She nodded sharply though, her gaze moving to the entrance to the lab as the secured doors slid open.

"Navarro, are you really going to make me look bad by refusing to accompany me down the hall, man?" Lawe Justice stepped into the exam room, and the fact that he seemed uncertain was almost amusing.

"How could I make you look any worse than you make

yourself look, Lawe?" Navarro asked conversationally as the other Breed stepped closer.

Head tilted, his long black hair free around the defined, sculpted planes of his face, Lawe looked as though he'd already been in more than one fight that morning.

Ah yes, Phillip Brandenmore.

Lawe's cheek was scraped with smears of blood on one side of his face, the other one was sporting what was sure to be a beautiful black eye come morning.

Lawe grimaced at the question. "Actually, it probably wouldn't be too damned hard," he grunted. "Come on, man, Wolfe is ready to murder because we're not producing you. He thinks we've gone and massacred one of his favorite enforcers. He and Jonas are presently exchanging insults, which is normal for anyone who talks to Jonas except his mate, but Wolfe has already accused him of having locked you up or buried the body where it couldn't be found. Let's go make a nice little appearance if you don't mind?"

Navarro could hear the exasperation in the other Breed's voice and didn't blame him a bit for it. Politics was alive and well, it seemed. It was just adopting a new member in the form of Lawe perhaps?

More and more Jonas seemed to be sending Lawe into the thick of conflicts and expecting him to actually work miracles.

"It's a good thing for you Dr. Morrey has her own intractable presence," Navarro informed him before nodding back to the doctor.

He turned back to Mica. "I'll see you later."

"Not if I see you first," she muttered. "I'm calling Dad. I'm going home. He can have an army transport here in no time flat—"

He turned on her so quickly it was shocking. His

expression dangerous, the warning in his black eyes almost frightening.

"Do you really want to push me?" There was that growl.

Her eyes widened. She, along with every Breed at Haven, was well aware that Navarro hardly ever growled. Until now.

She gazed back at him suspiciously, uncertain of the strength of determination in the sound. Exactly how far could he be pushed?

Arguing with her would serve no purpose, Navarro decided. Mica being stubborn meant, no matter man or Breed, active measures had to be taken immediately. Besides, he had to get the hell away from her. He couldn't get the image of her sucking his dick out of his mind. Each time he turned to her, it was there, and the hunger for it was only growing.

The pure, melting need to have those silken, pouty lips opening over the engorged crest of his cock was becoming overwhelming at this point.

"Let's go," he ordered Lawe gruffly as he turned away from her, hoping—hell he was praying—she didn't make the mistake of attempting to leave Sanctuary.

Not until he was certain that her trip to Haven—and she would be going to Haven—would be safe.

Striding past the other Breed, he ignored Lawe's smirk and strode to the entrance. The door slid open with a soft hiss, allowing him to leave despite the fact that the last thing he wanted to do was leave her.

"If I didn't know better, I would swear you'd mated her," Lawe commented as he followed him out and the door closed behind them.

"No kidding." Irritated and thrown off balance, he stared straight ahead as he headed for the vid-conference room on the other side of the underground facility.

"No mating scent," Lawe pointed out thoughtfully. "The two of you were aroused, but not to the point of insanity." Amusement laced his voice then. "Damn, seeing you now though, if you were mated, I'd be taking a vacation on the opposite side of the world. You're going to be a mite hard to get along with, aren't you?"

Navarro came to a slow stop before turning to stare at the other man.

"Weren't we trained to be quiet, and unobtrusive?" he asked the other man with grave deliberation.

Lawe's lips twitched. "Sure we were. Doesn't mean we have to allow those bastards the pleasure of thinking they succeeded though. Right?"

Navarro grunted in response. "Contact Ely, tell her I'll be back in the labs once we're finished here."

"You haven't mated her, Navarro." There was no amusement now, only the blunt truth. A truth that oddly enough had the power to piss him the fuck off.

"Mating heat is nothing but a contradiction and an anomaly with each pairing," he reminded Lawe, jaw clenching as he fought against the need to attempt to disprove the very truth the other Breed had stated. "You can't say that definitively at this time."

Lawe shook his head as he propped one hand against the holstered weapon at his side and seemed to contemplate what Navarro realized was a rather weak, desperate argument.

"Hell, I don't have time for this." Turning his back on the Breed, Navarro stalked down the steel-lined corridor, that damned unfamiliar rumble brewing in his chest again.

How many times had he heard that sound from other Breeds and commented mockingly that they were being "drama Breeds"? And now, he could more fully appreciate the almost helpless frustration in being unable to control the sound.

Lawe, Styx and even Wolfe had commented that they envied many of his recessed traits, especially that one. The animalistic responses in the form of the growls and, at odd times, the agonized howls that echoed around Haven hadn't been something Navarro envied the other Breeds for though.

He'd enjoyed his recessed status. He wasn't certain how to feel now that he could sense the animal rising inside him. Now that he could hear it.

The question was, if it hadn't made its appearance because of mating heat, then what exactly was it, and why had it only make itself known now that he was with Mica?

◆   ◆   ◆

Mica stared at the ceiling of the examination room as Dr. Morrey, Ely as she and Cassie had always called her, finished her examination.

"Are your breasts tender or sensitive?" Ely asked as she stood back and stared down at her curiously.

"Only when that damned Wolf is around," she muttered.

She must have managed to catch Ely by surprise, because she could have sworn the doctor's lips twitched with the beginning of a smile.

"I should have the blood and saliva tests completed soon." Ely frowned. "I don't expect a mating though." She inhaled slowly. "There's no scent of it, and no signs of it."

"Don't look so disappointed," Mica chided her in relief. "Can you just imagine being mated to that Breed? He'd make me crazy, Ely."

"They all make all of us crazy," Ely assured her with a tentative smile. "But they're just men, Mica. You should realize that by now. Or do you, like others, still believe that Breeds are all animals?"

"Give me a break, Ely." She almost laughed at the comment. "After all these years do you actually believe I would even consider such a thing?"

It was utterly laughable. She'd practically lived at Haven since the day it had become the Wolf Breed settlement. Before that, she'd spent more time at Sanctuary than she spent at home some years.

Her father had helped Cassie's father, Dash Sinclair, in many of the rescues of the more hidden labs that had created and imprisoned the Breeds.

"I don't know, Mica. You're twenty-five and you've never so much as gone to dinner with one of the male Breeds. Despite the invitations you've received since you moved from your father's home." Ely shrugged briefly, her expression less trusting than it had been before her life was threatened nearly a year before.

"So I'm automatically subconsciously prejudiced against the Breeds, and Breed males in particular?" Well, this was the last thing she had expected from the doctor. One who had known her almost as long as she had known Cassie.

"You're attractive, heterosexual, and you date human males often. It was a natural conclusion to draw." Ely wasn't defending herself, but neither was she backing down.

"Yeah well, most men aren't as arrogant as Breed males, and I don't care much for being ordered around. Breeds like ordering people around, Ely, as you very well know. And think about this one." She eased up on the gurney, swinging her legs over the side gingerly as irritation flared within her. "There are plenty of men in the military who have asked me out and I turn them down as well. Are you going to accuse me of being prejudiced against the military now?"

Ely's chin lifted. There was that Breed arrogance in the other woman. Her nostrils flared as her expression became detached, her normally warm brown eyes emotionally remote.

"Perhaps Jonas's research into your sexuality was faulty. Are you homosexual?" Then her eyes twitched as though on the verge of widening at some horrifying thought. "Are you and Cassie involved sexually rather than simply friends?"

Mica just stared back at Ely, uncertain whether she should be angry or amused.

"Ask Cassie." Mica slid gingerly from the gurney and headed to the bathroom, where she had stored her clothing before donning the paper gown she had been given earlier to wear during the examination.

"Wolf Breeds are possessive, even when they aren't in mating heat," Ely warned her, following behind her slowly until Mica stepped into the dressing room. "Having any lover, even another woman, would be unacceptable to him."

Mica rolled her eyes as she felt the instinctive distancing of her emotions. The subconscious knowledge that she was talking to a Breed with a heightened sense of smell. One created and trained for the science and the medicine she practiced. Mica was aware of the instinctive drawing back and the suppression of her emotions, which would make their scent much more subtle and harder to detect.

Cassie swore that the only time she could be certain of what Mica was feeling was when she slept, when those walls she'd built up over the years were thinner. Not dropped, but not as secure as they were while she was awake.

"Mica, ignoring me doesn't alter the situation." Ely's voice hardened as Mica pulled her clothes on slowly, trying to ignore the pain in her ribs and the tenderness of her muscles as she dressed.

She should have known better than to come down here with Navarro. She should have known better than to come to Ely for the examination period. There was a reason she had always gone to her own human doctor. Because she didn't have to worry about this incessant nosiness the Feline Breeds seemed to possess in much higher levels than Wolves. And Wolves were too damned nosy as far as she was concerned.

Still, she ignored Ely and finished dressing, wondering if there was any way to slip out of the dressing room and bypass the doctor completely.

Had she moved away from the door? Mica was almost too wary to open the door and check. There would be no playing it off if by chance Ely was still standing at the door. What excuse could she give her for simply peeking out and then closing the door firmly once again if she was still out there?

There wasn't one.

She inhaled slowly before releasing the breath and opening the door.

Ely wasn't standing there.

She was across the examination area that had been sectioned off, at one of the machines she used for whatever tests she ran. Vials and bottles of liquids sat at her elbow as she worked while she was recording something on a clipboard.

Ely's head lifted, her expression thoughtful as Mica closed the dressing room door behind her.

"I'll just be going now." A bright smile and a wave over

her shoulder toward the door, Mica indicated her intentions with breezy unconcern as she headed for the exit, intending to escape as quickly as possible.

"Not without an escort." Ely's tone was calm and unconcerned as Mica gripped the handle and tried to pull the door open quickly.

Smothering a curse and a twinge of pain, she turned back to stare across the room at the doctor's back.

"I'm quite certain Phillip Brandenmore is contained now," she said with little hope that it would do her any good.

"I'm sure he is, but those are Jonas's orders, and I tend to try to follow them now." The doctor's voice was carefully calm, almost too controlled.

At times like this, Mica would have loved to have all those Breed senses without actually being a Breed.

"I sent my assistant to the examination room next door to collect blood, saliva and semen samples from Navarro when he's finished with the vid-call from his alpha. I can have Lawe and Rule escort you up to the main house if you like. But just as a warning, unlike previous visits, you'll be confined to the house unless a team can accompany you outside."

Of course she would be. It didn't matter that she had practically been raised at Sanctuary. The recent betrayals by their own kind had damaged the trust they had even in one another, let alone a human they had practically helped raise.

"Lawe and Rule will work fine," she agreed.

Whatever it took to get the hell out of the examination room and away from Ely's too perceptive gaze and probing questions.

Mica watched as Ely lifted her hand to her ear, her fingers obviously activating the communications earbud.

"Lawe, Ms. Toler is requesting an escort to her rooms if you're still available," Ely said. "I'm certain that won't be a problem, but if it is, then he can come to me," she stated a few moments later. She listened, then said, "I'll let her know." She turned her attention to Mica. "Two minutes."

Okay, she might make it two more minutes.

"Lawe seems concerned that Navarro will be upset that you've left." Ely crossed her arms over her breasts as she leaned against the counter and stared back at her.

Maybe she wouldn't make it two more minutes before she became completely pissed off with the lot of them.

"Then Navarro can take it up with me," Mica fumed. "He's not my mate and no one sure as hell made him my boss."

Ely tried to suppress the wince that tugged at her face, Mica could tell she tried damned hard, but Mica caught it.

"What is with the lot of you?" Mica threw her hands up in exasperation before propping them on her hips and confronting Ely directly. "If he were Jonas, I could understand your reluctance to challenge him over anything. Hell, I could even understand with Callan, Wolfe or the Coyote pack leader, Del-Rey. But Navarro? He's just an enforcer, Dr. Morrey. You're acting as though he's a pack leader or something."

"He was once."

Mica wasn't surprised, and that was really troubling. The fact that she wasn't surprised, that Ely hadn't shocked her, should have worried her.

"He obviously still has the attitude, but not the title, but why are you so intimidated? He doesn't have the power without the title."

Ely's lips did twitch then. "Is that what you believe, Mica? That all it takes is the title? Do you believe the Breeds follow blindly?"

She stared back at the scientists silently.

"Mica, to follow a pack leader, a Breed has to have much more than a title. It's the strength, the ability to lead and the strength to lead properly. You may not see it, but I'm damned sure you've sensed it. And other Breeds feel it. As though the acknowledgment of such strength is coded into our DNA." A rueful smile tugged at her lips. "Some things are simply inherent, perhaps?"

Breed head games, she hated them.

"And some things are simply male, but, I'm not going to stand here and argue Breed points with you. I have to do that enough with Cassie when she's deliberating Breed Law and forming arguments for it."

Cassie was like a super genius when forming the legal parameters and arguments for Breed Law. But she still insisted on someone to debate her arguments with, and she never failed to insist on Mica to play devil's advocate.

"Be intimidated, Mica," the Breed doctor warned her confidently. "He's not a typical enforcer any more than he's a typical Breed. Don't make the mistake of believing you can control him as easily as you control Cassie."

A start of surprise jerked through her and she frowned, her lips parting to question the doctor indignantly regarding her statement.

She had never even attempted to control Cassie, and she wouldn't have succeeded if she had. No one controlled Cassie, even her parents.

"Fine, whatever." She gave a hard shrug and saved the anger for later.

She'd been doing that for years. Saving the anger for later. For when there were no damned Breeds around to smell it, become nosy of it and begin suspecting her of betrayal.

She didn't blame them for their paranoia. They'd been betrayed by friends, by those they called family, and by those they trusted their lives to. She simply didn't want to give them a reason to suspect, or a reason to bar her from Haven or Sanctuary and her parents from the safety the two Breed communities provided.

Her family was aligned with the Breeds; they would never be completely safe. Her parents were even discussing selling their ranch and moving into Haven to ensure the family's safety as her father grew older.

She couldn't endanger that. She wouldn't allow herself to endanger it. But if she weren't very very careful with Navarro, then that was exactly what she would do.

CHAPTER 7

Navarro sat on the steel gurney, the thin padding that cushioned the cold metal doing little to obliterate the reminder of the same gurneys once used at the Genetics Council labs. The only exception was the fact that the Council hadn't bothered to pad the steel, or to hang around the labs the bright, childish drawings that Ely had hung on the partitions surrounding her examination area.

He was wrong, the only real resemblance to the labs was the steel gurneys, but that was more than enough. Any reminder of those hellholes was too much for even those Breeds who hadn't suffered the full measure of the scientists', trainers' and guards' brutality.

The one he had been created in, high in the Andes Mountains, had been one of the worst.

His jaw tightened. Deliberately, he tried to push those memories behind him and focus on now and the question of mating heat.

He dressed once again, blood samples, saliva and semen

having been collected, as well as skin and hair scrapings, which contained the minute, all but invisible silken body hair Breeds possessed.

In the thirteen years since Callan Lyons had stood before reporters, his mate Merinus at his side, and revealed the secret experiments that had been going on for more than a century in the creation of the Breeds, mating heat had become an imperative secret.

"Let me get your blood pressure, pulse and a few other readings and we'll be finished," Ely promised as she came toward him, her assistant pushing a lab cart behind her.

He remained still and silent, forcing himself to relax, to accept the electrodes on his chest, at his temples and his back. To hold out his arm for the pressure cuff, and his finger for the heart rate monitor.

"What happened to the simple stuff? Blood, saliva and semen?" He stared down at the cuff, resigned to the fact that to get the answers he wanted, he would have to deal with it. He didn't have to like it. He didn't have to like the memories the tests evoked, but he'd been trained to endure them.

Ely gave a muttered little snort, a sound filled with both frustration as well as resignation. "Evidently you haven't been paying attention to your friends in the past few years, Navarro."

Oh, he had, he just hadn't wanted to admit what he was seeing.

His brow arched as though he was still unaware of that was going on. As though he was going to convince her he'd been living under a rock? It wasn't going to happen.

Her head lifted, her brown eyes so confidently know-ing he almost grinned. She knew he knew, but he wanted confirmation.

All amused knowledge and irritation aside, he knew

what they'd learned in the Andes, knew what he'd read in the files that had been stolen from the labs during the rescues. And he knew that the signs of mating heat from then to now were far different.

"Mating heat is changing," Ely finally revealed, her lips thinning as a hint of fear flashed in her dark brown eyes. "It's becoming very unreliable in its symptoms and progression, as well as its reactions from couple to couple. I don't know what we're looking at anymore, Navarro."

He could hear the hint of weariness, a fear for the future, and a sense of failure in her words.

"Have you managed to decode any of the files we sent from Haven?" In those files were years of research the Council scientists had done on mating heat at the Omega lab. The Omega Research Project had been a fully funded, closely watched project researching the mating heat phenomena that the scientists had been unable to grasp.

The aging delay, the higher human immunity and the strengthening of both body and senses of the human mate had fascinated the scientists, and pushed them to greater heights of depravity and pain than Navarro had seen before, or since. But what had especially fascinated them had been the rare times that they'd seen diseases disappear after a mating. The most notable, and the one that had infuriated the Council the most, had been the young scientist that had escaped with her Coyote mate. The scientist had been diagnosed with terminal cancer just weeks before. The members of the Genetics Council had been desperate to find them and to learn what drove the mating heat, as well as the anomalies that went with it.

"Bits and pieces. We've decoded nothing significant from them, but the files Storme Montague gave us are also giving us nightmares." Ely recorded the readings on blood pressure, heart rate and whatever the hell the electrodes were on his flesh for.

She was trying to avoid the memory of whatever those files had revealed. He'd seen it in Styx Mackenzie several weeks before, when Navarro had come to Sanctuary before heading to New York, just as he'd seen it in both Jonas's and Callan's gazes.

There was something in those files that had left a portal of dark fury raging in each of them, and Navarro knew exactly what it was: Breed mating heat research and the mated couples who had been tortured so severely, so horrendously, that even though they couldn't hear them, every Breed in those labs had sensed them, and raged inside for them.

Navarro stared across the room, ignoring Ely and the quiet assistant working with her as he once again pushed back those memories. He'd been a part of those labs. He'd sensed more than just their rage, their pain. He'd sensed that soul-deep darkness of an inner insanity that came with being unable to stop the destruction of their mate.

"Jenny, could you put a rush on those tests for me?" Ely asked, her tone more reserved as she spoke to the assistant. Suspicious. Ely would never be able to drop her suspicion of anyone who worked with her now.

How she had found the courage to choose another assistant after what the two the year before had attempted to do to her, he wasn't certain. They had nearly killed her, secretly drugged her, forced her to unwittingly do things she would have never done otherwise and nearly destroyed her mind.

She was stronger than he was. She had a new assistant; Navarro had yet to settle in one place, or to make more of a commitment than it took to remain at the Bureau of Breed Affairs as an enforcer.

He stayed on the move, never really making friends,

never allowing himself to acquire anything permanent. It was better that way. It kept the memories at bay, as well as the knowledge that he had failed the most important task of his life.

He'd once been a pack leader. More than a dozen Wolf Breeds and a few Coyote Breed trainers who had secretly turned against the scientists at the Omega lab had been a part of his pack.

He had worked tirelessly, commanded with confidence and strength, and in the end, he had lost the two most valuable members of his pack. He'd lost the very ones he and his pack had fought so hard to protect. He'd lost the couple that had secretly mated beneath the scientist's noses, and their unborn child.

It was a failure he was unable to forgive himself for, and something he'd been unable to forget.

"Perhaps you could give us a bit of your time to help decode some of the files while you're stuck here," Ely finally suggested as the last of the electrodes were removed. "You knew those scientists better than anyone, as well as their codes."

"No one knew those bastards, and their codes are a bitch. I've been studying some of them for years and I still can't make sense of them." Moving from the gurney, Navarro jerked his shirt from the end of the steel medical bed and pulled it on with restrained violence.

He could see Ely from the corner of his eye, her head tilting curiously to the side as she watched him.

"You're not as calm as you've always been. You seem moody, on the edge of violence, and restless. Those aren't Wolf Breed traits."

"They're human traits. I was created to be human, remember?" But the growl brewing in his chest was far from human. "Look, Ely, I'm ready to get the hell out of here—"

"And find Mica?"

He stared back at her silently.

"Her father and Dash are very close friends, aren't they, Navarro? They're loyal to each other. If you mate her, if he learns you've touched her, Dash Sinclair won't be pleased."

"Mike Toler might not understand, but Dash is well aware that nothing can change mating heat. Besides, I don't live my life to suit Dash Sinclair, or his friends."

"Would you live it to suit Mica Toler?" A questioning slant tilted her brows.

Navarro buttoned the shirt slowly before loosening his jeans, tucking the shirt in and neatly refastening the denim material. When he was finished, the fine cotton shirt and well-worn denim felt as comfortable against his flesh as the silk he'd worn at other times.

"What's your point, Ely?" he finally asked, knowing she wouldn't let it go, she wouldn't stop harping at him until she got whatever warning was itching her ass out of her system.

"Human's aren't the only ones who rely on a system of politics," she finally stated. "We have our own system of hierarchies, loyalties and understandings. Do you truly want to risk Dash Sinclair's displeasure for a woman that is not your mate? He wouldn't understand you touching her for any other reason but a mating."

And this was between him and Dash Sinclair. Ely had no say in it either way.

"Do you really want to risk my displeasure by continuing to poke your nose into my affairs?" he grunted testily.

"You seem to be forgetting there are still unwritten rules among the pride as well as the packs," she snapped back at him, the challenge in her tone raising his hackles just enough to piss him off. "Just because we're no longer in the labs doesn't mean that there isn't still a certain code we live by, Navarro. Dash is still your superior—"

"None but Wolfe could make such a claim. Make no mistake, Ely, Dash Sinclair is not my superior, but even more important, neither are you. Hierarchies and politics be damned, Dr. Morrey. I'd highly suggest you pull back." Savage and echoing with strength, his voice may have been low, but Ely recognized the latent command in it if the flicker of her gaze was any indication. Just as Navarro recognized the sudden guarded distance she instantly placed between them as her assistant scurried away.

Hell.

He was forced to restrain a curse. He could feel a growl tearing at his throat to be free, and at the moment, losing the hold he had on it could be more detrimental to his temper than Dr. Morrey could even begin to guess.

Ely's lips thinned, but the angry defiance in her expression and in her eyes eased away, allowing the primal instinct to suppress it to ease back into a relatively guarded position.

Where the hell had that come from? He hadn't felt such an overwhelming need to reinforce his own command since he had been in the labs and he'd been called commander rather than enforcer.

"I'll be at the main house when the tests are completed." Staying here wasn't happening.

"Just because you're a Breed male doesn't mean you have to display your arrogance and sense of worth like a damned banner, Navarro. You *are* still just an enforcer." Exasperation rather than anger filled her tone, but still, the words she used, and the insult behind them, set his teeth on edge.

He stopped in front of her slowly, his head lowering. Just because the confrontation in her tone had disappeared didn't mean her disrespect had.

He knew the moment she caught the scent of the fury raging inside him.

Her eyes widened as she swallowed tightly, the knowledge of his strength as well as her own lack of judgment flickering in her gaze.

"Never speak to me in such a way again." The growl definitely escaped. "I am not one of your pets here to plead for your help, nor will I ever be. I am not a Breed that you can speak to with such disrespect and expect that the memory and/or the guilt of what happened to you in these labs last year would convince me to allow you to take such liberties. I may no longer carry the title of commander, or of pack leader, but what you should well remember, Dr. Morrey, is that dropping those titles was by my choice, and there isn't a Breed alive that would have dared to attempt to force it from me."

Navarro turned sharply on his heel and stalked to the exit, the flames of such hidden anger building in that dark, icy pit he normally kept them locked within. He couldn't afford to lose the precarious control he had been holding on to since the moment he'd realized the danger Mica was in.

Activating the earbud communication device he wore, he snapped the code in for the locks that automatically slid into place each time the door closed.

This time, the locks slid free, allowing Navarro to jerk the door open and stalk through it before easing the heavy steel panel closed behind him.

Hell, ever since that bastard Brandenmore had managed to bribe two Breed physician's assistants to drug and betray Ely, she had had this attitude. She was changing before their eyes, and Navarro knew it greatly worried every Breed that called Sanctuary home.

They had hoped that once she came out of the padded cells that Jonas had been forced to lock her within for her own protection, she would heal. She had been so damned moody and confrontational, though, that even Jonas was having problems with her now. And normally, Jonas was the one person Ely refused to get angry with.

The subject of mating Mica seemed to be a particularly sore one with her, however. Ely seemed insistent on locking mating heat back into the parameters it had once existed within. The fact that nature was dictating its metamorphosis, rather than Ely predicting it, seemed to be throwing her off her game.

Navarro had warned Wolfe it would happen.

He had warned Callan and Merinus it would happen, and no one seemed to want to hear him. He had watched and listened as the scientists at Omega had fought with the conflicting and often confusing phenomena for years.

He knew just enough about it to get himself into trouble as the old saying went. Because he was damned sure nature wasn't finished playing with them yet.

What he did have was more than twenty years in the Omega lab, watching, listening, waiting. He'd spent his time there wisely once he'd matured into adulthood. He'd worked, along with his men, to contact those who could help them, who could provide the needed backup for escape. He'd gathered information, stolen as many files as possible, and fought to help those who mated within his own pack, of which thankfully there were few, to escape.

And through those years he'd listened to the agonized screams of those suffering the research that merciless scientists had conducted without guilt or compassion. Because he hadn't been able to help those that the Council brought in from other labs. There hadn't been a damned thing he could do to rescue them or to ease their plight.

He'd done whatever was possible to save those men and women he could, who were a part of the group he commanded. In the year before the rescues, the entire team had fought to protect one too small young woman and Navarro's second in command, the brother whose blood he shared. Nothing had mattered but hiding the truth of what had happened from the scientists, trainers and Coyote jailors.

He'd raised the girl, and his brother—

For a brief second his eyes closed in agony. He'd raised his brother alongside her, and now both were gone.

Opening his eyes, Navarro punched the button for entry to the secured elevator and waited until control identified him and the doors slid open slowly.

Stepping inside, he clenched his teeth until his jaw ached, suddenly so fucking impatient to find Mica he could barely stand it.

He got like this whenever she was around.

He knew when she arrived at Haven, whether he was told or not. It was as though his body became too sensitive, too aware of her. His response to her had always been confusing, uncertain. Even as a woman/child Mica had had an effect on him that had made him highly uncomfortable. An effect no woman could inspire.

It was the reason he had stayed away from Haven as much as possible, and the reason why he tried to remain indifferent now. When a man realized what he was doing to a woman as gentle as Mica, then it was time to fix it. Or it was time to mate her. And for whatever reason, the remnants of the animal inside him hadn't made the move to claim, and to mark, her as his alone.

Not that he wanted a mate, he assured himself as the elevator dropped him off on the second floor, just around the corner from Mica's suite. He hadn't gone out looking for what other Breeds considered the only consolation to be found for the suffering they'd endured.

And perhaps he even understood it now, because when he was with Mica, a part of him seemed to ease, to find a small measure of peace.

Mating heat. As Ely had said, it was changing, becoming harder to detect, harder to match and harder to treat the females with the hormonal therapy that had been created by the doctor that had helped Callan's pride survive outside the labs all those years.

And Navarro couldn't say that what he was beginning to sense himself wasn't mating heat, because she drew him as no other woman ever had.

And she was there, waiting for him.

He'd wondered if she would be.

She had friends in Sanctuary. She could have been anywhere on the property if she wished.

But she was waiting on him.

His stride slowed until he was pausing at the corner before turning up the hallway.

He closed his eyes. He didn't have a choice. The soft, subtle scent of her, heated and sweet, sent pure silken hunger piercing his senses and hardening his dick in a split second.

He rubbed his tongue against his teeth as he checked the glands beneath his tongue quickly once again.

The mating hormone that all Breed mates created

instilled a hunger, a need for the taste, the touch, the very presence of their mate until the time to conceive had passed. And even then, the need for that mate was high.

It never went away, he'd heard. That need was always fiery, an exquisite burn that wrapped a man in a pleasure so intense it bordered pain.

He didn't imagine mating heat could be much worse than what he was feeling. His hunger for her, even before he had kissed her, was like a fever only building inside him.

Before he realized what he was doing, he moved around the corner of the elevator area and headed to her suite.

Within seconds he was opening the door and stepping into the sitting room, his gaze moving to her, watching as she stared back at him, that sizzling burn reflecting in the warm depth of her eyes.

The arousal that flushed her face and created that subtle sweet scent of a summer rainfall tempted him as nothing else ever had in his life. And she was still furious with him. Anger and arousal building and peaking.

When she had mentioned sucking his dick in that damned examination room, he had nearly lost his mind. Nothing but sinking into the tight, wet heat of her pussy could be better than fucking those pouty lips.

"I knew I should have locked the damned door," she muttered as she uncurled herself from the low chair and rose to her feet. "You can leave the same way you entered."

Dark blond hair fell down her back like a heavy silken ribbon, gold and caramel highlights mixing with softer and darker blonds, sifting together in a rich fall of silk that only nature could create.

"Are you okay?" His gaze jerked to hers, holding the rich, soft golden green color as she crossed her arms over her breasts and faced him with such endearing confrontation that the recessed animal that would normally blink and grow irritated, remained calm inside.

She was no threat to him. Not that Ely had been, but there were ways to counter Ely's aggression that were far different than how he intended to counter Mica's.

"No, Navarro, I'm not okay." She was incensed and highly volatile, and he could practically smell the white-hot heat rolling from her.

"I will remind you I didn't actually lie to you," he pointed out, knowing exactly where this discussion was heading.

Pure disbelief filled the feminine little sneer that curled at her lips. "Navarro, do you really take me for a fool?"

Actually, he didn't, but she didn't seem inclined to believe him, so he merely watched, drawing in her scent with slow, even breaths to hide the fact that he was enjoying every damned second of the heated sweetness.

She fixed a level stare on him, the scorching look in her eyes almost searing his skin as she stared back at him.

Dressed in jeans, a soft, light gray sweater that fell loosely around her hips, and thick white socks on her feet, she looked as threatening as a kitten and so damned sexy he wanted nothing more than to push her against the wall and fuck her until she was screaming in release.

"I don't like that look in your eyes." Her hands went to her hips, her delicate little nostrils flared, and Navarro took a step forward before he could stop himself.

Mica took a step back.

Navarro couldn't help but let a grin tug at the corner of his lips.

"And what is the look in my eyes?" he asked her. He had a pretty good idea.

"I'm not having sex with you." Point-blank and without an ounce of the nervousness he knew she was feeling.

He couldn't see it, he couldn't smell it, much. There was a hint, a second here and there, but she had it covered damned well.

"Aren't you?" If she didn't have sex with him, then he was going to burn to cinders in the middle of her sitting room.

"No, I will not."

+   +   +

Mica had to forcefully restrain the urge to tighten her thighs, to ease the ache in her clit. The delicious, heady burn there was pleasure and a grinding ache. The need to clench her thighs on it was nearly overwhelming.

And there he stood, the reason for it, so damned male, so damned confident. And all she wanted from him was a touch. His hand stroking her, his lips covering hers. Just one more time.

"You're so self-conscious," he said then, pulling her out of the almost inebriated state she had been sinking into at the thought of him touching her.

"You're so crazy." She stepped back again, wishing there was some way to keep him from detecting the smell of her arousal.

"Yes I am. You would be, Mica, if you had any idea how soft your scent is, like silk and roses. And just how fucking hot it makes me."

Her knees went weak. Mica swore they went weak. They wanted to melt and take her right to the carpet beneath her feet.

"A strong breeze makes a Breed horny," she said, scoffing, hating the fact that from what she'd seen, that was close to the truth. They were very highly sexed, and very highly sensual.

Their sex drive was hard and driven, and the men at least had no problem whatsoever going after what they wanted. And the way he was looking at her now? Oh yes, he definitely wanted.

He chuckled at that. A low, wicked sound that had her stomach clenching with a tight, hard punch of sensation. Damn him, she didn't want to feel this. She didn't want to ache like this. The implications were too strong, the hunger was becoming something she knew she should be wary of.

"I would say it takes slightly more than a hard breeze," he murmured as he moved closer.

"And I would say you're simply playing with me." Dropping her hands from her hips, Mica moved away from him, keeping a wary eye on him as she stepped back. "You know there's nothing to this, Navarro. This isn't a mating."

And she should be happy about that. She was happy about that, she assured herself as she watched him carefully.

"Does it have to be a damned mating?" That flash of irritability was unusual enough in him that Mica's gaze sharpened on the pitch-black of his gaze, watching the glimmer of something in those dark centers as he stepped forward again. "I'm sick of hearing about a mating, Mica. It doesn't have to be a mating to make a man want a woman until his dick is spike hard and his balls torturously tight. Does that feel like I'm playing with you?"

His hand moved to the belt of his jeans, jerked it loose, and within seconds he was toeing off the ankle boots he wore and sliding the denim from his body.

Unashamed. She had always known he would never be the least uncomfortable, or the least defensive, in baring his body.

And why should he be? Hard muscle, corded strength,

and the thick, so thick, heavily veined, engorged flesh of his cock spearing out before him as he quickly unbuttoned and shed the white shirt he wore.

Naked, powerful. He was the quintessential male animal, literally. Dark-skinned, as though he had lived his life in the sun, the golden sheen giving the hard muscle beneath a rippling effect as he moved.

Like the dark, powerful Wolf he shared his genetics with, he moved with predatory grace and primal sexuality. Intent glowed in his black eyes and transformed his expression from wickedly sensual to completely sexually dominant. And it should have terrified her.

It had her pussy creaming, her nipples hardening, her womb contracting with a hard, sensual spasm that shouldn't have felt so damned good.

Before she could have moved, even if she had wanted to, before she could have avoided him, he crossed the distance and caught her wrist. She couldn't avoid him; there was no way to guess his intentions until she found her palm cupping the tight sac of his balls. Heated, the silken, tiny hairs that covered the flesh gave it a sensual rasp against her palms.

Weak. Yep, her knees went weak; she might have actually lost her breath as her head jerked back to stare up at him.

She couldn't break away, and she tried. She tried to force her fingers from the intimate position, but instead they curled against the heavy weight, testing, cupping as she fought to hold back a pleasure-filled moan.

"Does that feel like a game, Mica?" His head lowered, his lips brushing against her ear as he spoke. "Feel how hard you make me? Do you know I can't remember ever being this damned hard in my life."

The feel of his breath against the sensitive shell of her ear, the lightest brush of his lips, and she swore her juices were ready to pour from her pussy.

"Don't do this to me." She hated the thought of begging, she really did. "Don't hurt me like this, Navarro."

She was going to pray he had a conscience, that the plea, whispered with a voice roughened by the hunger tearing through her, would force him to back off.

"I would never hurt you," he promised as his lips nuzzled against her ear, the hand lying over her fingers urging her to caress the sensitive flesh as he sent electric thrills of pleasure chasing from the lobe of her ear across her body.

Her nipples hardened to the point that the rasp of her bra over them was an exquisite ache of pleasure. She was ready to clench her thighs, her muscles were tensing in preparation, when he suddenly pushed the heavy width of his thigh between her legs, as one hand cupped her bottom and pulled her closer, tighter against the muscular limb.

"You're not protesting anymore, Amaya." Both hands gripped her rear; they clenched, then with a smooth, powerful motion began grinding her against his thigh, pushing her pussy against her jeans, her clit rasping against the material as the heavy muscles pressed firmly against the swollen folds.

Protest? She was actually supposed to protest this? Oh God, she knew she was supposed to protest it, but she wasn't exactly certain why. She couldn't seem to remember how he was supposed to hurt her.

Her head fell back as he pulled her closer, lifting her against him until her legs wrapped around his hips and she began to tremble in reaction.

Yeah, that was it.

Thick, so thick and hard, his cock pressed against her

jeans, between her thighs. The engorged Wolf Breed cock, wide and powerful, a heated wedge of flesh that she had heard from some of the women in Haven stretched them with such delicious pain it bordered on agony. She could clearly see why. Feel why. She shivered at the prospect of taking him.

"I need you, Mica." Dark, a rough rasp of hunger against her ear, his voice stroked over her senses. "Do you remember how good it was, Amaya, at the hotel? How it hurt to stop?"

Of course she remembered. She would never forget.

"It could be that way again." He was moving. He was moving her, though she wasn't certain where until she felt her rear meet the hard, smooth wood of the buffet that sat at the side of the room.

"The bedroom," she whispered, forcing her eyes open to stare back at him, almost gasping at the sight of the Breed now standing between her spread thighs.

His face was tight, savage with lust; his black eyes gleamed like polished onyx and glowed with a hidden fire. Jaw clenched, his hands gripping her hips, his hair falling around his face, he looked like a sex god rising before her.

And she wanted him. She wanted him until her entire body felt on fire.

She swallowed tightly. "Is it the heat?" Mating heat. Was he her mate and their bodies just hadn't quite caught up yet?

"Not heat." His hands gripped the hem of her sweater.

Mica didn't fight. She couldn't fight.

God, he hadn't even kissed her yet.

Lifting her arms, she let him draw the light cashmere from her body before he tossed it carelessly to the floor beside them. Next, he flicked open the front clasp of her bra, drew it from her and tossed it to the floor as well.

Licking her lips, Mica told herself she wasn't disappointed.

"You'll break my heart." She could already feel the grief beginning to churn inside her. "When you leave me, when you find your mate—"

And those were the last words he allowed her.

CHAPTER 8

Mica had dreamed of Navarro over the years. She'd had fantasies, she'd made up daydreams, and she had imagined every way possible that he could touch her. If there was a touch she hadn't felt, a response she hadn't imagined, or a position that he hadn't taken her in during those fantasies, dreams and daydreams, then Mica couldn't find it in all the years she had been fantasizing.

But this, the way he was making her feel, equal parts erotic courage and sensual fear, she couldn't have imagined she could ever feel anything like this.

She hadn't felt this way the night she had lost her virginity, or at any time before or since.

As Navarro's fingers threaded in her hair and pulled it back, a low moan dug into her chest and her lips parted as his tongue stroked against them.

The nettled sensation of his fingers tugging at her hair sent a wash of echoing pleasure through every nerve ending in her body. Then his tongue pressed past her lips, found her tongue, and stroked.

It was there again, that hint of honey. Just a taste of it, so subtle and light it almost wasn't there. But added to it was a taste that reminded her of a midnight mist in the mountains. It was dark, seductive. It eased into her senses rather than tearing through them. His lips slanted over hers, his tongue stroking, licking, possessing her as Mica felt her hands moving up his chest, to his neck, burying themselves in his hair and holding him to her as though she were terrified he would stop.

She needed this. How could a woman need a kiss as though it were food or drink, if it wasn't mating heat?

Her tongue licked at his again as his stroked over hers. Tightening her lips on it, she could feel his surprise as she suckled at it delicately for the few seconds he allowed her.

From there, the kiss became equally as playful as it was lustful and driven.

With each second that their lips stroked and played, Mica could feel her pussy growing wetter, spilling to the sensitive folds and her swollen clit, moistening her panties.

Her body was preparing itself, knowing what was coming. Knowing the stretch and burn would be eased by the heavy slickness.

Arching against him, she tried to wrap her legs around his hips, add the exquisite pressure of his cock throbbing against her, even if it was separated from her by the denim she wore, for the moment.

Because she knew this was going to happen. After all these years, all the fantasies, all the years of wishing, hoping and fearing, it was going to happen.

His fingers pulled from her hair, causing Mica to give a

low, desperate moan. The sound of it shocked her, almost pulling her from the sensual undercurrents beginning to swirl around them.

The feel of his calloused fingertips stroking against her back stilled the little edge of fear. Lifting to him as much as possible, distantly thanking God and Ely for the shot the doctor had given her for the bruised ribs and the pain they caused. Because the pain wouldn't interfere now. It wouldn't break through the haze of pleasure or affect the swirling hunger.

It allowed her to wrap her arms tighter around his neck, to lift closer to him.

"Navarro—" The protest was torn from her as his lips slid from hers, though she dragged in much needed air, almost gasping as his lips slid to her neck, caressing down the sensitive column and over the reactive flesh of her shoulder. Once he reached the rounded curve, his teeth nipped with a sensual roughness that had her back arching and her breath panting.

Nerve endings sizzled in exquisite delight at the rough rasp of his teeth, her lashes fluttering helplessly as she fought to open her eyes, to find her balance amid the sensations spinning rapidly out of control through her body.

"I love the taste of you." The primal sound of his voice sent wracking chills of pleasure racing up her spine. "So sweet and hot, Mica. You could easily become my addiction."

His addiction, but not his mate.

The flash of pain that clenched her chest was confusing but did little to stifle the rapidly building need burning through her.

She ached for him. She'd been aching for him for years. His lips moved from her shoulder blade, spreading slow, heated kisses and hungry licks along a path that would lead straight to the straining tips of her breasts.

If she could wait long enough for him to complete his journey. The hunger beginning to twist through her threatened all that careful, certain control she'd had over herself for all these years.

"You make me dizzy," she whispered breathlessly as his head lifted, his gaze so dark, so velvet black and intent she felt as though she were sinking inside it.

"Just dizzy, my Mica?" Guttural, rasping with arousal, his voice was deeper, more animalistic than ever before.

Mica let her lashes drift over her eyes as she fought to block out reality, to block out the thought of morning when it came, and Navarro's mate when he found her. To block out the thought of the pain she would feel when she lost him.

She had the moment, the here and now. And here and now he was hers, and he wasn't pulling away from her.

It was going to happen, she could feel it. Navarro was hard, insistent, his entire being centered on having her. She could stop him, but she would be the only one that could do it. And she didn't have the strength to even attempt it. The will to push him away, to have him stop touching her, stop wrapping her in such incredible pleasure, was unthinkable.

She was helpless against him now, needy, as hungry for his touch as he seemed to be for hers.

Her hands moved from his hair as his lips returned to her. His palms cupped the sides of her breasts, the pads of his thumbs raking over the tender tips of her nipples as his lips devoured hers once again. Slanting across hers, his tongue pressing between, possessing her mouth as the subtle sweet taste of honey tempted her senses with a promise of more of its sensual sweetness.

Lost in the rioting sensations rushing through her system, Mica was only barely aware of being lifted against him, the lightest twinge of discomfort in her ribs quickly forgotten as Navarro held her to him and took the few long strides to the opened door of her bedroom.

He broke the kiss as he set her on her feet. They were both panting. It was a good thing the need for air was natural, otherwise Mica didn't know if she could have found the ability to remember how to breathe.

Her fingers were moving instinctively to the bare muscular expanse of his powerful chest. She could feel his heart beating, hard and insistent, almost as fast as her own. He wanted her. He wanted her, when as far as she could ever learn there had never been another woman within Haven that he had wanted, or that he had taken.

His fingers were at the snap of her jeans, releasing them, pushing them over her hips and helping her to remove them.

Mica was on the verge of moaning at the sheer carnal heat that flooded her body, and sent her juices flooding her pussy, as he knelt before her, his head at her lower stomach, his lips stroking across it as Mica stared down at him in dazed fascination.

She'd never felt, never experienced anything so incredibly sexy in her life. She'd never read anything this sexy. Never watched it. She hadn't believed it could exist or that she would ever experience it.

"I didn't fantasize about this," she whispered breathlessly. "I didn't know . . ." Her fingers landed on his shoulders, her nails biting into them as his lips parted and his teeth nipped her flesh sensually.

She couldn't believe it was happening. It seemed that as long as she had known Cassie Sinclair, she had known

Navarro Blaine, and for almost that long, she had been waiting breathlessly for this touch.

"Spread your legs, Mica." His hand pressed between her thighs, pushing at the inner muscle of one as she trembled before him.

"I don't know if I can stand up." Her knees were weak, tremors of pleasure racing through her and stealing her strength.

"I'll hold you up, baby." His fingers brushed against the swollen, slick curves of her pussy as Mica heard the pleading, needy little groan torn from her own throat.

Spreading her legs, she watched, barely daring to breathe now as electric, burning sensation sizzled everywhere he touched her. Parting the saturated curls that covered her pussy, his fingers stroked through the narrow slit, caressing, stroking down, then up and around her swollen clit, before easing back to the entrance of her pussy once again. Once there, he rimmed the opening, pressing and rubbing against it firmly.

"I'm going to push my fingers inside you, Mica." He teased at the opening as her gaze lifted to his, watching the black of his eyes as he stared back at her. "I want to fuck you with my fingers, baby. I need you ready. I need your snug little pussy so hungry that the pleasure borders pain, and taking me will be easier."

Her hips tilted forward, the unashamed pleading in the act bringing a rumbling growl from him as his fingers began to ease inside her.

She wasn't going to be able to stand. She couldn't. She could feel her legs weakening, becoming rubbery as she fought to stand in place, to take as much pleasure as possible.

As each digit pushed slowly forward, the delicate inner

muscles stretched and her juices spilled to his fingers, the pleasure stealing the strength from her body.

She was leaning heavily against him now, eyes closed, the whimpering cries tearing from her throat as her nails bit into his shoulders.

His fingers, the pads a bit calloused, the fingers lean and strong, forged inside her as his head bent, his tongue licking the tender flesh just above her mound.

His fingers pushed farther inside her, a deliberately dominative, quick thrust that filled her halfway and arched her back as a cry tore from her. His fingertips rubbed, caressed and set off a series of internal explosions of pleasure so intense she swore she would melt right there onto the floor.

Exquisite agony raced through her, tightening her pussy around his fingers, the muscles fluttering around them as convulsive orgasmic clenches overtook the snug inner muscles.

She could feel the moisture gathering and spreading in the narrow channel as he stroked his fingers inside, spreading her flesh, easing it, stretching it with slow, burning intensity.

Her hips writhed, thrusting against his fingers with slow, rolling movements, her breath panting from her chest.

"So sweet and tight." His lips brushed against her lower stomach as he worked his fingers deeper inside her, scissoring them, stretching her with an exquisite, unbearable pleasure pain.

His tongue licked over her lower stomach before laying in a series of hard, hot kisses that moved steadily lower. His fingers worked inside her pussy, scissoring, thrusting, his wrists twisting as he fucked her with smooth, delicious strokes that built the flames burning across her nerve endings.

"You're killing me," she cried out desperately as a firm

thrust separated and stretched her before his wrist twisted, screwing his fingers inside her and sending a burst of ecstatic pleasure surging through her system.

Rather than answering her, his head went lower, lips parting, and as she watched in amazement, his tongue pressed against her clit before flickering around it with quick, destructive strokes.

Digging her fingers into the heavy strands of hair Mica held on tight and pressed closer, gasping for breath as she tried to hold him nearer to her. To force his lips to her clit rather than his teasing tongue, as she fought to stay upright, to breathe, to maintain sanity.

Oh God, it was so good. The heated moisture of his tongue, the threat of his lips as he laid a perfect, suckling kiss to the sensitive bud.

The pressure sent shards of erotic sensation racing through her and clenching her womb in the desperate need to come. His fingers speared inside her pussy, stretched and stroked until that need was like a wildfire whipping across her flesh.

Her inner muscles flexed convulsively as the need throbbed through her. Her flesh was too sensitive, the need too intense, as hunger tore through her mind.

"I need you," she panted, forcing her eyes open to stare down at him. "Please, Navarro, let me come. I need to come."

That need was burning inside her. It flamed through her pussy, tightened her clit and clenched her womb as she strained to fall from the edge of the exquisite tension she seemed poised on.

He stared up at her, heavy, thick black lashes shadowing his midnight eyes as he let her watch. Watch his tongue as he licked at her clit with an edge of restrained rapacious hunger and a growl seemed to rumble in his chest.

Firm, latently powerful, his fingers moved inside the violently sensitive flesh of her vagina, working deeper, stretching her sensually as those wicked black eyes stared back up at her, watching as she cried out helplessly and finally felt her legs lose the strength needed to hold her on her feet.

Navarro caught her, one powerful arm wrapping around her hips as he lowered her slowly, so slowly, until she was straddling his bare thighs, the engorged, overly thick length of his cock pressed between them.

Helpless against the overwhelming hunger beating at her, Mica ground her pussy against the heavy shaft as Navarro gripped the back of her head, holding it still as his lips covered hers.

The taste of honey was an aphrodisiac to her dazed senses as she felt his hands grip her ass and he rose to his feet in a powerful surge of strength.

Her knees gripped his hips, her lips parting beneath his to accept the thrust of his tongue between them.

Need became a desperate hunger raging through her system as her skin felt flushed, heat surging through her as her juices wept from her pussy to coat the hardened shaft grinding against it.

Mica felt her back meet the bed, Navarro rising over her, his lips eating at hers as his tongue licked and stroked, spreading the heated almost taste of honey to her tongue.

And she wanted more than that almost taste. More than his cock grinding against her mound. More than just his kisses.

As his tongue thrust between her lips once again, Mica found her lips closing on it, sucking it inside as Navarro froze against her for her a heart-stopping second.

But it was there. That taste, so beguiling, mixed with

the heat and surging adrenaline born of a hunger she could no longer control. As she sucked at his tongue, that taste seemed to spread through her system, still light, with a heated nuance that had her moaning into his kiss as he began moving once again.

His hips shifted, the hard shaft dragging across her sensitized clit as the engorged crest raked over the swollen, slick folds.

He tucked against the entrance as Mica shifted her knees and felt the blooming ache, a sense of wantonness that filled her veins as the sensation of heat began to build.

Navarro tensed further, a muttered groan dragged from his chest; she could have sworn she heard a growl, a desperate rejection of something as his body jerked against her.

Then her breath caught. That heat that had begun at the entrance seemed to fill her vagina, at first bringing almost a sense of numbness before it became so sensitive, the nerve endings so incredibly acute, that nothing mattered but easing the internal ache building out of control.

"Mica. I'm sorry." The words whispered at her ear made no sense, but a second later, the feel of that heat suffusing her again, the feel of his cock flexing, thrusting into her, almost had her pausing.

She should be frightened of something. Wary. But there was too much pleasure, too much need. Her knees tightened at his hips, her hips shifting, pressing against him until the engorged head wedged inside the tender opening and sent pulses of exultant pleasure raging through her pussy.

The impression of heat surging through her, the flex of the wide head of his cock, the feel of the iron-hot flesh working inside her, rasping over the hypersensitive nerve endings, sent her senses spinning. Desperation was building inside her, incoherent pleas escaping her lips as she writhed beneath him.

"Mica." Hard, rasping, the growl that left his throat was primal, hungry. "Hold on to me, Amaya."

She was holding as tight as possible. Arching forward, she worked her pussy against the hard stalk of flesh beginning to penetrate her.

Then he was moving, his hips shifting, rotating, screwing the throbbing flesh deeper inside her as elation surged through her.

If pleasure could be violent, painful, then that's what this was. Each sensation was so sharp, so incredibly vibrant she wondered if she could bear it.

Each thrust stretched her farther, his hardened flesh raking over the tender muscle as he worked his cock deeper. The impalement was agony and bliss. Each stroke, each thrust that lodged him farther inside her sent her senses spinning further out of control.

"Please, please." She could barely breathe; there was no thought, no reality but the feel of him taking her now. "More, Navarro. Oh God, I need you."

She couldn't get enough. He wasn't deep enough inside her. She wanted more of him. Harder. Hotter.

The next thrust speared to the center of her and dragged a breathless, agonized cry from her throat.

She could feel his cock throbbing, heat spilling into her, and a distant part of her realized, knew what was happening. The unthinkable.

Her fingers clenched against the powerful muscles of his biceps, nails digging in as her hips writhed beneath him, her knees tightening further against his hardened thighs as he began to thrust inside her.

Spearing into her, the wide shaft of his cock began stroking, surging over tissue and nerve endings that screamed out for release. The burning ache that centered beneath her clit seemed impossible to sate, to satisfy. Each stroke only intensified the need, intensified the fire burning in the pit of her womb.

She couldn't get enough of him.

She wanted to scream in desperation, in a hunger that tore at her senses and had her thrusting desperately against him.

His hand locked onto her hips, and still she fought his hold.

She couldn't get close enough. He wasn't thrusting hard enough.

"Still," he commanded, his voice rough, so primal it stroked against her senses with the same reaction as to his cock stroking inside her pussy. It pushed her higher, yet she couldn't seem to fly, couldn't seem to find the release she was suddenly craving like an addict craving a fix.

She ignored the order to stay still, to simply take. Her hips jerked against his, fought his hold until suddenly, he jerked back from her.

"No!" She was reaching for him, her eyes flaring open to stare up at the savagely hewn expression on his face as he suddenly gripped her shoulders, pulled her to a sitting position, then flipped her to her stomach.

Before she could fight him, his knees spread her thighs, his hands jerking her hips to alignment with the thick penetration of his cock as he pushed inside her with a desperate thrust.

Mica's back bowed, a wail of pleasure tearing past her lips as she thrust back to him, following the hard grip of his hands at her hips.

She felt him cover over her, blanketing her with primitive possession as his cock shafted hard and deep inside her. His hips rotated, his cock stretching her farther, stroking desperate nerve endings closer now, pushing her higher, harder, until finally, she felt herself shattering and falling over the edge of rapture with explosive force.

The detonation tightened through her before the upheaval ruptured her senses and left only the barest minimum of thought for the sudden, agonizing, rapturous explosion that surged through her again, pushed higher harder, and stretched the delicate muscles of her pussy wider.

The pleasure destroyed her. But she knew, once her senses returned, it would be more than the pleasure that had suddenly changed her life.

◆　◆　◆

Navarro could feel the rejection of everything he knew was happening, but pulling away from her was impossible. Breaking the connection he could feel building between them wasn't happening.

The animal had awakened inside him, and there was no pushing it back to its corner to sleep again.

He'd felt the first pulses of pre-cum, the silky fluid that ejaculated into her at the first touch of the heat of her slick pussy against his cock head. As though the animal had known instinctively the moment when his cock was aligned with her, when the perfect opportunity had arisen to shock Navarro with the primal impulse.

The fluid enabled the delicate tissue of the feminine flesh to ease, stretch, to grow hungrier, to need more, to accept what would come when Navarro achieved his own release.

Still, he'd fought it. With everything inside him he'd

fought what was coming, a part of him begging, praying it wasn't happening, though he knew it was. And still, another part of him rejoiced.

Now, lying over her, the feel of his cock pulsing in release, the heavy, swollen Wolf Breed knot throbbing in the delicate, tight clench of the heavy muscles surrounding it, he could feel his Mica, his mate, her flesh rippling, sucking at the primal swelling in bliss as her climax shuddered through her exhausted body once again.

But even more shocking, more troubling, was his inability to pull his head back, to release the flesh of her shoulder from his teeth, despite the fact that there were no canines to pierce it. Still, he bit her hard, his tongue laving the area he held as hard shudders continued to jerk through his body.

For the first time in his life he was experiencing what other Breeds took for granted. The animal rising instinctively inside him, locking into him, seeing through his eyes, tasting with his tongue and living through each sensation, each scent, each sight Navarro experienced.

Like another entity sharing his body, one he wasn't familiar or wholly comfortable with. One that he could sense would refuse to ever become recessed again.

His body bowed as another wave of violent pleasure swept through him.

He'd never felt another resembling this. He'd never known such complete pleasure, such heady satiation. He wanted to lie here forever, locked to her, lost within the waves of pleasure that washed over him again and again.

He couldn't imagine ever being without it, being without her. He couldn't imagine a moment, so much as breath being taken, without the scent of Mica infusing it.

And he knew the dangers of that. He knew the folly of

what his body had just forced on both of them. He knew exactly what it meant, not just to him but also to several other Breeds within both Sanctuary as well as Haven.

He knew.

And he prayed as he had never prayed before that this time, he wouldn't fail.

CHAPTER 9

Mated.

She was mated by a recessed Breed that had shown absolutely no signs, not a single one, that he was even on the verge of mating.

But there wasn't a doubt in her mind that it had happened.

There was no way she could deny it, even if she wanted to, not after she'd felt him lock inside her, his already wide shaft thickening farther halfway up the heavy organ and fitting firmly inside the narrowest part of her sex.

And the moment he'd been able to remove himself, he'd come right out of the bed, dressed and stomped out of the bedroom.

So much for whispering sweet nothings, cuddling and doing all that growling and chest thumping "my mate" crap like she'd heard happened with other Breeds and their mates.

Wasn't it just her luck?

Her mate was out stomping, cursing and railing at fate because he had a mate.

Yep, it was just her luck. She should have expected it.

Rising from the bed, Mica moved to the attached bathroom, took another shower, dressed in jeans and a T-shirt and left the bedroom with a sense of resignation.

The anger was there, but she had spent so many years hiding her emotions that she barely felt it as she descended the curved staircase to the wide marble foyer.

Night was easing over the mountains, the cold rush of the evening air moaning outside the wide double front doors as it heralded a storm.

Rain or snow? At this time of the year, it could be either or a mix of both.

She shivered at the thought of any of those options. The thought of rain only reminded her of that mad dash through the dark streets of New York City, while the thought of snow in the mountains made her wish she had simply stayed at her parents' ranch in Colorado rather than returning to her job at the paper after she finished at Haven.

"There you are." As Mica stepped from the stairs, Merinus stepped from the kitchen entrance farther along the foyer.

Still slender despite the two children she'd had, and the fact that she had passed her fortieth birthday, Merinus still looked the same as she had the day she stood in front of those journalists by Callan's side while he told the world what he was, and what he was created to be.

"Yep, here I am." Mica pushed her hands into the pockets of her jeans. "It's quiet here today."

"There's a storm moving in." Merinus's smile was quiet, confident.

She was the pride leader's wife and mate, the prima they called her, and she carried her title well.

Moving toward her, Mica suddenly felt self-conscious, wondering if Navarro had spoken to this woman after he left, if she knew what had happened in the bedroom Mica had slept in whenever she visited, since she was a child.

"Come on into the kitchen. There's coffee and chocolate cake. I've been indulging today."

Turning, Merinus led the way back into the spacious, cheery kitchen, the jeans and sweatshirt she wore looking incredibly comfortable when paired with the thick, white socks on her feet.

Stepping into the kitchen, Mica almost breathed a sigh of relief at the fact that Merinus was the only one there.

"Cassie called earlier," Merinus stated as she poured coffee and slid a cup across the wide center island, as Mica took a seat on one of the high bar stools in front of it.

"I lost my cell phone," Mica sighed. "I'll have to see if Jonas will get me another."

The Breed-secured sat phone she carried had been in her purse along with her ID, cash and credit cards.

"Cassie told me to assure you she was taking care of things in regards to cards and so forth," Merinus stated as she pushed the cake across the counter. "She assumed that since the sat phone was disconnected that something had happened."

Mica gave a short nod. It was an agreement they had. If the other even suspected that somehow one of them had been hurt, robbed or taken, then they'd take the precaution of canceling all credit cards. The last thing they wanted, or needed, was some bastards cashing in after they'd possibly been killed by one of them.

"Callan, Jonas, Kane and Navarro are at communications headquarters going over mission stats," Merinus told her. As though she needed to know, Mica thought resentfully as she dug into the cake.

"I just need to know when the heli-jet will be here to take me home, Prima." Mica stared back at the other woman questioningly. "As much as I enjoy Sanctuary, I think I'd feel better if I were at my parents' ranch."

"Your parents are at Haven, Mica," Merinus revealed gently. "The ranch was hit at the same time you were targeted in the city. Your father and mother were, thankfully, not at home at the time."

Mica inhaled slowly, carefully. "Does Jonas know why they were targeted? Does he know why I was targeted?"

Merinus gave a quick shake of her head. "I know he's working on it. I promise, we're doing everything we can to figure this out and to get you safely home. But the key word is safely. We're not certain that even the heli-jet would be a secured means of transportation at the moment. Until we know for certain, it's not a chance we want to take."

Mica took another bite of the chocolate cake, sipped at her coffee and simply allowed the information to settle inside her.

She couldn't leave yet. She was stuck here, which meant the support system she would have counted on at any other time wasn't available.

Hope, Faith and Charity, and especially Cassie, as aggravating as she was sometimes. They were her friends, her support system. She could have talked to them, and they could have helped her figure out which way to go at this point, with a Breed mate MIA only hours after said mating.

NAVARRO'S PROMISE **163**

"Does Jonas have any idea how long it will take?" Mica finally asked Merinus.

"I'm sorry, Mica." Merinus shook her head, her shoulder-length brown hair emphasizing the compassion in her expression. "I do promise you, he's not the only one working on it. Callan, Kane and Navarro are investigating as well. I'm certain it won't take them long."

What was she supposed to say at this point?

She wanted to go home. If it was up to her, she would have gotten in a car and simply driven. She was one woman, and as long as no one saw her leave, then there would be no one to report it to whoever the hell was out there looking for her.

That wasn't going to happen though, and she knew it. She wouldn't make it to a vehicle, let alone past the gates of the compound, before Jonas, Navarro, and any number of Breeds who had watched her grow up, would stop her.

"Cassie asked that you call her whenever you have time." Merinus leaned against the counter and sipped her coffee. "She said to remind you to beware of contentment?" It was obvious Merinus was very curious as well as partly amused.

Mica sipped her coffee.

She was going to strangle Cassie.

The moment she had the chance, she was going to wrap her hands right around her friend's throat and just start squeezing.

Cassie deserved it.

She was hiding the truth of whatever she had sensed that day from Mica, and Mica knew she was.

"You're not going to explain the contentment reference?" There was an edge of laughter in Merinus's tone.

"I might explain it if I understood it myself." Forking another piece of cake, Mica shot Merinus an irate look. "Do you always understand what Cassie's talking about?"

"Sometimes." Merinus didn't sound as confident as Mica was certain she wanted to. "Does that idea of contentment have anything to do with the repeat mating tests Navarro insisted Ely run this morning?"

Yeah, that was Merinus, right to the point there.

Mica sighed wearily. "According to Cassie, she has no idea what it has to do with. As for the mating tests, Navarro simply wanted to be certain."

"I see." Merinus nodded somberly. "And that would have nothing to do with him nearly losing his sanity when Brandenmore escaped confinement and managed to pin you against the wall either? Or how he threatened to kill Brandenmore after he managed to free you from him?"

Merinus was more perceptive than many wanted to admit.

"What do you want to know, Merinus?" Mica asked quietly as she pushed the cake and coffee back.

She could tell when someone was fishing, and at the moment, Merinus was throwing dynamite in the water.

"Are you his mate, Mica?" she asked.

She wasn't going to lie to Merinus. Mica had lived her life amid lies, deceptions and double-talk, and she hated it. She could mark her life divided by one event. The years of contentment and safety before the night Cassie Sinclair and her family arrived at her father's ranch. The years filled with double-talk, lies and danger had been every day thereafter.

She understood, she truly did. There was only so much you could tell most children. But Mica hadn't been most children, and the resentment had only grown over the years.

"So it would appear." She shrugged, the attempt to appear

casual, unconcerned, took nearly every ounce of control she possessed.

There were times she forgot Merinus wasn't a Breed herself. She'd been a mate for so long, the mating hormone now so firmly entrenched in her body, that her senses were so much more sharply advanced that she could detect emotions herself, if not scent them.

Although Merinus was by no means a Breed. Yet.

She continued to watch Mica, making her extremely uncomfortable as her dark gaze remained intent. She wasn't a Breed, but she was developing the senses of one, which meant she was no longer a person Mica could pretend to be calm around.

"How long have you known?" the Prima asked.

This was no longer the friend who had sheltered Mica along with Cassie when they were kids. She wasn't the woman that cut Mica's hair the first time, or the one that taught her to use makeup when she was a teenager, when her own mother refused to so do.

She was now the Prima, the dominant feminine force within Sanctuary, and there wasn't a Breed male or female within the compound that didn't inherently recognize her quiet, intuitive strength and power.

Mica glanced at the clock on the microwave. "Oh, two hours maybe?" she answered blithely. "Could be a minute more, could be a minute less. So let's not get into the whole psychological mishmash that goes with it quite yet, if you don't mind? I'd like another minute or two to adjust."

There was the odd situation or two when her need for truth was almost outweighed by her need for privacy.

Breeds and their mates were just too damned nosy. And she couldn't tell Merinus to mind her own damned business as she would most other Breeds.

"You'll likely need more than a minute or two to adjust," Merinus said ruefully. "It's been fourteen years since I met Callan and I still can't say I've adjusted."

But she was happy. Mica could see the happiness as well as the contentment in the Prima's gaze. She might appear now no more than twenty-four or -five, but she was fourteen years older and wise well beyond her years, Mica often thought.

That didn't mean she wanted to discuss with Merinus something as private and as confusing as what had happened in her bed earlier with Navarro though.

"I wondered what was going on when Navarro stomped downstairs and out the front entrance." Picking up the plates and cups, Merinus deposited them on the sink counter before turning back to Mica, leaning against the counter and bracing her hands on the edge behind her. "I don't think I've ever seen Navarro stomp before."

Mica was quite certain no one had ever seen Navarro stomp before, simply because he so rarely stomped.

Just as he so rarely kept the same lover for longer than a week or two.

She imagined he was stomping because it wasn't as easy to walk away from a mate as it was a one-night stand.

Poor Navarro, she thought mockingly.

Her shoulders almost slumped in dejection, "poor Mica" was more like it. She was the one sitting here alone with Merinus rather than trying to figure out exactly how she was going to keep her father from killing Navarro.

It would be hard, especially considering the fact that at the moment, she wouldn't mind killing him herself.

After he fucked her again.

She wondered what it would take to convince him to fuck her again just before she killed him?

She glanced at Merinus as the other woman watched her compassionately. And that compassion grated. As though someone should feel sorry for her. They should feel sorry for Navarro, because her father really wasn't going to be happy.

"Did you and Navarro argue before he left?" Merinus finally broke the silence between them.

"No." She brushed her hair back from her face as she gave Merinus a tight smile. "There was nothing to argue over." Moving from the bar stool, Mica tucked her hands into the back pockets of her jeans.

The sudden memory of Navarro's hands cupping her rear, lifting her to him, flashed through her mind as a shiver chased up her spine.

Just as quickly, her womb clenched, a second before a rush of heat flashed through her pussy.

Mating heat.

Swallowing tightly, she jerked her hands from her pockets and stared around wildly for a moment, thrown so off balance that she knew Merinus couldn't help but realize.

She could feel herself flushing, knowing that if Merinus's sense of smell was anywhere close to a Breed's, then she would know what had just happened.

Mica hated this. There was nothing worse than allowing anyone at all to realize something as intimate as her arousal.

"There's always something to argue over if mating heat affects you. And I can imagine Navarro, as quiet as he is, could be a force to be reckoned with if he became angry." Merinus sighed as though she had no idea of the sudden flames of aroused heat that were beginning to burn inside Mica.

"Navarro wouldn't hurt me." Mica shook her head dismissively.

She just wanted to escape. She wanted to run to her room, or outside, get away from Merinus's too perceptive gaze or her possibly too sensitive ability to smell.

"No, Navarro wouldn't hurt you," Merinus agreed. "But, in mating heat, even the most self-controlled Breed can become unpredictable."

"Merinus, I really hate to be disrespectful, because I have the highest regard for you," Mica stated as she struggled to hold on to her patience now. "But I don't understand what you're getting at, and I don't understand why we're having this little chat. So if you would be kind enough to either explain it to me, or excuse me, I would really appreciate it."

Because she didn't think she had the patience to be social much longer.

"Your father is threatening to arrive at Sanctuary," Merinus said then. "I need to know, Mica, if he arrives, will you be able to suppress your own anger, or any emotions that would upset him, long enough to reassure him and keep him from feeling the need to take you from Navarro at the moment? We both know how dangerous that could be."

Oh yes, she knew exactly how male Breeds could be where their mates were concerned. She'd seen it for years; each time one mated, the possessiveness, the dominance and the pure overprotectiveness.

They were more overprotective than her father.

Mica turned her head away before shaking it slowly. "You need to convince Dad to stay away," she stated as she turned back to the other woman. "I don't know if I can deal with his overprotectiveness as well as Navarro's at the moment."

And he was overprotective. So much so that Mica often

felt smothered in his presence. Growing up around him had been almost impossible. If he could, he would have kept her a child for the rest of her life.

She wouldn't have had her first lover, let alone a chance to allow a Breed to actually mate her, if her father had had his way. And if he arrived here and had to face Navarro sleeping in her bed without the benefit of marriage, then he was likely to do something stupid. As Merinus feared, there was a very high chance he would indeed attempt to force her back to the ranch, or to Haven.

It wasn't that he didn't love her. It wasn't that he didn't want her to be an adult.

He wanted her to marry a man he believed to be the kind of man she needed. He wanted her to settle down in a nice little house and have babies and be bored out of her mind.

He didn't consider a Breed acceptable, and not because he disliked them, not because he was prejudiced. But because he knew the danger that came with being a Breed's mate.

"Mica, I can help you."

She paused at the kitchen doorway before turning back to Merinus. "Have you found a cure for mating heat?"

"You know we haven't," Merinus said softly. "But that doesn't mean I can't help you through this. I'm always here, Mica. All you have to do is tell me what you need. I'm your advocate here."

"Until a cure is found to mating heat or male dominance, then I'm screwed, and we both know it," she said bitterly.

"And is mating heat so abominable?" Merinus asked. "Is Navarro such an unworthy mate, or lover?"

"He would have been a perfect lover," Mica answered

truthfully. "But I wasn't looking for a mate, Merinus. I wasn't looking to confine myself to Sanctuary or Haven for a man that doesn't even love me. One that doesn't even want me but for mating heat."

With those words she left the kitchen, unwilling to hear any more arguments for mating heat or Breeds as mates. She sure as hell didn't want to see the acknowledgment in Merinus's eyes that she was right.

The only reason Navarro would stay with her now was because of the heat, not because he was willing to fall in love with her. Not because he wanted to love her. But because of some biological reaction. Because something had matched in their hormones, their pheromones or some other bodily element that now bound them together.

She rather doubted though that it was as Cassie had always claimed, that their bodies knew what their hearts weren't yet willing to accept.

She couldn't accept that excuse, despite the arguments Cassie had to back up her theory. The fact that all Breed mates, all pairings had ended up being perfectly matched. That they loved. That they were devoted partners. That not once in all the years that mating heat and mates had been recorded had nature ever created a less than perfect couple.

There was always a first time for everything. And mating heat didn't release the couple. It created a sexual pleasure that became addictive, as Mica understood it. An addict would never betray the addiction, especially if it was approved by the surgeon general, she thought sarcastically. And mating heat was definitely approved by both the Breeds as well as the humans who were aware of it. A much higher endorsement than the surgeon general's, Cassie had once told her with a laugh.

Moving to the front entrance, Mica dragged a heavy

jacket from inside the nearby closet and pulled it on quickly before leaving the house. She expected at any minute for the Breed watching silently to stop her, or for Merinus to come from the kitchen and call her back, which would have the guard moving to stop her.

Fortunately neither of them seemed to care, and Mica wasn't in the mood to be told no.

Wrapping the overly large quilted jacket around her, Mica ducked her head against the chilly wind whipping from the mountains.

Sanctuary was one of the most beautiful places she had ever seen in her life, summer or winter. The old, heavy pine trees looked even more gorgeous at this time than at any other.

They were laden with a heavy covering of snow from the night before, which glistened in the cold air, and pine needles lying on the ground beneath them cushioned Mica's footsteps, while the silence that surrounded her seemed almost eerie.

Sanctuary always seemed to have an otherworldly feel to it, but now even more so.

As though the world itself was awaiting the moment that the warmth of spring would finally show its face and melt the cold around it.

"You shouldn't run off like that, not someone letting someone know where you're heading and when you'll be back."

Mica swung around at the sound of Navarro's dark voice, glaring back at him at the reminder that there was no way to hide in this damned place. There was especially no way to hide from him now.

"Reporting my possible activities wasn't high on my list of priorities."

"It should have been." There was something about the look on his face, the set of his expression, that had her watching him warily.

She knew Breeds, and she knew this one wasn't pleased.

"Fine, the next time I'll sign out like a good little girl before I leave the house. Now, if you don't mind, I'd like to enjoy a little peace and quiet for a change." Her gaze flicked back toward the estate house in silent invitation.

She didn't want him around her right now. She needed a chance to clear her head rather than giving her body a chance to grow even hotter. And it was. As though simply having him around her was enough to make her pussy begin weeping in arousal and her heart begin racing in excitement.

She needed him.

She wanted him, but that was really nothing unusual, she had been wanting him for years now, but she hadn't wanted him like this. Forced. Bound to her by a hormonal reaction he couldn't control any more than she could.

She pulled the jacket tighter around her as she felt her body sensitizing further, nerve endings and erogenous zones growing in interest by the second.

"Trade me jackets." He shrugged the leather jacket he wore from his shoulders, revealing a black silk shirt tucked into well-worn jeans.

Jeans that were filled out exceptionally well by the heavy erection beneath them.

Flames suddenly licked over her skin as she concentrated on the jacket he was holding out to her and tightened her fingers on the one she was wearing.

"I like the one I'm wearing just fine." She'd seen Merinus wear this one before, earlier in the fall when she had been there with Cassie for a weekend.

"As much as I like Callan, I don't like the scent of him on my mate," he suddenly growled.

Micà rolled her eyes, lips parting, teeth clenching in irritation, but she jerked the jacket off, barely feeling the chill in the air as she extended it to him.

But rather than taking the jacket he extended to her, she stalked away instead, heading back to the house and hopefully as far away from him as possible. And as quickly as possible. She would absolutely love it if she could get far enough away, fast enough, that the heat building in her body would simply evaporate.

She just didn't need this.

But that didn't seem to matter, because he moved in beside her as though her quickened stride were no problem to keep up with at all.

"We can't run away from it," he stated, his voice dark, heavy as she came to a stop, turned and stared back at him warily, angrily.

"And who ran from it this morning?" she questioned heatedly, wishing she were cold rather than steaming in arousal, because that steam was beginning to build to a full roiling boil.

She could feel it taking over, cell by cell, inciting not just a physical, but also an emotional response she had no hope of defeating.

The problem was, she'd wanted him before mating heat. She'd been close to falling in love with him before that first kiss. But for him, there was nothing more involved than the physical, and now more of that than he wanted too.

"I'm not running." His eyes seemed to burn with black fire.

"And I'm not a *wham bam thank you ma'am* kind of woman, and I'm sure as hell not a few one-night stands that you can slip out on the next morning." She sneered. "I'll tell you what, Navarro, when you're ready to ask for more than a nice little fuck, then let me know. I'll see what I can do for you then. Until then, I think I'd prefer the hell of mating heat for company."

Stalking away, Mica cursed her tongue, her temper and Breeds in particular as she stomped toward the main house, determined to get away from him before she ended up begging. Begging him to fuck her. Begging him to love her.

"It's not that easy."

Before she could even imagine he would try to stop her, his fingers wrapped around her upper arm, pulling her to a halt and, before she could stop him, pressing her firmly against the wide trunk of a bare tree.

His warmth seemed to blanket her as he pressed against her, the heavy length of his cock imprinting against her lower stomach through their clothing.

It was cold around them, she knew it was, but she couldn't feel it. All she felt was the flush of need as it began to overflow through her, saturating her pussy, hardening her nipples and sensitizing her skin.

All she felt was the irrevocable need she couldn't resist any more than he could.

"It's just that easy." She was breathing heavily, her voice much too weak to be as commanding as she wished she could be.

Her breasts were rising and falling harshly, her hard nipples raking against her sweater where his chest pressed tight against her.

"Is it, Mica?" he asked, his hand lifting, fingers brushing back the heavy strands of hair that had fallen across her face.

The touch was so gentle, the stroke of his fingers along her cheek causing her breath to catch at the need that was so much more than physical, so much more than simply the need to fuck.

"Do you really want to run?"

She did. She wanted to run. She wanted to breathe. She wanted . . .

She just wanted to hold as much of him as he held of her.

She wanted more than just his body.

· C H A P T E R 1 0 ·

Navarro stared down at her, wondering if she knew how the walls around her emotions were slipping. There had been a time when he couldn't have cracked those walls in any way. When she could have tucked those emotions so far out of sight that he wouldn't have had a chance of scenting them.

The intriguing mix of subtle scents that emanated from Mica were like an ambrosia to him. Even the scent of her disappointment, her anger and her emotional pain were slight enough that they only blended with those of heated rosemary, a field of wildflowers, a hint of brown sugar. All the sweet, soft scents of the compassionate, honest woman she was. Scents of her arousal, and a hunger that went far beyond the physical, were like a soft, sweet hint of a coming day.

She wanted more than the physical pleasure that came with the mating heat. The hunger that raged inside her was for far more than just the sex.

Mica wanted love, commitment. She wanted a man whose affection would warm more than just her body. And he'd sworn long ago he'd never let himself step into the treacherous waters of emotion.

Even for his mate.

"I would run if I could," she finally answered. "You ensured that wasn't possible when you mated me."

He cupped the side of her face with his palm, amazed at the silky softness of her skin even as a twinge of amusement filtered through the arousal, and the irritation with that arousal, and had him restraining the tug of a grin that would have pulled at his lips.

"I could say the mating was more your fault," he stated. "I wasn't having a problem with any other woman until you."

"That is such a screwed argument." The dark frown she angled up at him was accompanied by the disbelief that glittered in her gaze. "Only a Breed would say something so asinine. Sorry, Navarro, but only Breeds have the ability to mate. That cancels me out."

She had him there. But he noticed the confrontation was increasing that hint of a summer rain as her pussy grew wetter, hotter.

The remembered taste of that soft flesh had the glands beneath his tongue swelling further, the mating hormone spilling to his mouth in increments as he fought the need to kiss her.

Not yet. He wasn't ready yet.

"Amaya, you are never canceled out," he assured her. "I believe perhaps it's a two-way street if we're placing blame. Because as I understand it, only you could have awakened that ability within me."

"Go ahead, pawn the blame off." Her hands flattened

against his stomach above the silk of his shirt. "You're good at that Navarro. I've noticed you never take the blame for anything."

"But, Amaya, there's so many so very capable of taking the blame," he drawled.

Amaya. Night rain. This was what she reminded him of. A soft, sultry summer night's rain. Soft, warm, caressing. Stroking not just the flesh but also the senses.

"I'm not one of them." Her lashes drifted over her eyes as her expression softened and her face flushed with the pleasure rising inside her.

Stroking his fingertips down her neck, he came to the loose neckline of the sweater and hated the clothing covering her nakedness from him.

He wanted her here, and he wanted her now.

"I followed you when you left the house," he told her. "As you walked here, I could smell the sweetest hint of summer in the air."

The rush of dampness between her thighs teased his senses.

"That's enough," she whispered. "Don't do this to me. Don't make me ache like this, Navarro."

"Should I ache alone then?" Trailing his fingers over her breast, down, he tracked a path to the hem of her sweater as he watched the rise and fall of the soft mounds increase.

Pushing his hand beneath her sweater, he fought soft, feminine flesh.

He could take her here, he told himself. Turn her, press her to the trunk of the tree. He could push inside her and warm them both with the heat of her need.

Her pussy would milk him in, suck at the head of his dick until he found himself fully seated inside her.

The thought of it was enough to have his cock throbbing

beneath his jeans. Or rather, throbbing harder. He'd never lost the hard-on he'd been packing before he fucked her earlier. Hell, he'd come like he was dying as he was locked inside her, and still the erection hadn't abated.

"See, this is why Breeds were on my 'no date' list." She was huffing with charming irritation. "You never pay attention."

"I would pay more attention if you weren't rubbing your pussy against my thigh, Amaya."

Her eyes widened as surprise glittered in the golden green depths. Her hips paused; the sensual little motions she'd been making against his leg had been about to drive him insane. The heat of her pussy had been like a brand against his thigh. He missed the feel of it grinding against him and the invitation inherent in the motions.

She inhaled slowly, deeply, as his knees dipped, placing his cock against the juncture of her thighs as his hands gripped her hips, lifted her just enough and notched his cock against the sweet pad beneath her jeans.

"I could take your jeans down, lift you and let you ride me." He swore his cock thickened impossibly at the very thought of it. "Or I could turn you and just ease your jeans to your thighs and take you from behind. Do you think, Mica, that the chill of the air would ease the heat that will burn inside us?"

He didn't think it possible that anything could ease the heat torturing him at the moment, or the rain of liquid fire he knew was spilling between her thighs.

Her head fell back against the trunk, her breathing short and jerky as she stared back at him.

"I think this is a very bad idea," she answered, her voice weak as his finger moved to the snap of her jeans.

"I've decided what I would prefer," he told her as his

head lowered to her lips, brushing against them, "I'd prefer to have you ride me, Amaya. To have your hot, snug pussy lifting and falling on my dick as you work yourself on it."

His fingers moved to the snap and zipper of her jeans, releasing them as he allowed her to settle on her feet once again.

They were secure here in the shelter of the pine forest. No eyes could see, and the chances of anyone slipping up on them were next to zero.

He'd been seen following his mate, and Breed security would ensure they were protected. Not that he trusted anyone else with her life.

"Ah, Mica." His hand slid into the opening of the fabric, pressing in to find the soft, swollen folds and saturated curls of her pussy.

With one hand he pushed the jeans down over her legs to her ankles, halting their journey as he wrapped his arm around her hips.

Lifting her, Navarro stared down at her, then he jerked her sweater above her breasts and guided her knees to his hips, as he released his cock and felt the engorged head pressing against the hot curves of her pussy.

"Ah fuck!" Heat surrounded the very tip of his cock, blazing, an inferno of lush, slick juice easing his way as he began to press inside her.

Turning, he braced his back against the tree and lowered his head to catch the ripe fullness of her nipple between his lips to suck. To draw the overly sensitive bud between his lips and tongue it erotically.

She shifted in his grip, the image of her face, delicate and flushed with need, imprinting into his brain as she began to work her pussy against the thick, heavy length of his cock pressed inside her.

There wasn't enough foreplay, he knew there wasn't. For some reason the seminal fluid that usually came with Wolf Breed matings, to ease the female mate's clenched muscles, hadn't developed. But still, he could feel her taking him. Her juices were thick and heavy, coating his cock and allowing her to work it inside her as a tremulous cry pierced the silence of the trees surrounding them.

He was only barely aware of the snow that had begun to fall outside the stand of pine. A thick, heavy fall of fluffy white enclosed them in their own wonderland, one of sensuality and erotic promise.

Her hands clawed at his chest as she tried to get closer, her cry turning to a heavy, hungry moan as she moved against him.

His lips surrounded her nipple, sucking at it, drawing her deeper into his mouth as his tongue lashed at the tender peak.

Navarro could hear his own growls rumbling in his chest as he pierced and parted the tender flesh of her pussy with his cock, separating the clenched tissue and easing forward as she worked her hips against him, slowly, with peaking pleasure. He was forced to pull his head back from the tender nipple to clench his teeth in agonizing ecstasy.

"Ah fuck, sweet Mica," he groaned, his hands gripping her ass, palming it, parting the delicate curves with greedy hands as he helped her move on him. "I could stay inside you forever, just feeling you fuck me like this, rising and falling against me."

After that first, wild cry, she began to restrain the sounds, as though she were frightened of being heard.

Being heard was the least of her problems, but he allowed her the illusion, at least for now.

How could he not? Her nails were biting into his shoulders, her head thrown back in ecstasy, and she was giving him more pleasure than he had ever known in his life as he took her.

The desperation that filled her scented the air with a unique, delicate scent as it blended with the arousal and the varied emotions that raged through her. The unique scent it created was an aphrodisiac to his senses. It filled his head, made him high, made his dick harder, his heart race, his body dampen with perspiration as he fought to hold on to enough control to allow her to set this pace.

Until he could figure out why the seminal fluid wasn't present, the slick, sensitizing, muscle-relaxing fluid that was ejected into the vagina from the tip of the Wolf Breed's cock and eased the mate's flesh for penetration. He couldn't risk hurting her.

Wolf Breeds were taught from their first sexual instruction that the unique design of their cocks could be either an instrument of pleasure or one of pain.

And his Mica deserved nothing but pleasure. Nothing but the sweet cries of hunger that spilled from her lips as he felt the walls of her cunt grip and flex around the head of his dick as it penetrated her fully and began to make way for the heavy shaft.

Thick and pulsing, the heavy veins standing out in stark relief beneath the darkened flesh, his cock ached like a wound. It was all he could do to keep from taking over, to keep from taking her fully and pounding into her.

The need for just that was ripping through him as she'd barely taken two inches of the length.

"Navarro. Oh God. I need you. I need you so much," she whispered, barely able to speak, let alone breathe as he finally slid inside her halfway, stretching her until she felt on fire, burning with the rippling pleasure surging through her.

She could feel her cunt flexing, rippling with need as instinct had the muscles rippling around him, sucking him in deeper as though desperate to milk every inch of his cock inside her.

"Take me, Mica," he groaned against her, his head lowering as Mica stared unseeing at the canopy of evergreens above them.

She felt secure, so heated and warm. The engorged strength of his erection penetrated her by slow degrees as Navarro allowed her to take him at her leisure, at her pleasure.

His body strained, the tension evident in the corded strength of his muscles against her as she felt the wicked nip of his teeth against her shoulder, then a slow, erotic lick over the mark he had left on the flesh between her neck and shoulder earlier.

Each rasp of his tongue over the abrasion had her jerking in his hold, her hips writhing against the impalement of his cock as streaks of sensation whipped from the bite mark to her womb, clenching it violently.

Tension rose inside her. The need to feel him thrusting hard and deep inside her obliterated any other thought that may have threatened to penetrate the ecstatic pleasure surrounding her.

Whimpering with rising need, Mica fought the jeans at her ankles until one leg slipped over her ankle, pushing her shoe from her foot, allowing her to part her legs farther, to wrap them around his hips and find the position needed to allow her to take him more fully.

It was like climbing through flames to reach the explosive center of the sun. She was burning, on fire from a pleasure so intensive, so extreme it was nearly unbearable.

Wrapping her arms around his shoulders, using his hips as leverage, she lifted, rising along the stiff stalk as incoherent whimpers left her lips. His hands clenched on her ass, helping her lift as rapid-fire ecstasy began to throb in her womb, her clit.

Poised at the crest, Mica opened her eyes, her lips parting at the savage pleasure in Navarro's expression. Black eyes narrowed and glittering with wild intensity, lips pulled back from his teeth in a feral grimace.

"Slow," he growled as she fought against his hold, desperate to feel him shoving inside her, taking her with the fierce, hard strokes she was beginning to crave.

"No. Harder," she demanded fiercely, but she was willing to beg.

A hard growl tore from his chest as his head jerked forward and lowered, his teeth biting into the shoulder he bared by stretching the loose neckline to the side.

Mica shuddered violently as she bore down on the heated erection piercing the entrance to her pussy. Pleasure raced through her like a wildfire fever. It pierced her womb, her clit, the sensations racing up her spine and spreading through her body with a rush of heat intense enough to steam the air around them.

Her pussy clenched on the engorged head of his cock, the width of it stretching her with a shock of fiery sensation that was both pleasure and pain.

Bit by bit, he allowed her more. Inch by inch, slipping inside her, as Mica felt her flesh giving beneath the iron-hard erection pushing into her.

She struggled against him, needing more, and needing it harder. She wanted those desperate hard thrusts that would send each surge of pleasure tearing across her nerve endings.

Crying out with the need, with the sensation of his teeth biting into her neck, his tongue laving the mark he had left earlier, Mica tightened the inner muscles of her pussy on the thick wedge of his cock as her hips writhed, her knees digging into his hard hips as she bore down, struggling against the hold he had on the cheeks of her ass.

She couldn't have anticipated his next move. She couldn't have guessed the sudden loss of control that would herald the hard, powerful thrust that buried him to the hilt.

A shock wave of ecstatic sensation raced up her spine and spasmed through her womb. Flames crackled over her flesh as electrical sensitivity raced through her veins.

She could feel his fingers on the cheeks of her rear, his palms cupping them, gripping them firmly as he began to move her in sync with the powerful rhythm of his hips.

Fierce, hard thrusts, deep and fiery, as he buried himself to the hilt before pulling back and thrusting deep again. Each powerful stroke stretched, burned, pushed pleasure to its limits, to the border that teased pain and amplified each sensation.

With her head thrown back, gasping for breath, Mica felt the tension rising, each fiery stroke pushing her higher, burning through her, clenching the muscles in her pussy, her womb, until she felt the pleasure implode with an explosive, furious detonation that dragged a strangled cry from her throat and arched her convulsively in his hold.

Within seconds, the fierce, rumbled growl tore from his chest and she felt the first spurt of his release jetting inside her. A second later, a low, delirious moan slipped from her lips as ecstasy built, rose and erupted into a harder, hotter orgasm that went through her system as his cock throbbed, swelled, and locked inside her with vicious pleasure.

His fingers clenched in her ass.

His body drew tight, his teeth tightened at her shoulder, a grating sound between a growl and a snarl vibrated against her flesh and heralded another, hard pulse of his release inside her. Another surge of explosive pleasure, the involuntary tightening of her inner muscles around the hard, throbbing knot locked inside her. Another pulse of his release and it began again.

Mica shuddered, trembled, a kaleidoscope of pleasure raging through her as she collapsed in his arms, gasping for air as each shudder, each hard contraction spilled a release of ecstasy to flood her senses.

Held against him, she fought against the need to lower the fragile barrier between pleasure and emotion, between the bonding of the flesh and the bonding of the soul.

Because only her soul would have reached out. Only her heart was bound it seemed.

"I won't let you get away from me, Mica," he whispered as he sat her on her feet, seconds before she watched in shock as he went to his knees in front of her.

Lifting her bared foot from the cold ground, Navarro drew her jeans leg back over her ankle before slowly, almost hesitantly, dressing her. After fixing the snap and zipping the jeans slowly, he knelt before her once more and held her leather running shoe to her foot as she pushed it on.

"I guess things could be worse," he stated quietly as he stood to his full height, staring down at her. "We could have hated each other."

Mica gave her head a hard shake.

"And how does that change the situation?" As far as she was concerned, it only made it worse.

It would have been easier, she thought, if she hated him. Then perhaps she would have found a way to deny him, to survive when she forced herself to walk away from him.

She wasn't born to be a Breed's mate and nothing more. And Navarro refused to love. She needed love, devotion, the qualities she had seen with her married friends, both human as well as Breed.

Her parents were a great example of the type of relationship Mica wanted for herself. Her mother shared with her father even the most mundane details. They were a couple, a unit, and the thought of settling for less had her heart clenching in dread.

Because with mating heat, she had no choice. She was forced to settle for what nature had given her. A mate that neither knew how to love nor wanted to learn.

"Are you okay?" Navarro could sense more coming from her than the scents of her alone.

Emotions were roiling inside her, but she was keeping them so tightly contained, so carefully hidden, that even with his advanced senses, he couldn't define them.

It was a scent that was just almost there, a knowledge the animal inside him was awakening to yet hadn't yet managed to decipher.

"I'm fine." She swallowed tightly, averting her expression from him as she continued straightening her clothing. "I think you're right though, it's time I return to the house."

To hide.

He knew what she was trying to do, what her uppermost desire at the moment was, now that the sexual needs had been sated. She just wanted to hide.

He had noticed that about her years before, when she was younger. Mica tended to hide whenever she was in Sanctuary. Though that had been wise of her in the past years; otherwise, this mating would have occurred long before now.

"I was going to invite you to go into town with me." The words slipped from his lips before he could call them back, causing him to clench his teeth in self-disgust.

That was no way to place any distance between them, he told himself sourly.

She gave her head another hard shake, causing the dark blond strands of her hair to ripple around her. "Not today. I'll just return to my room."

"Our room."

He could tell she didn't think much of his comment, by the stiffening of her body and the frown that creased her forehead.

"I am not moving into your room." Fiery stubbornness gleamed in her eyes now.

Navarro tilted his head in acknowledgment. "I assumed you would want to keep your bed. That's the reason I had my belongings moved to your suite instead."

He laid his fingers over her lips in warning as they parted, and for once, her scent was unmistakable. Pure feminine outrage.

"You can argue until hell freezes over," he warned her, his tone darker than he would have liked, as though instinct were giving her the only response he was capable of. "But the plain and simple fact of the matter is that I'm not sleeping without my mate. You can deal with that however you like."

Possessiveness wasn't a part of him, he'd always assured himself. He was dominant. He knew what he wanted. But he'd learned long ago to never be possessive. It was far too easy to have what he thought belonged to him taken away.

Until now.

The possessiveness rose from within, surprising him with the fact that it had been so carefully hidden until now. She belonged to him, and he'd be damned if he'd allow her to hold herself back from him.

He couldn't keep her, and he knew it.

But he also couldn't let her go, couldn't remain distant from her, no matter how hard he tried.

"We'll see about this." Lips thinned, teeth clenched, Mica swung away from him and began marching furiously down the incline that led from the pine thicket to the main house.

He let her go this time. Chasing after her would only incite both their tempers, and he knew exactly where that would lead. With his dick buried deep and hard inside the velvet heat of her pussy for the third time that day.

He grimaced, fixed his own clothing, then raked his fingers through his hair before moving back toward the main house himself.

He had work today. There were any number of projects that he should be working on while he was at Sanctuary. This wasn't a vacation for him, though he clearly didn't have his head where it should be in regards to his job.

A job he should have taken care of years before, he admitted, as he headed back to the labs and the files awaiting him on the horrors of the Omega Project. A project Phillip Brandenmore had funded and overseen.

The project that had killed Navarro's brother, Randal, and the mate Randal had adored. The project that had inspired the vow Navarro had made to ensure Brandenmore died at his hand.

❖   ❖   ❖

Ely moved among the equipment in the lab, her gaze studying with a frown the readings that came through, as the steel doors slid open and her personal irritant and bodyguard, Jackal, entered the room once again.

In his hands he carried a heavy tray filled with what was obviously lunch.

Her favorite.

Ham and cheese sandwiches made with the homemade bread Sanctuary's cooks had prepared.

How amazing it had turned out to be that Breeds who were trained to kill, to stain their hands with blood, could also cook and bake with such perfection as to bring tears to the eye.

The sandwiches were piled high with ham, several different kinds of cheeses and with them were a variety of vegetables, along with roast beef, turkey and chicken luncheon slices.

Chips and pickles completed the meal along with frosted glasses of sweet, sweet iced tea.

Strong and muscular, Jackal should have looked out of place as he carried the tray of food dressed in his black heavy-metal-band T-shirt and worn jeans, his dark hair cut close to his scalp.

He didn't though. She'd determined over the past years that nothing could make Jackal look out of place, and few things could make him feel out of place.

"How are the tests going?" he asked, his baritone voice a deep, almost Breed-like growl.

She gave a heavy sigh as she moved to the sink and washed her hands thoroughly before stepping over to the table and taking the seat he pulled out for her.

"That sigh isn't exactly an answer," he drawled, the Texas accent filled with concern.

"The tests aren't exactly conclusive either," she told him as she accepted the plate he lifted from the tray and set it in front of her. "It doesn't matter how many tests I run, the final results remain inconclusive. There's a mating, but they're not mated."

She hadn't seen anything like it and still couldn't make sense of it.

"You may have to explain that one to me, Ely." He watched her expectantly as he bit into his sandwich with strong, white teeth.

"Who will explain it to me then?" she countered with the same frustration that had pricked at her for the past hours since beginning the tests.

"What's the problem with the tests?" he probed further, obviously becoming impatient with her refusal to explain the situation.

She took another bite of the sandwich as she tried to figure out the best way to explain it.

"I'm not a moron, Ely," he assured her, obviously reading her look, and he was very good at that actually.

"The tests are positive for mating," she finally stated. "But I've never seen such weak results during an active mating. All the hormonal requirements are there, but they're in such small quantities, that I wonder if Navarro couldn't easily walk away from Mica without suffering for it. Once the hormone, weak as it is, reaches Mica's system, it seems to grow stronger though." She frowned again, still bothered by the hours she'd spent attempting to figure out the problem. "The test results are responding differently to different stimuli as well. Such as the weakened hormone, once introduced into Mica's system, becoming stronger.

The mating hormones in their blood are different, and in different levels than those in his semen and the natural lubrication in her vagina. Just as it was when we tested the saliva. But if I introduce other parameters to the tests, such as a variable of the hormones created during certain emotional responses, then the mating hormone in Navarro's specimens explode."

Jackal's head tilted to the side as he frowned back at her questioningly. "It has to do with the emotional responses during mating heat then?"

Ely nodded again, chewing another bite before continuing. "Most Breeds are actually looking forward to finding their mates. They see it as a gift that God has arranged just for them, for their survival. So despite protestations or the levels of anger, fear or just sheer stubbornness, that need and that hunger are there to begin with, and the mated Breeds don't have the subconscious desire to suppress those emotions. Once they find their mate, possessing her means everything. But I know Navarro and Mica well. Neither of them would have come within ten feet of the other if they had suspected this would happen, no matter how intense the attraction or the need. Mica, because she was already aware of the emotions that would build and grow within her and she feared the consequences of them. Navarro is a little different, and harder to define. Suffice to say, he has no intentions of loving her, and he just might have the training and the strength to suppress those emotions."

"That doesn't make sense. How can not wanting to mate, or a subconscious desire not to love, affect whether or not they do it? As I understood it, it's supposed to be impossible to deny it." There was a definite growl of suspicion in his voice, as well as a reluctance to believe what she was saying.

"Because Breeds were created to have no emotions. Our very genetics were altered to ensure the Council's ability to train any chance of those emotions out of us," she reminded him. "And we were trained to put aside any emotion that slipped past the creation process. We were lucky to maintain any feelings at all; still though, we were taught how to hide what we were feeling, to push it aside. Navarro, perhaps more than others, was taught this lesson with savage determination."

Navarro Blaine was an Infiltration Level 5 Breed. He had been created for recessive Breed genetics. He was still stronger, faster, his senses more advanced than any human's, but there was no way to detect those genetics.

He had been created to infiltrate the corporate and political world and to work it to the advantage of the Genetics Council.

"Then it's Navarro's ability to lock out those emotions, and the resulting hormones, that could allow him to walk away from this when no one else has been able to?" Jackal asked.

She gave a sharp nod. "And, until he or Mica or both acknowledge those emotions or they lose the battle to fight them, then they may never be fully mated."

"Or fully free," he said.

"Or fully free," she agreed.

And she blamed this on Navarro. When she wrote up her statement later, she would be certain to include that.

"Poor Navarro," Jackal finally grunted as he lifted his glass for a drink.

"No, poor Mica," she argued. "She'll receive the brunt

of the pain if Navarro manages to walk away from her. She'll be the one that suffers. And that leaves me in a very untenable position. Do I use this unique response to search for a way to ease mating heat, perhaps grow closer to curing it? Or do I instead attempt to convince Navarro to understand, before it's too late, because Mica may never be free of him?"

And the suffering wasn't easy. Mating heat demanded touch, it demanded a kiss. And now with Mica and Navarro it seemed to demand love and the mate.

"I should warn Mica," she sighed. "She needs to know what the possible outcome to this can be."

"No, don't."

She stared back at him in surprise. "This isn't your call, Jackal."

"And it's not yours either, Ely," he stated, his tone harsh as she stared back at him in disagreement. "Stick to the science of mating heat, and leave those two to figure out their emotions alone. They won't thank you for interfering, and you'll only end up hurting yourself if you don't stay out of it, and blaming yourself if you don't attempt to see what effect Navarro's control of his emotions could have on future mates, or the world's discovery of mating heat."

"Just let him break her heart, Jackal? Is it worth following this if she lives her life in pain?" she questioned him bitterly.

"It doesn't sound to me that you could help either of them either way, Ely. Let them have a chance to find each other's heart. Just because you're determined to deny it yourself doesn't mean Mica should."

Ely stood to her feet slowly. She was finished at this point. She'd be damned if she would be drawn into this argument again.

"I don't deny anything, Jackal. Nor do I avoid it. I leave that to the rest of you."

She turned and walked away from him, shaking on the inside at the confrontation and wondering if this time Jonas would finally give her a new bodyguard.

The next morning Mica was waiting for Navarro at the elevator entrance of the floor their suite was located on.

Leaning back against the wall, her arms crossed over her breasts, she watched as he turned into the small corridor and then came to a stop in front of her.

His dark gaze went over her, remaining impossibly distant, before meeting her eyes.

Slowly, Mica arched a brow as she reached over and pressed the old-fashioned button to send the order along the lines to the elevator, telling it to rise to meet them.

She didn't speak, but she didn't break his gaze either. She had sworn she wouldn't beg him, and she meant it.

"Did you sleep well last night?" he finally asked her with all discretion of a falling wall.

"Perfectly well," she lied, and she did it effectively.

His nostrils flared as he drew in her scent to check for the lie she was certain he knew she was telling. The lie she knew was well hidden.

She may have spent an absolutely miserable night, but she was rather calm this morning if she did say so herself. The night hadn't been one of her more pleasant, the symptoms of mating heat had driven her nearly insane. At one point she had actually found herself outside his bedroom door, shaking, so desperate to feel him inside her that she was ready to demand her rights as his mate.

Hell, he'd moved his stuff into her room. Everything but him. What the hell was going on here?

Pride had finally kicked in though, a second before her fist landed on the door. Thank God. She couldn't have borne the shame of it otherwise.

The elevator doors slid open, and with a graceful roll of her shoulders Mica pushed herself from the wall and entered the compartment.

Sliding into the far corner, she kept a wary eye on Navarro and cursed her body at the same time. She was supposed to have a handle on this arousal stuff for the day. She'd finally taken one cold shower too many the night before, chilling her body until the heat abated.

And now it was rising once again, with a strength that had her groaning silently as she stared at the back of the man that claimed to be her mate.

"Have you eaten this morning?" he asked as the old elevator made its way to the labs nearly ten floors beneath the estate house.

"Nope. I know better," she assured him. She hadn't been coming to Sanctuary all these years for nothing.

He was silent then, his back tense as Mica wisely remained silent as well.

As the elevator came to a stop, Mica had to steel herself to actually step from it. The memories of Brandenmore and his attack the day she arrived were still very fresh in her mind.

As she took the first step, Navarro turned back to her, his black eyes watching her closely.

"Everything okay?" Flashing him a bright, confident smile, she stepped forward as two Breed Enforcers made their way down the long hall.

"Everything's fine." His smile was tighter.

"You have the look of a man who has something pricking his little mind," she commented, mockery and anger mixing into the arousal burning inside her.

"Navarro always has something pricking his little mind." Josiah Black sniggered teasingly as he stepped up to them.

His arm was in a sling, obviously still healing from the confrontation with Brandenmore and Navarro the day before. His eye was still bruised, but healing quickly.

Breeds tended to heal quickly, and Josiah seemed to be proving the theory.

"Be nice, Josiah, Navarro's having a bad day." She threw Navarro another calm, confident little smile.

If he thought she was going to kiss his ass and beg him to touch her, then he could think again. She was more likely to attempt to *kick* his ass today.

"You're treading on thin ice, little girl," he warned her, his voice low enough that the words carried no further than her own ears.

"What are you going to do, Navarro? Spank me?" She winked at him as she let her gaze slide over his body then back to his eyes. "I might enjoy it."

Josiah snorted behind her, while Cougar shifted beside her as though uncomfortable. Only one thing could make a Breed of Cougar's ilk uncomfortable. The threat of danger from a Breed he was unwilling to fight.

Navarro stood watching her, black eyes focused completely on her, his face more still than normal and completely devoid of expression.

The danger was coming from Navarro?

Oh, he might be feeling dangerous, but it wasn't violence he had need of. And she wasn't in the mood to pamper him, whatever seemed to be his problem.

"So, are the two of you escorting us to Ely's lab?" she asked as she shoved her hands into the back pockets of her jeans and turned to the other Breeds. "I'd like to hurry and get this over with if you don't mind."

She did have better things to do at the moment. Things such as washing her hair, cleaning floors, masturbating maybe? The masturbating part was rumored not to help, but she was getting desperate enough to try it.

Cougar spoke up then. "Josiah will escort you to Ely. She doesn't need Navarro today." He turned to Navarro. "Callan and Jonas would like to see you in the vid-comm room ASAP."

And Navarro didn't like the idea of that much at all. Mica could actually feel the denial emanating from him.

Poor Navarro. Wasn't that just too damned bad?

"Well, Josiah, looks like you're it. You get to babysit me." Sliding her hand to the bend of his elbow, she urged him up the hallway. "You know, I think the black eye I gave you when you were eighteen looked much nicer than this one. Are you getting old, or did I just have a hell of a stroke of luck then?"

She swore she could feel Navarro's gaze boring into her back as they moved up the hall; intent, dangerous, he didn't like her familiarity with another Breed. He sure as hell didn't like the fact that she had some connection to Josiah, no matter how innocent.

And she didn't like his determination to see her suffering in her room alone all night either. And oh, he knew. He had to have known. He was in mating heat just as she was, she wasn't suffering alone when he stayed away from her, which meant he knew very damned well exactly how the mating heat was affecting her.

He knew she was hurting, and he'd done nothing to fix it, even though he was hurting as well.

What the hell did he expect her to do? Beg? Fight?

She was a grown woman; she knew what she wanted, and she knew what she was willing to fight for. And despite her anger at Navarro's arrogant attempt to move into her room the day before, a mate that willingly stayed away from her wasn't something she wanted to fight for.

"Are you trying to get me killed now, sugar?" Josiah asked as they turned the corner and headed toward Ely's examination room. "You don't mess with a mate like that. He could have taken my head off if he were any other Breed."

Mica rolled her eyes. "Man up, Josiah. The most he's going to do is growl at you a little bit, if he can work up the interest to do that much. So chill already."

He glanced at her from the corner of his eye, his expression disbelieving.

"What did he do? Refuse you coffee or chocolate? I've watched enough of this mating shit, I know it had to be one or the other."

Oh, it was far more important than chocolate or coffee. And if he was a Breed, why couldn't he smell the hell her body was going through right now? She was so aroused she felt as though she were burning up from the inside out.

"Josiah, no one refuses me anything," she informed him, more out of pride than simply because she rarely asked anyone for anything. "I'm a grown woman; I know how to go out and buy it, how to buy it online and call in orders. It's all really simple, honey, I promise. Besides, I haven't needed permission to do anything since I lived with my parents."

And she wasn't going to allow anyone to treat her like a child again, especially not the Breed who had decided she was his mate.

"Then what's the problem?" Sincere concern filled Josiah's gaze as she glanced up at him. "I can tell the mating heat is bad, but I can sense more than that."

So much for whether or not he could smell her arousal.

Josiah was a friend, but she didn't discuss her personal life with anyone outside Cassie. And last she checked, he wasn't channeling Cassie.

"The problem is my business," she told him lightly, as they turned up the hall that actually housed Ely's examination room. "Your job was to get me here, and you've done that with flying colors. You can leave now, Josiah."

Ely opened the secured double doors as they paused in front of them.

"Leave, Josiah," she repeated Mica's request as an order to the Breed. "And be certain to check in at the vid-comm room so Navarro can concentrate on his meeting rather than the fact that you're with his mate."

"Yes, ma'am." Josiah just about jumped out of his skin when Ely snapped at him.

Turning sharply on his heel, he hurried back through the halls to carry out her orders.

"You should know better than to draw another Breed into your quarrel with Navarro, Mica." Ely stepped back to allow her to enter. "I've been watching you on the cameras since you entered the elevator. I could have sworn you'd know better by now."

"Ely, I'm not quarreling with Navarro." Mica looked back at her, a small kernel of resentment beginning against the scientist.

Ely was harder now than Mica remembered her being. Harder and less compassionate and understanding than the last time Mica had spent any time with her.

Ely's lips thinned, but she stepped back and allowed Mica into the examination room.

"So what kind of torture do you have in store for me today?" Mica questioned her, maintaining the sense of cheerfulness as Ely glanced back at her.

"Today will be fairly simple," Ely stated. "A few questions, urine and blood samples. How long has it been since you and Navarro had sex?"

The doctor asked the question impatiently. She was probably wondering why her patient smelled like a walking sex hormone. "Almost twenty-four hours." Mica glanced at the clock on the wall. "Twenty-two hours and forty-five minutes maybe?" She flashed the doctor another bright smile. "Just before we came in yesterday to be as precise as I can get."

Ely seemed to freeze in place as Mica relayed the information.

Did the good scientist think she wasn't aware of the fact that it wasn't exactly normal Breed mating behavior?

"I see," Ely finally said musingly. "Was Navarro in meetings or called away?" She picked up the electronic pad and began making notes.

"Are you asking why it's been so long since we've had sex?" Mica questioned defiantly. "Why, I have no idea, Ely. Do you?"

She hadn't meant to allow that fiery flash of pain to strike at her chest. It struck with precision though, tearing through her heart before she could rein it in and push it back into the darkened corner where she hid all her emotions.

Ely's head jerked up as though she sensed it. Her nostrils flared and a frown creased her forehead.

"Are you feeling the symptoms of his refusal to relieve the pressure of mating heat?" Was that compassion in the good doctor's gaze?

"Am I horny enough to hump the bedpost?" Mica asked. "Not quite yet. Should I consult with you first, Doctor?" Sarcasm lay thick and heavy in her voice.

"I believe a consult would be a very good idea." Ely nodded with mocking solemnity as Mica lifted herself onto the gurney. "You never know what you may end up hurting if the act isn't done properly."

Okay, so maybe the good doctor wasn't just a little bit colder and harder than Mica remembered. She was definitely more distant, but Mica could understand that. It hadn't been a good year for Ely in terms of being able to trust those around her.

Still, Mica couldn't stop the grin that tugged at her lips, and she wasn't the only one. Ely seemed to be struggling with her own amusement.

How strange was that? Her clit was throbbing like a toothache, her vagina clenching to the point that it was nearly spasming, while her womb felt as though it were on fire, and still, two women could find a way and a reason to inject a little filthy humor into the situation.

"God!" She lowered her head, her eyes closing as she whispered miserably, "I can't beg him, Ely." Lifting her lashes, she stared back at the doctor. "And I'm not far from it."

"I've tried to develop a hormonal therapy for you." Ely

sighed roughly as she pulled the small stool from the edge of the gurney to her and sat down, facing Mica compassionately. "But there are too many anomalies to the tests, and I haven't been able to isolate enough of the mating hormone to develop a therapy that will aid it."

Mica wondered if she could get the good doctor to speak in English.

"Maybe if you repeat that very very slowly and enunciate clearly, I might understand it," Mica stated wearily. "That, or use layman's terms?"

"There isn't enough of the mating hormone in Navarro's saliva, blood or semen to have a base to begin testing a hormone therapy that will be effective. I'm sorry, Mica. I've never seen anything like this in all the years we've been testing for mates. It's not the first anomaly, just the first one of its kind. This seems to be a year for Mother Nature to screw around with Breed hormonal reactions and mating heat."

Not enough mating hormone?

Mica struggled to make sense of the words.

"So, Navarro isn't a walking hard-on this morning," she whispered.

Ely shook her head. "Yesterday, yes. The day before, definitely. But somewhere in the past twenty-four hours the emotion-based hormones that drive the mating heat seem to have begun disappearing from his system. They've become amplified within yours though, driven and made stronger by whatever emotions you keep bottled inside you." Her gaze was somber. "I am so sorry, Mica, that it had to be you who seems to be proving my theories that the mating heat reacts in large part to the emotions, both conscious and subconscious, of the mates involved."

"So Navarro has no emotions." She felt blank inside. As

though everything she knew about herself and the world had been stripped away from her overnight.

"I'm certain he has emotions," Ely said, her voice soft. "But I know his creation, his training. He was trained to annihilate even a suspicion of any emotions beyond hatred. And he would have succeeded perhaps, if it weren't for the fact Navarro wasn't raised entirely at the labs. He was there during the rescues by choice, Mica. An attempt to save his brother and his brother's mate before the scientists there learned of the mating. Navarro was taken from the labs by his grandparents."

"Morton and Elsie Blaine." Mica remembered them. She'd actually seen them from a distance a few times when they had come to Haven to see Navarro.

"Yes." Ely nodded. "After the age of ten, he was raised by his grandparents. Unfortunately, he had a Council-trained nanny. And that nanny was a monster, as was the butler the Council managed to get into the Blaine household. Navarro didn't have a chance to develop the emotions that were bred out of him, Mica. The fact that he's as compassionate as he is is surprising."

The Blaines' daughter had been kidnapped by the Council and used as a breeder. Navarro and Randal were a result of that union, but the Council refused to allow Morton and Elsie to buy Randal as they allowed them to buy his twin, Navarro. They had never seen their other grandson before he was killed during the rescues.

Randal had been their insurance against the Blaines striking back at them.

And Mica believed they would have. Morton Blaine might not have been able to destroy them, but with his financial empire and the powerful friends and favors he had gained over the years, he could have hurt them, if nothing else.

That, or destroyed all the Breeds by making sure the world learned of them in a more threatening light than had occurred with Callan Lyons announcing their presence.

"So, simply put, he realized he might be beginning to feel something for me, and destroyed it?" Mica asked with bitter sarcasm.

Ely nodded hesitantly as Mica felt her chest clench with the hurt that suddenly exploded inside her, which even she couldn't hide.

She swore she saw Ely flinch as well as the emotion struck through Mica's soul, rending it in half.

"So Navarro is no longer in mating heat?"

Once again Ely nodded. "All but the smallest traces of the hormone are gone from his system."

Mica's fists clenched around the edge of the thick pad beneath her as she fought the need to rock in agony.

A distant part of her couldn't believe the horrendous pain welling inside her now. It was like a wildfire, sucking the life out of everything in its path.

"And that leaves me where?"

"A mate, without a mate," Ely stated, her voice incredibly gentle, her brown eyes filled with pity.

She pitied her. Ely was watching her and feeling sorry for her, Mica thought.

She swallowed tightly. "Let's get this over with then." She had to force the words past numb lips as she realized she was nearly gasping for breath. "You need samples, right?"

"Blood, saliva and vaginal." Ely clasped her hands in her lap. "You should be prepared, Mica, it may be very painful. And there's nothing I can do to ease the pain.

Most female mates seem to have a horrible physical reaction to even a female touch during the strongest phases of mating heat."

Once again Mica nodded shortly, as Ely reached for the supplies in the small basket at the end of the gurney. "I'll get the blood first, then we can do the rest."

As Ely took the blood, Mica could feel no pain. There was a heavy layer of discomfort, a feeling of disgust and loathing each time Ely was forced to touch her, even through the latex gloves she wore, but the extreme physical discomfort was absent.

She was a mate without a mate.

"There." Several minutes and four vials later, Ely pushed back from the bed. "Change into one of the gowns and we'll get the rest of it finished as quickly as possible."

Mica moved from the gurney, feeling the ache of loneliness and the loss of what she hadn't even dared to hope for, but had fantasized of, Navarro's love.

Pulling one of the soft cotton gowns from the small rack in the bathroom linen cabinet, Mica blinked at the moisture in her eyes, uncertain why this seemed to be affecting her so strongly.

It wasn't as though she hadn't been fully aware that Navarro had no intention of loving her. That this heat stuff was something he would escape if he could.

But she hadn't believed he *could* escape it, any more than she could.

Sucked to be her. Navarro was escaping and she was burning alive with the need for his touch.

Typical.

She should have never expected less.

Hell, she should have expected just this.

◆   ◆   ◆

Navarro sat in the vid-comm conference room, relaxed, leaning back in the comfortably padded chair, arms relaxed casually on the rests at his side, watching Wolfe Gunnar; Del-Rey Delgado; their mates, Hope Gunner and Anya Delgado; and their seconds in command, Jacob Arlington and Brim Stone on the large screen. Now joining them were Dash and Elizabeth Sinclair, to assess the information coming in as the video conference, Navarro hoped, was winding to an end.

"How much longer, Callan?" Wolfe questioned as his gaze sliced to Navarro from the mounted large-screen video communications board.

"As soon as Jonas can get the heli-jet here safely," Callan stated with no regard to the fact that Wolfe was all but ordering him to make it happen. "I understand your concerns, Wolfe, but moving Mica at the moment simply isn't possible. We believe the risk is too high."

Wolfe grimaced as he turned to Dash Sinclair, the Wolf Breed who had arrived to assess the present danger and decide the next course of action where his goddaughter was concerned.

Dash was presently staring a hole through Navarro, and the angered, knowing glitter in his amber eyes would have been enough to have any other Breed sweating.

"What aren't you telling me, Callan?" Dash turned his gaze to the pride leader.

It seemed all eyes turned to Navarro, and in each case there was a sense of confusion and perhaps a hint of a question.

"At the moment, Dash, the only thing you're not being told is information we're not certain of." Callan turned back to the screen and the other Breeds' intent look. "As soon as I have the information and can verify it though, then you'll be the first to know, I promise you this."

"And if Mica were to find a mate while she's at Sanctuary?" Dash asked coolly. "Would you tell me immediately, Callan?"

"Dash, the minute I verified and Dr. Morrey reverified the tests, then you would know," Callan assured him sincerely. "That is not information I would keep from you."

Now there was a load of shit if Navarro had ever heard one. He slid a look in Callan's direction, expecting to see a warning in the Feline Pride leader's gaze to hold to the lie. Rather than the warning though, what he saw was somber confusion and, amazingly, pity.

"And you, Navarro?" Dash asked then. "Would you tell me if Mica had mated?"

Navarro's brow lifted.

"Dash, Navarro doesn't carry the mating scent. I give you my word on it if that's what you're questioning," Callan spoke up.

Navarro was careful to show no reaction. No surprise, no confusion. He'd never known Callan to outright lie in such a way, especially in front of witnesses. It was such a gross disregard of the agreements between Sanctuary and Haven that even Navarro questioned the decision.

"There are rumors he mated her, Callan." Dash frowned back at both of them. "I can't disregard those whispers."

"We'll figure it out on our end and get back to you," Callan promised. "Would you trust me to do that?"

Dash stared at the pride leader for long moments before turning back to Navarro to give him a probing look. Finally, the other Breed rubbed at the back of his neck in irritation before giving a tight nod. "I'll trust you, Callan.

But remember if you will, Mica is family, and she's an only child. Her parents . . . worry."

Yeah, they worried their little princess would end up getting fucked or worse yet, horror of all horrors, mated by a Breed. It wasn't that they were prejudiced or even disapproving of the Breeds. It was simply that they believed their daughter deserved better.

And with that thought came a surge of possessiveness Navarro barely caught in time to tamp it down and dispose of it. The night before had been relatively comfortable. The agonizing arousal that had marked the time since he'd first mated her had eased.

The realization that he'd taken her as an animal beneath the trees had shaken him to his soul. He'd wanted nothing more than to push her to her knees, press her shoulders to the forest floor and fuck her until she was screaming for him, begging for him as he rocked into her from behind.

The image of that, even now, had the power to slip past the walls he had built around it and cause his dick to harden with need.

Hell, he was getting tired of sitting here. The more he listened to them talk about Mica, the harder it was to deny his need for her.

Thankfully, the conversation ended, the vid-comm darkened, and then, uncomfortably, all eyes turned to him as the door to the conference room opened and Josiah walked into the room.

Anger spilled from the Breed in waves.

His eyes snapped with steel gray blue flames as he raked his fingers through his shaggy dark blond hair and glared at Navarro.

"Did you know the presence of the mating hormone in you is now negligible?"

Surprising. Hell, the day was just getting more interesting by the moment, wasn't it? Negligible? That meant Mica would no longer be his mate soon. That had happened only once before with Callan's pack sister Dawn and her mate, Seth Lawrence, but it had taken ten years and the complete removal of Seth from Dawn's life during that time for it to happen, not ten fucking hours.

Should he regret it?

He could feel the need to claim her once again trying to rise inside him and he fought it. Mica didn't need this. If the heat was receding, then it would be a blessing for her. She had dreams, plans, desires that he knew did not include a Breed. It didn't include the hell their lives could become if public sentiment turned against them.

"You're acting as though it's a crime," he stated as the others continued to stare at him as though he had somehow deliberately caused this.

It felt like a crime against nature.

He hadn't neglected her as the need burned between them. He'd taken her, satiated her, stilled the hunger raging inside her until last night, just before going to her, he'd realized he felt . . . normal.

He wasn't iron-hard and hurting with a sexual pain he couldn't make sense of. Oh, he wanted her, he hungered for her, but it was no longer that desperate, amplified lust that he couldn't control. And that lack of control had been destroying him to the point he'd actually feared the animal he could feel crouched and waiting inside him.

Just waiting for Navarro to drop his guard, to relax his attention and give it a chance to jump free. And it would—straight in the direction of the petite, too stubborn, too independent woman he believed he had mated.

Even now, he could feel that snarl brewing in his chest,

an unquenched fury threatening to spill from the tortured center of his soul that he only rarely acknowledged.

That didn't mean he didn't want an explanation.

Rising to his feet, he didn't bother to excuse himself—rather he stalked to the door with every intention of leaving and garnering those explanations immediately from the doctor herself.

"Let her go." Josiah was suddenly blocking his way, a snarl on his face, his gaze filled with his anger as Navarro stared back at him with a sudden, icy fury.

Behind him, Navarro could feel the others rising from their chairs, the tension in the room building to a smothering point as he faced off with the other Wolf.

"Back off, Josiah," Navarro warned as he felt the adrenaline surging through him, a wild, burning hunger for action, to take out his enemy, to go for the throat and to taste blood.

The genetics of the Wolf. The animal was awakening again. If it awoke, if he allowed those instincts to rise inside him once again, then nothing, no one he cared for might ever be safe again.

"Back off?" Josiah sneered, his Wolf flashing in the snarl at his lips and the dilation of gaze. "Fuck you, Navarro. Stay the hell away from her. If she's lucky, real fucking lucky, then rather than rising inside her and torturing the hell out of her as it did last night, maybe the heat will dissipate in her as well."

"No." Navarro gave his head a hard shake. "I would have smelled her pain, her arousal."

It wasn't possible. His senses rated off the charts. There was no way to even measure his ability to detect scents, to sense disturbances, and he hadn't sensed Mica's? That wasn't possible. He refused to believe it.

Josiah scoffed. "As if you didn't. Even I scented it, Navarro." Rage clouded the Wolf's voice, roughened and rasped it until it was more animal than human. "You're not a worthy mate and you should be barred from approaching her."

Navarro felt as though his brain were clouding for the briefest moment before he fought back. Instinct, hunger, rage and animal fury threatened to overwhelm him before he managed to get control of them. He forced them back, restrained them as he had all his life. Since birth. Since before birth.

Navarro turned slowly to Callan, Jonas, and Dane Vanderale.

So far, the current Vanderale heir and hybrid Breed had remained silent—watching and amused, but silent. But Navarro knew if Dane took a side, then that side would be sure to win, against all odds.

Navarro couldn't take that chance. He wouldn't take that chance. The very thought of any of them taking her from him had rage threatening to shake his control.

"Attempt to bar me from her and there will be a war," Navarro promised them.

"Ely believes if he is barred from her, then there's a chance Mica could mate with a Breed willing to take on the responsibility of loving her," Josiah snapped. "I request he be barred from her long enough to learn if she'll be compatible with me. I'll claim her." His gaze raked over Navarro with insulting emphasis. "And he can go to hell!"

Shock resounded through Navarro.

A snarl slipped past his throat as he turned on the other Breed, fury spreading through his system with the force of a tidal wave.

He'd be damned if he'd allow any other Breed a chance to do any such thing.

"She's still my fucking mate," Navarro informed them all with icy rage. "She carries my scent."

Josiah's arms crossed over his powerful chest as a smirk curved his lips. "No, Navarro, she doesn't. She smells of heat and arousal, but her scent is still her own. She has not taken your scent. Dr. Morrey believes nature would allow Mica to choose another mate, as you've so obviously rejected her. She's Breed compatible and mate hungry. And I have no problem whatsoever fixing that little problem."

Breed compatible and mate hungry?

Navarro sneered back at him. "If she had wanted you, whelp, then she would have claimed you years ago. What makes you think you can claim what's mine now?"

"Because you so obviously don't know how to do the job right." Josiah smirked.

That smirk, the confidence and male gloating in his eyes, seemed to snap something inside him, something primal and vital, and before Navarro could restrain it, that unknown something disappeared from his grasp beneath the anger surging through him.

"Get the hell out of my way." Navarro went to move around Josiah.

He was finished with this conversation.

"If the doctor is right, then perhaps we should consider what Mica has to say first, Navarro," Dane drawled with a hint of amused interest. Enough so that Navarro knew the other man was entirely serious about asking Mica's opinion. And Navarro was certain it wouldn't be in his favor.

Navarro froze for the briefest second before turning to face the Vanderale heir, a man he had considered a friend until this moment.

"Go to hell!"

Turning back, he pushed past Josiah and slammed out

of the vid-comm room to stride furiously up the hall to Ely's office.

He'd be damned if anyone would take his mate.

He didn't have to let the animal free to claim her. No matter the mating hormone that no longer filled his system, he could still claim her.

He'd already claimed her. He'd left his mark on her, and he'd be damned if he'd allow another Breed to replace it.

But to keep her, could he release the animal struggling to awaken inside him?

It was a question he wasn't willing to answer.

But, he feared, it was one he would have to face. He could feel some unnamed emotion, a burning sense of awareness flaring inside him that he was unable to fight, unable to define. And for both his and Mica's sake, he prayed it wasn't the animal finally breaking free.

CHAPTER 12

Cassie had been amazingly silent since Mica's little adventure began, but as she stepped into the bedroom and closed the door behind her, the first thing Mica spotted was the sat phone and note left on the coffee table.

Moving to it, she couldn't help but smile.

Cassie's having a meltdown and threatening to leave Haven. Please call her—Merinus.

Choosing the contacts option, she was thankful to see Merinus had added Cassie's number. Remembering phone numbers was her weakness. She used speed dial for a reason.

"I'm sorry," was Cassie's answer before the first ring ever went through.

Mica felt her lips tremble. Cassie didn't cry often, but when she did, her voice had a particular sound, a raspiness that was unmistakable. And from the sound of it, Cassie hadn't been simply crying, she had been sobbing for long periods.

"Cass, stop crying," Mica ordered as she fought her own tears now.

God, she wished the other woman were here. At the moment, she needed a shoulder to cry on herself, and she needed someone to help her figure out exactly what was going on.

"I can't." The sound of Cassie's tears tore at her heart, and at that part of her that couldn't understand what had happened.

"Look, I can't cry." Mica blinked desperately to hold the tears back. "You have to get control, Cassie. If I start—"

If she started crying, she too wouldn't be able to stop.

"I sensed it," Cassie sniffed. "I sensed he was your mate, and I sensed he would betray you, Mica. I sensed it, and I didn't warn you."

Mica sat down slowly, resting her head in her hand as she listened and fought to just hold the tears back.

"I could sense the mating heat on you, but I knew something would happen, that he would turn away from you, Mica. I knew it. I knew because I could feel the presence of another Breed. Maybe he'll be your mate, Mica. Oh God, maybe you should just hate me," she sobbed. "I should have told you."

Mica wanted to laugh. Her only fear was that the sound of it could possibly be more hysterical than amused. This was so Cassie. Knowing and not telling, fearing that the telling would somehow change what the future was supposed to be.

Somehow though, Mica had always thought Cassie would warn her about something like this.

"Say something," Cassie sobbed. "I keep feeling your pain, Mica. I feel it clawing at my chest and I can't stop it.

And I keep hearing a fucking Wolf howl and no one here is howling this week."

"Stop crying, Cassie," she whispered. "It's okay, I promise."

"I was at Dr. Armani's office when Ely called her earlier. I know what he's done. I didn't know before, Mica, I swear I didn't know. I had no warning that Navarro could walk away from mating heat so easily."

"I know." Mica wrapped her arm across her stomach and rocked forward. "It's okay, Cassie, I swear."

But it wasn't okay. Because even she didn't know exactly what Navarro had done, or how he had managed to do it.

Cassie was silent for long moments, the sound of her heavy breathing and occasional sniffs all Mica heard.

She held the phone to her ear though; as fragile as the connection was, she needed it desperately.

Cassie finally spoke again. "Dr. Armani is going over the tests results Dr. Morrey sent her. Dad spoke to me this morning though, he's already heard there may be a mating. I pretended not to know anything. The last thing you need is our fathers heading to Haven right now."

Mica cringed. "Thanks, Cass. That's definitely the last thing I need right now."

Her father would likely rupture a blood vessel. She could hear him screaming now, she could hear the anger, the concern, but even more, the fear that his baby girl would be harmed in some way.

He loved her. He just didn't know how to let her grow up. In his eyes, she was still that child that he needed to protect from the world.

"Have you spoken to Navarro since you were with Dr. Morrey?" Cassie asked, her voice still rough, weary, but thankfully she was no longer sobbing.

"No." Mica shook her head. "I haven't seen him, but it's only been a few hours."

Long enough to allow the truth to sink in. To realize that somehow Navarro had been so against mating her that he had managed to escape it.

He had done what no other Breed had been able to do. He had been able to reverse the mating hormone.

How? How could he have done it?

"He fears what he carries inside him more than he fears losing his mate," Cassie said softly as that thought brushed through her mind.

Mica froze. "What did you say?"

"Aren't you listening, Mica?" Cassie asked gently.

"I missed part of it." Her heart was racing now. How had Cassie known?

"I said, Ely told Dr. Armani that Navarro fears what he carries inside him more than he fears losing his mate. I think I believe it. I know he's recessed, but he sometimes appears more human than even a recessed Breed."

Mica was on the verge of breathing a sigh of relief. God help them all if Cassie ever developed the talent to read others' thoughts. She would single-handedly start World War III.

"It doesn't matter what he fears," Mica finally said, the weight of the rejection pulling at her, exhausting her until she just wanted to curl into a corner and weep herself. "He started this, Cassie. He mated me. I didn't ask for it. Now he thinks he can escape it?" Bitterness welled inside her. "He obviously wants to escape it."

"I don't believe that, Mica," Cassie sighed. "But I'm not there either. You always told me you were woman enough to know when a man was yours and when he wasn't. You'll know if you should fight for him, or if you should see if all those vicious little mating hormones can become compatible with another Wolf Breed. Just think, girlfriend, you could set a precedent yourself by showing all Breed females, and perhaps later the world, that no one has to be a victim of mating heat. Right?"

"Yeah, right. How about I just swear off Breeds period? I think that would be the better course of action, Cassie." All she wanted to do was find ease and sleep. She wanted to sink against Navarro's flesh and find the comfort, the satisfaction she'd known earlier.

"And I think we both know that's not possible," Cassie reminded her sadly. "If I could help you, Mica, I would. I wish I were there with you. We'd give them so much hell they'd regret the day either of us was ever born."

Mica guessed that may have already happened. They'd terrorized the Breeds at Haven and in Sanctuary for years before they'd become adults.

"I know, Cassie." She wished her friend were there as well. It was just her luck that she was left to face it alone instead.

Somehow, she'd always suspected this would happen, and that when it did, she would have to face it without help.

"Call me, Mica, if you need me," Cassie whispered. "You know I'm always here."

"I know." Mica felt her lips trembling again. "I promise, Cassie. Now I better go. I have a few things to finish here, then I think I'll go to bed."

"I love you, Mica," Cassie stated, the regret and compassion in her voice nearly breaking Mica as Cassie fought to hold back the loneliness and the fear Mica could hear building inside her.

"I love you too, Cass," Mica promised. "Good night."

She disconnected as she breathed in a hard, ragged breath.

She couldn't let herself cry. God only knew if she would ever stop if she started. There was too much pain built inside her, too many long, lonely nights of wondering what was wrong with her, why it seemed that even making friends was so difficult. Let alone lovers. Before Navarro, she'd only had one previous lover, in college, and she'd awakened the next morning to find him gone. He'd never even called her back, after spending months chasing her.

She'd moved to New York to escape her father's rule and learned that the big city was less than friendly. Making friends was nearly impossible for her.

She'd never seen herself as an unlikeable person.

She was friendly. She was reasonably attractive. Sometimes, she even knew how to carry off a joke. Yet she'd spent the better part of her life alone, except for Cassie and her parents.

Alone and wondering why.

Now she was mated and her mate had rejected her in the most elemental way, proving once and for all that something was indeed wrong.

Rising to her feet, she moved slowly across the room to the windows on the other side. Standing before them, she stared into the gathering darkness, hands shoved into the back pockets of her jeans, and faced the knowledge that she would spend another night alone.

Aching.

Hurting.

So flawed that even her mate didn't want her.

◆　◆　◆

Ely paced the exam room portion of the labs as she nibbled at her thumbnail and fought to find a way to help Mica out of the hell she could be entering if they didn't find a way to fix whatever was going on with Navarro.

If they didn't find a way to force him to release the primal, more animalistic side of his genetics.

That had to be the answer. The recessed genetics were more or less a block between the man and animal, separating them and keeping the man from accessing some of the animal genetics inside him. Though Dash Sinclair had waged this fight for years in his mating with Elizabeth, it hadn't seemed to affect his sanity. It also hadn't seemed to allow him to walk away from his mate.

But walking away wasn't something he seemed capable of doing either, if the confrontation in the lab earlier was any indication.

Moving back to the holo-comp, the holographic computer she'd finally convinced Vanderale she so desperately needed, she once again pulled up the files from the Omega labs.

Project Omega had dealt with mating heat and the variables the scientists had found within the four mated couples they'd managed to detect.

The horrific experiments that had been done on the couples still had the power to give Ely nightmares. She forced herself to go through them again, praying she could find in time the answers Navarro and Mica needed.

Everyone thought she had grown cold and hard inside. That she no longer cared.

She cared too much, but she was so much more aware of her limitations now than she had been before.

The low though nonetheless strident buzzer from within Phillip Brandenmore's cell pinged again.

Ely turned and stared at the activated partition, the

glass that had been darkened to keep Phillip from seeing out or anyone else from seeing in. It had been activated all day while she tested Mica and ran the tests for answers.

Answers she had yet to find.

The strident summons came again.

What would it hurt?

The man was crazed, she knew. A psychopath slowly dying while the senses of the animal were being born inside him. Seeing the progression from a scientist's standpoint was incredible. Watching the tortured destruction of the man would give her nightmares for years to come.

The sound echoed through the labs once more as Ely gave an exhausted sigh and moved to the control panel.

The glass cleared, revealing Brandenmore as he sat huddled in the foam chair, his knees drawn to his chest, his face staring back at her through saddened, pain-filled eyes.

The old, diseased man was slowly regaining his prime. A thick head of hair had been brushed casually to the side. He was muscular and fit beneath the loose scrubs he was given to wear.

So handsome, and so corrupt. Even before he had injected himself with the devil's brew he'd concocted to return his body to its former condition and his mind to its once crystal clarity.

Before he'd injected a baby with it, and forced the Breeds to halt the freedom he had so very little time left to enjoy.

"I hear whispers," he told her as she activated the two-way communication between the rooms. "I hear a Breed has mated a human, and has now unmated her."

It didn't surprise Ely that he knew, despite the fact that he shouldn't have. The guards knew now, and sometimes the small slots were left open in the door of the cell to facilitate the guards' ability to hear his screams if the pain returned. It also allowed him to hear what they gossiped about. She had no doubt the gossip was flowing now. Talk of the Breed that had reversed mating.

"You shouldn't listen to whispers, Phillip," she reminded him as she returned to the holo-comp. "You know how deceptive they can be."

Sometimes, the whispers he heard were in his own head.

"The whispers keep me company," he said and sighed.

It seemed the day was one of his calmer ones. They were becoming few and far between.

"Have you figured out how to save me yet, Ely?" he asked conversationally, as though they were talking about anything other than his death.

"I haven't yet, Phillip." She shook her head. "I told you, I need your help."

She had to have the recipe he'd used for the formula he'd injected himself with. The recipe he'd injected Amber with. He refused to tell them, certain that if he held that information back, then they would have to figure out how to save him, to save the child.

That theory wasn't working very well. They couldn't figure it out. The drug seemed to have mutated inside him, whereas they could no longer find traces of it inside Amber.

In a matter of no more than eight weeks, the changes that had been wrought in Phillip Brandenmore were horrifying. But other than a few anomalies, Amber seemed to be thriving as any other infant would be.

"What if I wasn't certain?" he mused when she said

nothing more. "What if the recipe was one I found, the notes indicating success?"

Ely froze.

She stared at the files she'd pulled up on the holo-comp's grid and prayed he'd continue with his musings. Sometimes he did, sometimes he didn't.

"Are you listening to me, Ely?" he asked.

"I'm listening, Phillip," she assured him with apparent absentmindedness as she continued as though she were concentrating on the files on the grid.

She heard him sigh heavily.

"I'm dying Ely," he stated. "I wasn't supposed to die."

"You killed yourself, Phillip," she reminded him.

A rough chuckle sounded from him, a wheezing, ugly sound.

"Angels await me," he sighed.

"Last I heard demons inhabit hell, Phillip."

"Fallen angels, beauty and grace, the most beautiful of God's angels. Then man thought he could be God, and create a creature in his image. Beings of beauty and grace. And they betrayed us, as do all beings betray their maker."

She shuddered at the reverence in his tone and the sense of omnipotence in his words.

"If we couldn't control the creations, could we become the creations?"

Ely turned slowly.

He was watching her. Sly. Knowing. He knew she was listening to every word that passed his lips.

"Project Omega." He nodded to the file on the screen. "It came from there. From where her Breed was created. From where he was trained. From where his brother died."

Ely knew that. Brandenmore had funded that lab. He had researched there. He had tortured Breeds there.

Ely turned back to the files, staring at them. He always talked about the Omega lab. It was his favorite of those he'd worked within and those he'd funded. It was there the mated couples they'd found were taken, and there that the breakthroughs in mating heat had been made.

The answers to the formula he'd injected himself with had to be there. It could save him, and she wasn't certain she was doing anyone a favor in saving him. But in saving him, they would save Amber as well.

"He controls his animal," Brandenmore sighed. "Ahh, such training. Such insight into the Breed mentality and creation there, even all those years ago. Insight into the genetics, into training, into the psychology and physiology of each Breed. They were the masters of genetics."

He rambled and Ely let him. Unobtrusively she turned on the lab recorder rather than relying on security video and audio alone.

And as she pretended to ignore him, pretended not to believe him, for the first time Phillip Brandenmore gave out a few clues, just enough for her to start working on, just a few directions to lead her to the answers she needed.

And, she prayed, at least a clue as to the direction to take to save Mica.

◆   ◆   ◆

What now?

Navarro paced his suite, the restlessness he'd fought to contain building inside him despite his attempts to hold it at bay. It was like a million electrical pinpricks racing beneath his flesh. Irritating, the reminder that there was more to him than he wanted to admit. That his genetics were those of an animal, a predator. And that predator wanted out. It wanted free.

It wanted its mate.

Recessed genetics were rare in Breeds, or perhaps it was that known surviving recessed Breeds were rare. Most Council scientists had terminated recessed Breeds in the womb if they were detected. If not, then they were usually terminated at birth.

But there were those few who had used the recessed infants for further research. They had kept some, others had been given to adoptive parents and kept under close supervision. Others, like Navarro, lived between the two worlds.

He'd been placed with his birth mother's parents after his tenth birthday. His nanny had been Council, his bodyguard had been a Council trainer, and his pediatrician had been a Council scientist. And he'd always known, always been aware that each day of his grandparents' lives hinged on his perfect adaptation of the Breed they wanted him to be.

The Infiltrator. The Breed with the ability to move between both worlds. The human world, and the world of a Breed assassin.

He raked his fingers through his hair, grimacing as he inhaled roughly, searching for the scent of her, the action unconscious, primal. And he couldn't stop it.

He couldn't smell her. Not the scent of her or the arousal of her. He was at this moment truly recessed in ways he had never been.

Protection.

It was the only way to rein in the animal searching for her, the one intent on throwing him back into mating heat.

It was mating heat, or lose her.

He'd seen it in Callan, Jonas, and Dane Vanderale's gazes. They'd actually considered Josiah's suggestion that he should be banned from her. No doubt they were discussing it now.

Like hell.

There wasn't a chance in hell he was going to allow it.

Pulling the sat phone free of the holster at his hip, against his better judgment, he put a call through to Dash Sinclair.

It was the height of idiocy and he knew it, but he was damned if he knew who else to talk to at this point. He had no idea what was left.

"Navarro," Dash answered the call quickly. "Talk to me."

There was a wealth of suggestion in his voice, a controlled command from a man, a Breed, who had known nothing but command for most of his life.

"She's mine!" There was no other way to put it. "If they try to ban me from her, there will be a war."

Silence filled the line.

"I know from Dr. Armani that the mating heat has disappeared," Dash said. "Your genetics are making you crazy. It feels as though there's something beneath your flesh threatening to break free. As though those genetics are creating an animal inside you that's fighting to be free." He paused, and Navarro remained silent, waiting until Dash continued. "Why do you think I asked if you had mated her, Navarro? Why do you think you've been watched so closely around her?"

"You could have told me."

"And have you hoping for a mating that might never happen?" he asked. "Just because I mated didn't mean you would. It doesn't mean any other recessed Breed will. I had hoped you'd come to me once you experienced the first symptoms."

Navarro grunted at that. "Who knew? I kissed her the night of the attack against Haven and there was nothing."

Frustration roughened his voice. "There was nothing, Dash. I assumed she was safe."

"Safe?"

Navarro grimaced again. "Hell. Yeah. Safe. I won't say I haven't wanted her, we both know I have. Bad. But I tried to keep her out of mating heat. I came in slow, Dash. Touches here and there, a kiss to the cheek. A kiss to the lips only. I tried to keep this from happening."

"And I warned you, you couldn't expect normal mating symptoms as a recessed Breed, Navarro," Dash growled with an edge of anger.

"You didn't say to expect no symptoms at all," Navarro snarled.

The primal rasp had him stilling instantly, the loss of control a warning so deeply ingrained he couldn't ignore it.

"Do you want to lose her, Navarro? Is it what you want, to have the one thing you could call your own taken from you?"

"And if nature is taking that out of my hands?" He felt as though he were numb from the inside out. The mocking laugh was more a grim sound of disapproval than anything resembling amusement.

"She's loved you since she was sixteen years old," Dash stated. "We've all sensed it, Navarro, we've all known it. All but you. You've ignored it, just as she ignored it every time you came around. Letting her go won't change what's going to happen, or what has already happened. You're changing, just as she is. Your genetics are becoming active rather than recessed, and denying it, or fighting it, will only end up hurting both of you in the end."

"It happened to you." It had to have. There was no way the other man could have known all this if it hadn't.

"It happened," Dash admitted. "And it had the potential

to steal my mate from me. I felt, at the time, that I could make the choice, Navarro. I could be unencumbered; I could accept what my heart was longing for, what my soul needed to survive, or I could let that part of me die forever. Are you willing to lose the only person that could mean anything to you?"

"The question is, am I willing to destroy her?" he asked.

He definitely wasn't willing to stand here arguing it, not when he could smell Josiah nearing, sense the other Breed going to Mica.

As though the bastard could take his place.

A growl definitely rumbled in his chest this time. A low, dangerous sound that would have shocked him, would have had him pulling back in a desperate attempt to rein in the animal he could feel surging forward.

But it was too late.

Just that fast, he went from recessed genetics to full, raging beast, in the blink of an eye.

The door was jerked open hard enough that it bounced against the wall as he released it. The resulting crash was loud enough that as he stalked from the room, several doors opened along the hall.

Taber Williams stepped from the suite he shared with his mated wife, his broad chest bare, his jeans obviously hastily pulled on.

Behind him, his wife, Roni, stared into the hall in surprise, her fingers gripping the robe tight at the top of her neck as her disheveled hair fell around her delicate face.

"Problem, Wolf?" Taber drawled, his green Jaguar eyes knowing as Navarro moved past him without speaking.

He would get to Mica's door before Josiah, but the other Breed would be there before Navarro could get inside her room.

Perhaps.

As he made his way to her, the most intriguing scent met his senses. A dark hint of a raging storm as it rolled in across the ocean. A taste of honey, a hint of cinnamon and spices. And heat. Pure wild heat so addictive he wondered how he'd survived the past hours without tasting her.

His tongue became sensitive, swollen. He could taste the hint of spicy sweetness in his own mouth, feel the adrenaline coursing through his veins, raging through his body.

He'd felt it that last night he'd taken her as well though. Then the next evening it was as though the mating had never happened, as though it had never existed.

Until now.

It was flames tearing through his senses. It was a rush of heat, of hunger; it was being infused by the lush, earthy scent of her and the determination rocking through him.

He couldn't even say he was himself at the moment. Hell, he knew he wasn't himself. He was a creature bent on one thing and one thing only.

A mate.

His mate.

CHAPTER 13

A cold shower didn't help.

A hot shower didn't help.

And she wasn't even about to try masturbation, no matter how badly she needed to.

Walking from the bathroom, a robe wrapped around her, no one could have been more shocked than she was when the door was shoved open, the panel crashing against the wall as she froze and stared at Navarro in shock.

He stepped in and slammed the door closed before turning the lock.

Mica blinked.

He looked . . . different.

The sensual Asian features of his face were suddenly sharper, his eyes darker and gleaming with surprising, shocking hunger. A physical need that matched her own, that could even threaten to surpass it.

Staring across the room at him, her gaze locked by his,

held by it, Mica found herself unable to break that invisible line, the hold those deep black eyes had on her.

She could feel that touch inside her. It wrapped around her clit, tightened her womb and the tender tips of her nipples. A ghostly caress raced up her arms, stroked across her swollen breasts. It was like being wrapped in the most incredible heat. For the first time since the mating had begun, Mica actually felt as though there was more flowing between them than just his lust and the love she had fought to keep hidden for so long.

"What do you want?" She shook her head as she tried to shake off the dazed, drugging hunger flowing through her now. Before, it had just been heat. It had been lust. Now it was something more.

Something had changed. She could see it in his face, in the ink black of his eyes and the violent tension raging in his body.

Her breathing escalated, her breasts rising and falling heavily as the blood began pumping hot and wild through her body.

"Mica, are you okay?" Her gaze jerked to the door as the sound of Josiah's concerned voice came through the panel. "Just say something, baby. I'll get Callan and Dane, Mica. You don't have to let him touch you."

Mica blinked again, shock resounding through her at not just the tone of Josiah's overly familiar words, but also the offer and the suggestion that Navarro would somehow demand something she wasn't willing to give.

For a moment, she wondered when she had managed to step outside reality into this perverse "almost" world and the Breeds she was facing now because of it.

"Would you like to tell me what's going on?" she asked

as Navarro's head turned, his teeth snapping at the closed door in a completely un-recessed-Breed-like way.

What had happened to the icy, determined-to-walk-away Breed she had seen that morning?

"Josiah wants to die." Navarro turned back to her, a tight smile curving his lips as his eyes narrowed on her. "I hope he wrote out his will. I heard he had some impressive art hidden away." This time, the smile showed teeth. "He even offered me a piece if he died. He didn't say how he had to die, and I think I'm ready to collect."

"Not a chance, Navarro," Josiah snapped from the other side.

Mica licked her lips nervously, then her breath caught at the expression that appeared on his face. If the savagery reflected there was anything to go by, then Navarro was definitely going to attempt to collect that piece of art.

"I want that hot little tongue on my body," his voice grumbled. "I want to feel it stroking my dick, Mica. Licking it like a favorite treat as you go down on me."

So explicit, and so sexually exciting she nearly orgasmed where she stood.

Her gaze went down; the bulge at his thighs, heavy and engorged beneath his jeans, was impossible to miss. The effect of his words and the image implanted in her mind were impossible to resist.

His cock was so thick it would fill her mouth. It would be hot, throbbing against her tongue, rubbing against it as he fucked past her lips. Would it be hard thrusts? Would he do it with deliberate, controlled strokes? How much more could he make her want him?

She had a feeling it would be a hell of a lot more.

"That sounds interesting," she whispered breathlessly, refusing to allow herself to melt beneath the power of the arousal rushing through her. At least, not quite yet. "Do I get the same in return?"

She wanted that and so much more. His tongue on her pussy, stroking over her flesh.

Her stomach tightened, sensation clenching spasmodically at the sudden thought of his tongue thrusting inside her, stroking inside the aching center of her body.

His gaze stroked down to the juncture of her thighs, spreading a wave of intense sensation over her. Her clit throbbed, her pussy pulsed as she nearly whimpered with the sudden intense need for touch. A hard, dominant touch. A thrust that stretched her muscles with blistering pleasure that raked over her flesh with flaming intensity.

"Mica, sweetheart, just give the word. I'll have him removed." Josiah called out to her again, his voice attempting to cajole, sounding concerned as it raked across her nerves and had her grimacing in irritation.

"He wants to die," Navarro suggested quietly as his eyes moved from her swollen breasts to lock with her eyes.

She had entered the Twilight Zone or something. This was unreal. There was no doubt in her mind that Josiah was playing some game; she had never been his sweetheart, his baby, or any other endearment. And she was coming very close to stepping out and shooting him herself. If he didn't stop messing with her pleasure, and messing with it now, then he was going to be in a world of hurt. If Navarro didn't beat her to it.

She swallowed tightly, her breathing rough as Navarro took a step toward her.

"Mica, honey, I'm going to go get Callan and Leo. Just give me a few minutes, I'll be back. I'm not going to let him get away with this."

Her lips had parted to speak, to inform Josiah she was

fine when Navarro turned, jerked the door open and went
nose to nose with Josiah.

"She's fine, you fucking mutt!" he snarled in Josiah's face.
"Get the hell away from my mate and go find your own."

The pure fury in his voice, the rough animalistic growl
and the tension amped with the threat of violence had her
eyes widening in concern. This could become a problem if
Josiah refused to stand down.

Josiah crossed his arms over his chest and glared back at
Navarro with a snarl. "She's not your mate, remember? No
more mating hormone, Navarro. And for all we know, she
is my mate. It's time you move to the side and give someone
else a chance."

The snarl that came from Navarro's lips would have
been damned impressive even if he was a full Breed rather
than recessed. For a recessed Breed, it was bordered on
frightening.

"Fuck off!" Navarro seemed taller, broader, more imposing. His whole body was tense, the aura of danger pulsing
around him like a volcano preparing to explode.

This was really quite interesting, but Wolf Breeds didn't
posture for the hell of it. They didn't posture at all. Right
now, he was at his most dangerous.

"Excuse me, boys." She stepped between them as the
growls began to deepen and become more alarming. Two
Wolf Breeds fighting was not a pretty sight, and Dash Sinclair had once told her that Wolf Breeds would fight to the
death for a mate, just as wolves did in the wild.

Now if she could just figure out what the hell Josiah
was up to.

"Mica, you don't have to deal with this, sweetheart,"
Josiah assured her, his voice gentling. "Come on, we'll talk
to Callan."

He made the mistake.

Mica tried to avoid it. She tried to move back quickly, to get out of the way of the hand reaching her before it actually touched her. The last thing Josiah wanted to do was antagonize Navarro further at the moment. Blood would be shed, and it wouldn't be Navarro's.

But she wasn't fast enough.

His finger curved around her arm. First discomfort, then a flare of pain that shot up her arm and caused her to cry out at the shock of it. She wasn't expecting it. There hadn't been a problem until now. But now there was a serious problem.

◆　　◆　　◆

Navarro felt it explode inside him.

If he thought the animal genes had awakened earlier as he left his room, then what they did now was more like a wave of shocking intensity rushing through him. He literally felt the animal he had been bred to be awaken with a surge. It leapt beyond his control, broke the bonds of restraint that had been wrapped around it since his birth and broke free.

He threw Josiah back from his mate, one hand clamping on the other Breed's wrist to ensure the fingers that touched Mica didn't tighten or jerk her along with him.

Josiah fell back as the door slammed in his face, and the next thing Mica knew Navarro had her in his arms, his lips coming down on hers, the incredibly sensitive, swollen flesh of his tongue sinking inside her mouth.

It was like lightning, like fusion, like being immersed in the most pleasure that any one man could endure. It was silk and silken velvet as his tongue found hers, stroked against it, then hers pressed into the caress, stroked over the glands that had swelled beneath his tongue with such tight need, before her lips closed on them and sucked the mating hormone from them with greedy abandon.

It was fiery. Wild flames screamed across his flesh as his arms wrapped around her, pulling her close. A sense of how delicate, how fragile she was sank into his mind. Sank deep. He could feel it. The frailness of her bones, the tenderness of her flesh. Like waves of knowledge mixing with the hunger and the pleasure, the knowledge of how easily he could hurt her, how easily he could break her, seemed to sink into the very heart of the genetics he'd been fighting to hold back.

It was there now. In the forefront where the animal inside him now ruled, demanding, intent on claiming his mate so irrevocably that no man or Breed would dare to touch her.

When the glands beneath his tongue seemed to ease, Navarro tore his lips from hers, the need to feel her hot little mouth sucking his dick too strong to resist.

"Take off the robe, Mica. Don't make me tear it off."

He was tearing at his shirt, jerking buttons from their moorings, pulling it over his shoulders and dropping it to the floor before toeing off his low boots and removing his jeans.

His dick was so hard it was painful.

And Mica didn't hesitate.

Her fingers stroked down his stomach as her lips and tongue began to move down the hairless flesh, stroking, tasting him, her sharp little teeth nipping as she moved inexorably closer to the straining length of his dick.

He watched. Sensual and as beautiful as anything that could have been created, past or present, she was the fantasy that he'd not known he had until she was sixteen.

Sixteen and so fucking beautiful, and a part of him had known. He'd looked at her and felt the animal stirring inside him for the first time in his life.

"Ah fuck!" His hands jerked from his side to bury themselves in the heavy length of her thick blond hair as her fingers wrapped around the base and her tongue licked over the engorged head of his cock.

The broad head pulsed, shards of pleasure raking through the heavy length as ecstasy ripped through his balls and a spurt of the heavy pre-cum spilled against her lips.

She was his mate.

She was—

His thighs tightened as her lips parted and she sucked the nerve-laden crest into her mouth, filling it, wrapping silken heat around the engorged crest and sending sensation exploding through his body. Flames shot up his spine, filled his brain and burned through his senses. It was beyond pleasure. It was the most sensual, most sexual pleasure he could imagine at the moment.

It was all he could do to hold back another spurt of the pre-cum as his fingers tangled in her hair, loving the feel of it against his fingertips, like warm, living silk caressing his flesh.

Watching her, God, loving her as she loved him, and he'd never let himself admit. Couldn't let himself admit it, until his primal genetics had taken the decision out of his hands. Until the knowledge that he could lose her, that she was in danger of slipping from his grasp and he would never touch her, never have her again.

He couldn't allow that to happen.

"Enough."

Pulling her to her feet, Navarro lifted her into his arms, carried her to the bed before following her down.

His lips moved over hers, his tongue sinking past her lips for a kiss that sent the flames ripping over him again.

He wanted more of her. His lips moved down her neck,

licking and nipping, tasting her with each greedy lick, each desperate kiss, until he reached the soft, silken curls of her pussy.

Parting the swollen, slick folds, his tongue licked through her slit. He flickered it over and around her engorged clit, tasting the heat and the need flaming through her.

Covering her clit with his lips, he gave it a deep kiss, sucking it into his mouth, his tongue stroking around it. The sweet, summer rain taste of her was an aphrodisiac to his senses.

Filling his senses with her, he pushed as far as he could. He tasted as much of her as possible before he was forced to draw back and rise between her soft, silken thighs.

He rose over her, his cock pressing between the swollen folds of her pussy.

Tight. Hot.

Inch by inch he pumped inside her slow and easy, each spurt of the pre-cum easing her, making her wilder, hotter. He could feel her pussy tightening, clenching around his dick like a slick, hot little fist. Each clench and flex around his iron-hard cock was an exquisite agony, the ecstatic pleasure rushing through his senses like flames gone wild, making him crazed to fuck her with enough force to throw them both into a violent rush of release.

Her pussy flexed around his cock, sucking him inside, as he began to move faster, to thrust harder. Inch by inch he stroked inside her, filling her, shafting inside the snug tissue of her pussy with heavy thrusts as he felt the wild, uncontrollable rush of heat beginning to consume him. Like a drug overtaking him, stealing his control of himself, overwhelming his senses.

He was only dimly aware of his teeth locking in her shoulder, his hips moving with heavy, quickened strokes as the pre-cum jetted inside her, mixing with her juices, making her slicker, hotter, destroying them both until he felt her coming. Felt the deep, hard contractions of her pussy milking his dick, stilling the pre-cum only to tear through his body with the hard, powerful spurts of come as he drove in deep and felt the rush of incredible, intoxicating rapture overtaking him.

His cock pulsed and swelled further. The heavy swelling in the middle of the shaft stretched the heavy muscles of her pussy, locking him inside as each spurt of his come began to shoot straight to her womb. The Wolf Breed knot locked him inside her, holding him deep and tight inside her as the thick, heavy swelling throbbed with rapturous pleasure, spilling his cum inside her, and he swore, releasing more than that throughout his system.

He could feel something primal, something dominant and possessive, tearing from him as he spilled inside her, spurt after spurt of seminal fluid ejaculating from his cock followed by a hard, heavy flush of semen and a surge of wracking pleasure.

He was consumed by her. By her pleasure, reflected in her inarticulate cries. By her touch, her nails digging into his shoulder, the taste of her on his tongue where his teeth latched onto her shoulder, the scent of her invading his senses, and he was possessed, even as he possessed. Even as he lost himself in her, a part of him knew not only would he never be free, but he never wanted to be free.

◆　　◆　　◆

Mica wrapped her legs around Navarro's lean waist, her hips writhing beneath him, working her pussy on the hard knot throbbing in the thick, agonizingly sensitive muscles that gripped him tightest.

Rolling and jerking against the impalement, the thick penetration working inside her as she began to moan, gasping for more as she felt another hard spurt of his come spill into the greedy depths of her pussy.

His teeth were at her shoulder, locked inside her, holding her, marking her. His tongue lashed at the small wound, spilling the mating hormone from his tongue into the tiny wound, knowing this would tie her to him in ways she couldn't fully comprehend.

"I love you." The words were torn from her. "Oh God, Navarro." Her arms and legs tightened around him as the words escaped her lips. Words she should have never allowed free.

She felt Navarro freeze against her, felt his hard, corded body as the words torn from her settled in the air around them.

What had she just done?

Oh God, what had she done?

She should have known better. She should have controlled the emotions she had promised herself she would never allow free. But it didn't quite work that way. All those years she had kept her emotions tightly inside, kept the words, the feelings hidden, even from herself.

This was the most dangerous game she could play, and Mica knew it. Navarro didn't want to love, and she knew, he didn't want her love now.

He didn't speak.

His teeth released her shoulder slowly, his tongue licking over the sensitive flesh as she felt the knot that had swollen in his cock ease, allowing him to pull back from her.

She couldn't stop the low, pleasure-filled moan that left her lips or the tightening of her arms around his neck as he began pulling away from her.

She let him go.

There was no way to hold on to him, no way to steal his heart as he had stolen hers.

Just how dumb had she been in her inattention to the words that spilled free from her lips?

"You were supposed to be protecting your emotions," he said flatly as he sat at the side of the bed.

Mica opened her eyes and then wished she could close them back, because he was staring at her, those black eyes seeming intent on unlocking her very soul and slipping inside.

"It was pillow talk." She cleared her throat cautiously. "I'm sure you've heard it before. You know how women can get." Her throat tightened. Too emotional. That was what women were like. They were too emotional, and she was damned sure not as intelligent as she liked to believe she was; otherwise, she would have never allowed those words to slip past her lips. "Besides, you're my mate, aren't you? What does it matter, Navarro?"

It was too late to stop feeling it. She'd been feeling it since she was sixteen years old and she'd given up hope of ever tearing the emotion out of her heart. And she was supposed to love her mate. Her mate was supposed to love her. Wasn't he?

His gaze was too intent as he stared down at her, and she had a feeling he was waiting for something, watching for something. What more could he want from her? What more could she give that she hadn't already given him?

She breathed in slow and easy. Damn him. She didn't need this. After all the warnings against loving him, about allowing him too close.

"It matters," he growled, tension emanating from him as she stared back at him in confusion.

"Oh yes, I forgot, the mate that isn't really a mate," she

mocked painfully. "So sorry, Navarro. Please excuse me for complicating your delicate little life."

"Don't push me, Mica." There was a roughness to his voice that sent a shiver of awareness chasing up her spine.

"Don't push you." Pursing her lips, she nodded slowly. "I'm you're mate, but I'm not supposed to love you. Mating lasts forever, but for some reason you're escaping what you're doing to me." She shook her head as she watched him intently, pushing back the anger and pain as she always did.

It was harder this time. This time, the pain was rising so sharp, so hot inside her that battling it back took every ounce of control she possessed.

"That's not the way it is, Mica," he began to protest.

She lifted her hand sharply, palm outward. She didn't want to hear his excuses. She didn't need them. "I have things to do. Thank you so much for relieving the pain though. It was becoming a bit of an irritation. And do forgive me for that lack of discretion in the emotion department. I won't let it happen again. You can leave now, Navarro. I'll let you know the next time I need you to perform."

She was so glad Cassie wasn't here. If the other girl ever learned she had said anything so corny, then Mica would never live it down.

And on top of it, she had just asked her mate to forgive her for promising him her heart. Before she knew it, she would be promising him his freedom if she could give it to him.

It was killing her though. The pain was driving a wedge so sharp and deep inside her soul that she swore she could feel herself splitting apart inside.

"A bit of an irritation was it?" he murmured. "I don't think I meant to simply scratch your itch, Amaya."

She almost shivered at the rough quality of his tone. It wasn't a growl, but the rumble was a distinct warning.

Her teeth clenched until her jaw hurt. It was a warning to stop whatever she was doing to irritate the animal, to awaken it inside him. She could feel it, like a premonition, an instinct, and it demanded she submit to him. A demand and a submission as primal as the genetics that went into his creation.

"A bit of an irritation," she agreed as she rose from the bed and grabbed her robe. "And if you'll excuse me now, I believe I have things to do."

She could feel adrenaline racing, surging through her. That primal demand for her submission was just pissing her off. Where the hell did he get the nerve to demand she not love him, to demand that she not be a true mate to him, while inside it felt as though she were still dying for his touch?

Her pussy was still heated, still aching. She felt as though her flesh was desperate for his touch. Not so much a sexual touch, but a touch. A stroke.

She wanted that touch so desperately she knew that if she didn't get the hell away from him, she was going to end up begging for it. To keep that from happening she pushed herself from the bed, her movements jerky, the emotions tearing through her threatening what little control over revealing them she had left .

"Where do you think you're going?" He caught her wrist, his look domineering and so sexy in its arrogance that she sincerely wished she could find a defense against it.

Whether he was pissing her off, breaking her heart or making her scream out in need, he still had the power to make her want to laugh with him, to hold him, to feel his arms around her.

"I have a few things to do," she told him. "And spending twenty-four-seven here in my suite isn't exactly my idea of a fun time to be had." Especially when he was so rarely there with her.

"You appeared to be enjoying it enough," he stated, that dangerous calm intensifying.

The look of wounded male pride that flashed for the barest second in those deep black eyes had the feminine side of her almost giving in with a weakening gentle amusement.

"Of course I was enjoying it." She shrugged, refusing to let her heart break just yet, or the softening that threatened to fill her, free. Damn him, he wasn't going to get by that easily, that quickly.

Not yet.

She didn't have time to deal with a broken heart and she didn't have time to deal with a confrontational Breed either. Especially her mate. Breed males could be very unpredictable while in mating heat, or if they believed their mates were in danger. If they were mated that was. She was beginning to wonder if Navarro was even her mate, despite the signs he showed of it.

Pulling her wrist from his grip, she shot him a dark glare. He had no idea what he was doing. No idea that the feelings, the need for emotional vengeance was about to tear them apart.

"What the hell are you up to, Mica?" He rose from where he sat on the bed, his dark face savagely intense as he glared at her, naked, powerful.

"Doing something besides sitting here alone and waiting on you?" she suggested with mocking sweetness.

Damn him. She should hate him. She really should. He shouldn't be able to do this to her, to make her so crazy for him that she could barely breathe just minutes after him telling her that she shouldn't love him. Where was the fairness in this?

And double damn him, he was still hard.

She cast an irritated glance at the fully erect flesh he was currently covering as he pulled his jeans over his powerful legs and buttoned and zipped them with arrogant confidence. And not once did he take his eyes from her, staring at her as though with the silent command in his eyes he could will her to do whatever he wished.

Oh boy, he better rethink that idea. He'd known her long enough to know that simply wasn't going to happen.

Besides, she really did have things to do today.

She'd decided to find out exactly what was going on with her life. Why was she mated when her mate wasn't? And what had Josiah been after as he stood outside her door calling her by endearments he had never used with her before?

She was going to have to figure out what this was, and how to deal with it, if she was going to find a way to live with it.

"Why does a person have to be up to something simply because they're not bending to their knees to kiss your ass?" she asked, wondering just what it would take to distract him.

"I don't require that, as you well know," he stated flatly as he pulled his shirt on and began buttoning it. "But I know you, Mica. I know you well. You're definitely up to something, and I want to know what it is."

"Really? Can you smell it?" Okay, she sounded definitely mocking, perhaps just a little bit snide, but she assured herself she had the right. After all, it wasn't every day a woman got tied to a man in the way she was tied to him, right?

"I can smell the anger."

The anger? Oh, he just had no idea. If he could smell the anger, then it was a hell of a lot stronger than she thought she was.

Or rather, she wasn't hiding it as well as she hoped. He was breaking her control, and she hated that, because it was evident she wasn't touching his in the least.

She wasn't to him what he was to her.

She stared back at him, wondering how that could be? How had it happened? Why did nature hate her this much? She couldn't understand that. Why was she the only woman mated to a Breed who wasn't mated to her?

Well, at least not fully mated.

"What the hell have you managed to pull off here?" The words were out of her mouth before she could stop them. And once she'd started, she finished. "How did you get so lucky to have escaped the mating heat, the symptoms and the ties you forced on me, Navarro? Tell me, how did I get lucky enough to get the only Breed who could beat mating heat?"

She couldn't believe it had happened to her, and she wanted to know why. She wanted to know how. And she wanted to know how to fix it, one way or the other.

Either he mated her fully, became as desperate for her as she for him, loved her as deeply, or she wanted a cure. And she wanted it now.

The only Breed that could beat mating heat?

Where the bloody hell did Mica and Ely come up with this crap? Simply because the hormones in his blood weren't at the level they should be didn't mean he wasn't being driven insane by it.

"I'd like to know how the hell you and Ely can assume I've beaten anything." Navarro glared back at her, amazed at the scientist's deductions and Mica's assumptions. "Wolf Breeds only knot their mates, or have you forgotten that?"

He sure as hell hadn't forgotten it, and he was damned tired of feeling guilty over something they were only assuming. Or imagining.

Damn them, he felt mated, didn't that count for something?

Evidently it didn't.

"And Wolf Breed males show the hormone in their own systems, they feel the same pain their mates feel."

She stopped, swallowed tightly and told herself she wasn't becoming overwhelmed with emotion.

He could almost feel her pain himself as it sliced across his senses, sharper than a scent, more intense than any smell could ever become. It dug sharp, vicious claws into his chest, clenched it, and made him wonder if it wasn't physically tearing into his heart.

Never had he felt another's pain as he felt hers now. He hadn't even had a connection this sharp with his twin. "And you think I don't feel your pain?" Then what the hell was he feeling? It damn sure wasn't warm and fuzzy.

Rather than answering him, Mica shot him a glare as she forced herself not to rage at him before swinging around and heading to the large walk-in closet that held all the clothes a girl could want, and they were all in her size. There were shoes, stockings and boots. There were scraps of lace and silk parading as panties, bras, leather belts and lacy socks. Merinus had always taken care of Cassie and Mica whenever they were here, and she had done so once again.

It was too bad a cookie couldn't fix her hurt feelings anymore though.

It was too bad one of Merinus's warm hugs couldn't make her feel like everything was going to be good again. And it was really too damned bad that Navarro couldn't get a clue and wouldn't hold her himself and at least attempt to comfort her.

"Stop!" His fingers curved around her upper arm, drawing her to a stop. "I don't understand why I didn't sense, didn't feel your arousal last night. I assumed your reaction to the mating heat would be the same as mine. I assumed it had calmed and eased for you as well."

"Then you assumed wrong, didn't you, Navarro?" Her

voice was rough, and she hated it. Her emotions were there; that meant she wasn't hiding them. She wasn't as calm and controlled as she had hoped she was.

She was hurt and she was angry, and she felt betrayed. She felt as though everything had been taken away from her when she had learned she was suffering alone and Navarro was as content as he had been before he had ever supposedly mated her.

"Why?" She stared up at him as she fought back as much as possible, fought to hide as much of the pain as possible. "Why did you bind me to you, yet I couldn't bind you?"

It was the betrayal. Nature. Navarro. They had turned on her together and left her out in the cold. She didn't like being in the cold. She didn't like this feeling. She didn't like feeling alone at a time when she was supposed to be a part of something. The one time when she had been certain that she would have someone to hold on to.

"Do you think I'm not bound to you, Mica?" He frowned down at her, his expression somber as his fingers stroked down her arm, caressing the sensitive underside.

That stroke, so light it was barely there, seemed to sink inside her. Gentle and caressing, it stole past her defenses with the unexpectedness of it, threatening to leave her in tears.

"I think I don't know what's going on anymore," she informed him bitterly as she stepped back from his touch. As much as she needed it, ached for it, she couldn't afford it at the moment. "What I do know is that I need to figure this out and I need to decide what to do from here."

"What to do about what?" Confusion colored his tone. "You're my mate; it's that simple, Mica. I don't give a damn what Ely or her tests say."

Mica could only shake her head. "Just because you say it doesn't make it so," she whispered hoarsely. "The mating heat is going away in you, Navarro, it's only rising in me."

"I mated you, Mica. That knot wasn't a figment of my fucking imagination. I don't care what Ely's damned tests say. Once we return to Haven we'll have Dr. Armani run her tests. Ely knows Felines dammit; she doesn't know Wolves." Mica could frustrate him as no other woman ever could. She had the power to make him crazy and to tempt his control in ways it had never been tempted before.

"It wasn't a figment of my imagination either." Shaking off his touch, she entered the closet and chose the clothes she wanted to wear that evening.

Jeans and another soft sweater, this one a bright scarlet red, soft cashmere socks, silk panties and bra and a silk sleeveless tank beneath the sweater.

Navarro watched as she carried the clothes to the shower and carefully locked the door behind her. As though a locked door would ever stop him. As though it could stop him.

In this case, it wasn't the locked door, it was the pain centered so deep inside her that he had no idea how to face it. Even more, he was afraid Mica didn't know how to face it. She was fighting it with everything inside her, pushing it back as far as she could push it and struggling to come to grips with just the small amount that was slipping past her control.

Son of a bitch, how was he supposed to handle this? What the hell was he supposed to do?

Mating heat was just changing a bit, that was all.

Or was it?

Ely couldn't answer his questions, and the research he'd found on the Omega Project hadn't been decoded enough that he could find even a hint of how to fix this. Hell, he'd never faced anything like this before. A mate that wasn't a mate. An anomaly that prevented the hormone from showing in the male's blood while driving the female mate through the gamut of mating symptoms. None of it made sense.

And now, Mica was hiding. Hiding and hurting, and she didn't want his comfort.

Where the hell did that leave him?

He wished they were at Haven. It was just his damned luck to be stuck in Sanctuary with a Feline specialist pouring over his tests when he should be at his own base, with Dr. Armani, the Wolf Breed specialist attempting to make sense of this.

As she told him earlier that day, it could be something as simple as a single recessed gene holding back the full power of the mating heat. Something she couldn't say for certain until she examined him and Mica herself.

He stared at the door and grimaced at the pain that still swirled from her and seemed to spear straight through him. In his chest, in the deepest pit of his soul, he swore something wild swirled and howled in rage before he could shut it down.

That was why he had always been so drawn to Mica. She was one of the few humans that could do as he had learned early to do. To shut her emotions off, to keep them put away where they wouldn't or couldn't affect the Breeds around her.

But that wasn't the reason she did it.

He'd never truly learned why she did it. But she wasn't able to do it now, and he knew the pain was tearing ragged holes into her soul as she was losing that control.

Moving from the suite, he headed downstairs to search

for Merinus, and to hopefully learn why. He knew she talked to Merinus. Merinus had known her since she was a young girl. She would know far more than what little information he had been about to drag out of Cassie over the years.

It wasn't Merinus he found in the parlor downstairs. It was Josiah.

Leaning back comfortably in one of the heavily padded chairs arranged in a conversation area, sipping at the liquor in a short glass, the other Breed watched him with brooding unconcern.

"Pack Leader Blaine," he murmured as Navarro entered the room. "So damned commanding and full of himself." He smiled tightly. "You think you have this one won, don't you?"

"She's my mate," Navarro reminded him. "No one takes what's mine and survives it."

"She doesn't carry your scent. All she smells of is sweet, hot need." Josiah sat the glass on the table, each movement carefully controlled. "You don't carry a mating scent either, Navarro. You can't claim her without it."

"She carries my mark," Navarro informed him as he felt adrenaline beginning to flood his veins, his muscles tensing with the need for violence. "Don't try to trespass, Josiah."

He didn't take the warning further; there was no need to. He'd said all he needed to say. The warning was implicit in and of itself. He'd stay away from her. It was that simple.

Josiah may have decided they were enemies for the moment. Perhaps forever. Navarro didn't give a damn. He'd made his position clear. If Josiah attempted to touch what was his, then he'd pay for it.

"Navarro. We need to talk."

Turning, Navarro watched as Jonas stepped from the

office farther up the foyer. Dark, icy cold, the director of the Bureau of Breed Affairs looked as imposing as hell and not in the least pleased as Navarro moved to the end of the wide foyer and stepped into the office.

"What the hell are you up to?" Jonas growled as he closed the door behind them.

"Hell if I know." Turning to face him, Navarro crossed his arms over his chest and wondered exactly what burr Jonas had up his ass this time. "You'll have to be more specific, Director."

"Why did you return to the labs after leaving earlier? And why were you attempting to access Phillip Brandenmore's cell?"

Navarro stared back at him in surprise. Now here was a new one. With the security in the labs it should have been pretty damned evident he hadn't been in the labs since that time he'd been there with Mica for those damned inconclusive mating tests.

"I haven't been back to the labs, Jonas. And I've definitely not attempted to access Brandenmore's cell. I have far better things to do than to fuck with him at the moment."

Jonas stared back at him with icy suspicion. Navarro knew the director's inability to scent deception from him was a sore point. Jonas's sensitivity raked off the charts as well, making it impossible to know exactly how sensitive his sense of smell could be. The difference was, as director of the Bureau of Breed Affairs, Jonas's inability to confirm any of his enforcers answers as truth or lie was a problem.

Finally he grimaced, a sign that he was willing to trust, but only for the moment.

"Your access code was used to attempt to breach Brandenmore's cells an hour ago. We have it logged."

"And I was with my mate an hour ago," Navarro stated with icy distain even as he began to feel a cold edge of premonition beginning to run through him. "Change my codes," he told Jonas. "Something's not right here, Jonas."

Jonas watched him for long, careful moments, though this time, there was no suspicion marking his expression. There was instead a barely glimpsed hint of calculation in his gaze.

"Someone breached the cells the other day when you went down with Mica for the first mating tests. We had the protocols changed to log all access codes into the hall leading to his cell. Someone released him. He didn't get himself out."

"What do the security camera's show?"

"An error notice that an electronic jammer was being used. That message alerted us to the problem but by the time we managed to get to the cells, whoever it was was gone. But your access code was the last one entered into the security panel at the time."

"It wasn't possible." He shook his head again. "I was with Mica and before that I was involved in a confrontation with Josiah that began in the labs. He's an asshole, but he'll tell you where I was." His lips thinned then. "Has it occurred to you, Jonas, that perhaps if you didn't allow the humans within Sanctuary's secured areas, that perhaps you wouldn't have nearly so many spies?"

"It occurs to me every fucking time one of them betrays us." Jonas cursed. "But isolating ourselves isn't going to solve the problem. We'll only become easier to frame. And the problem is becoming more Breed than human. Our spies, Navarro, are our own people."

And wasn't that the truth. Breeds who had been too

strong to maintain the normally high level of genetic animal coding. Their human genetics had instead taken precedence, and greed and prejudice took over.

"Then what options are left to you?" Navarro asked bitterly. "The humans begin the problems, Jonas. You're sacrificing Sanctuary for the sake of world opinion?"

"Not hardly." Jonas grunted. "It's taken us a while, but we're finally uncovering them. We were aware it was possible we still had one or two working with Brandenmore, but until now, we weren't entirely certain."

"I'm going to pretend you didn't suspect me of this then. This time," Navarro stated roughly.

"I suspect everyone, Navarro." And there was no doubt Jonas didn't have ample cause to do just that. "No one is beneath my suspicion except my mate and my child. Remember that. And remember what's important in your life."

"Meaning?" Jonas was always all about the advice.

Jonas let a rueful grin tug at his lips. "You're used to being alone, You've not had to worry about anyone but yourself. You've not had to watch anyone's back but your own since the rescue of the labs. Having a mate, having that responsibility, changes things."

"I don't need a mating lecture."

Jonas brows lifted. "Then how about a friendly warning. Get your head out of your ass and get your mating scent on your woman before you lose her forever. Until then, I want you in the labs with me and help me figure out what the hell is going on there and why someone is trying to make it look like you're aiding Brandenmore in an escape."

Jonas left the office, leaving Navarro to watch his back until he jerked the door open and disappeared along the foyer.

The mating scent still wasn't there?

What the hell was nature doing to them now?

And who the hell thought they could frame him for Brandenmore's release? He'd see the bastard dead before he'd ever see him free.

CHAPTER 15

She wasn't going to put up with it.

Mica could feel the anger beginning to build inside her the more the knowledge of Navarro's hold on her penetrated her senses.

It was her fault as much as it was nature's that she'd become mated to him though. She'd been the one stupid enough to fall in love with a Breed when she had been too damned young to even understand the implications of it.

And had she let go of it as she grew older? As she'd realized exactly what she would be facing if the worst happened?

She hadn't.

She'd remained distant from him. She hadn't pushed the situation. But it hadn't been because she hadn't wanted to. It had been because she'd been too frightened of loving a man, a Breed, whose very genetics would demand everything she had and then more in a life that would be more dangerous than it ever had been.

Loving a Breed and enduring the lives they lived required a strength Mica was never certain she had.

Navarro wasn't blameless in this though. Pheromones, biology, physiology, chemical matches, whatever the hell the science of it wanted to label the phenomena, it was still a bonding, a connection, not that different from any other relationship. Mating heat simply refused to allow the Breeds, who had been trained not to feel, to dream or to love, to walk away from the man or woman that would love them with the depth it took to continue their species.

Man had created them, but God had definitely adopted them, and he had made the decision that they would survive.

It was a decision, that in their case, Navarro was attempting to cancel.

Ten days after arriving at Sanctuary, after being mated by the stubborn, taciturn Wolf Breed, Mica was still looking at full-blown mating heat while Navarro was skating by with diluted symptoms and the ability to walk away from her.

Oh, this wasn't going to work for her.

It had taken her a while to find her footing, she had to admit, to find her "mad" emotion, but Navarro had no idea just how pissed off she was over it as she stood watching him the next afternoon.

She'd heard his warning to Josiah, and though she hated the fact he'd done something so possessive with nothing to back it up, she at least appreciated the effort. He claimed her, but he didn't want her love, nor was he inclined to give her his love.

Lips thinning, she debated the best course of action in demanding his heart. She had a feeling simply making the demand wasn't exactly going to work.

"You look like a woman with a grudge." Merinus

slipped out on the back porch where Mica stood watching him with Callan and Jonas as they met several of the pride commanders in the backyard.

"You could call it a grudge," she said in agreement as she turned to Merinus. "Tell me, Prima, how do you secure a mate?"

"Secure his heart." Her answer was quick, certain.

Perhaps she was the wrong person to ask.

"It should already be mine." She turned and looked out to where he stood with the other men once again.

Merinus sighed deeply. "I believe he loves you more than he'll ever love anyone, Mica, but he holds that part of him that couldn't survive if he lost you back from you. I think it's losing you that he fears, not loving you."

"And that's how he's managed to hold back the mating," she decided.

She was aware of Merinus crossing her arms over her breasts as they both watched the men then. "Ely agrees with me actually, as does Dr. Armani," Merinus stated.

Nikki Armani, the Wolf Breed specialist had been telling her for years that the Wolf Breeds were far more stubborn and independent than the Felines, and Mica hadn't believed her. After all, in the animal world, it was the predatory cats that were far more independent and less social than those of wolves.

"It was their training," Merinus continued. "It was horrifying for the Felines, but for the Wolf Breeds, it was even more so in many cases. They weren't considered as valuable or as intelligent. They were used as research subjects more often, and the files I've read have given me nightmares for weeks. No Wolf Breed mate will have it easy."

"So how do I seduce my mate's heart?"

Merinus gave a little light laugh. "I would say, Mica,

you know Navarro far better than I do. What's his weakness? Even more, what is his weakness where you're concerned? What would force him to give up that part of himself that he's holding back?"

"It's according to the part he's holding back." She sighed.

"Mica, he's your mate," Merinus chided. "What part of Navarro do you never see? Never sense? What part needs to be seduced?"

How easy that answer should have been. "The recessed genetics," she murmured. "Every time his inner animal begins to push forward, he finds a way to push it back."

"Every Breed fights that inner animal in one way or the other," Merinus agreed. "Recessive genetics are a bitch. If Ria and Mercury were here, they could tell you how that inner animal can destroy the Breed if they don't allow it free."

Wild and free.

The Breeds were men and women who carried the animals inside them. Animals that demanded freedom, that demanded supremacy over the human that fought to contain it.

"Recessed Breeds have a greater battle," Merinus continued. "Mating awakens those genetics and changes everything for them. These aren't men and women who adapt well to such change, or such loss of control. They've not had to deal with their animal, and dealing with it is something they will fight at all costs."

"Even losing their mate?" Mica glanced sideways at the other woman.

Merinus was silent for a long moment before she glanced at Mica regretfully. "There have been times. I feared it would come to just that with Mercury and Ria. But his circumstances were unusual. Though"—a rueful grin pulled at her lips—"they're all rather unique, aren't they?"

"Women need a damned rule book to deal with them." Mica sighed again.

"And where would the fun in that be?" The love Merinus felt for her own mated husband, Callan, was reflected in her voice. "You'll never be bored, you'll always be loved and warm, and above all things, they will do whatever is necessary to protect you."

And that was the promise he had made to her, that no matter what, he would protect her. He was protecting her just fine. From everything but the mating heat.

"Callan says you're fighting the arousal," Merinus said then. "That you're not going to Navarro, you're waiting for him to come to you."

"I'm not going to beg," she gritted out. She felt as though she had been begging him as long as she'd known him. She would like, at least once, to see him come to her.

"And the heat is there for a reason," Merinus stated. "Use it, Mica, or risk living in the hell you're in forever, and perhaps losing Navarro in the process."

Merinus turned and left then, entering the house once again and leaving Mica to watch Navarro thoughtfully.

The heat was there for a reason.

The emotions tearing through her, the anger she kept biting back, the emotions she kept such careful control of. They were all there for a reason.

Just as it would be for him. The genetics that would cement the mating heat were all there, and he was holding them back. He was denying them both, and she was tired of sitting back and hiding everything she felt, everything she craved.

Her lips thinned at the thought. For too many years she hid her emotions, always frightened that the anger and pain she felt would backlash if the Breeds suspected that because of it, she was capable of betrayal.

She'd seen Wolfe Gunnar ban several humans from Haven when he had sensed a family member's hatred of the Breeds. Her fear of costing her family the protection Haven afforded terrified her.

Dash wouldn't allow it.

Cassie wouldn't allow it.

She had to hold on to that thought, believe in it as Cassie had always sworn she could.

Somehow, her friend had to have suspected what Mica was doing over the years, because she had promised her that no matter how angry a situation made her, she could always trust in her friendship and in her father's.

She had to trust in it now, because it was the only way she was going to force Navarro's animal out into the open. Wolf Breeds were incredibly protective, so much so that a mate's pain could drive the Breed to violence simply because the animal genetics they carried inside went haywire.

Rather than hiding her pain, she was going to have to release it. She was going to have to force the animal inside him to tear free rather than attempting to convince Navarro to let it be free.

As she watched him, he turned slowly, his black eyes looking up at her from the rims of the dark sunglasses he wore.

Slowly, teasingly, he winked, surprising her at the flirtatiousness of the gesture, but also, the challenge.

Narrowing her eyes on him she let her tongue run slowly over her upper lip, dampening it, wondering if it would affect him as that little wink had her.

And it did.

She saw his expression before he cleared it.

She watched the slow shift of his body as her gaze dropped to the proof of his erection behind the denim of his jeans.

She felt her heart rate double, her stomach clench and a feeling of breathlessness sweep through her as she fought to hold back the rush of her juices, failing horribly.

Her pussy creamed furiously, heated, her clit swelling with a force that had her aching to moan with the need for release.

Just that fast. He could do it to her just that fast.

There wasn't a hope in hell of being able to survive without his touch, and Mica didn't even bother to tell herself she could. Staring back at him, watching him, awaiting him, she could only hope that she could one day own half as much of his heart as he held of hers.

✦   ✦   ✦

He could feel her.

Navarro hadn't imagined he could feel so much from one person with the distance that existed between him and Mica. As though they were connected in a way he'd hadn't imagined possible.

He felt her heart break, and there were no words, no way to tell her how much he regretted that pain, how he would ease it if he could.

He felt her arousal, her need for touch, her hunger for something, though he knew figuring that one out was something he hadn't quite managed yet. He'd been trying to figure out that hunger for years and hadn't managed it.

But he knew why she hurt, and he knew he was the cause.

She should have protected her feelings, he thought. He'd

tried to convince her of that from the beginning. She needed enough of an emotional distance that the distance he kept himself wouldn't hurt her. That it wouldn't break her heart.

It had hurt her anyway though, and knowing that somehow the mating hormone wasn't as strong in his system as it was in hers, hurt even worse. Hell if he knew why. Dr. Armani had her ideas on it just as Ely did, and strangely, they were closely related.

He refused to let his emotions free.

Dr. Armani had gone even further to say that the reason was because his animal was recessed inside him. And unlike Dash Sinclair, he refused to allow that sleeping animal inside him to be free. Or perhaps, it wasn't that he refused. Maybe the animal simply didn't exist inside him as it had inside Dash. There was always the chance that his genetics weren't actually recessed, but non-existent. It could be that he truly was simply human, with a few advanced senses.

Those advanced senses hadn't helped him to save his brother's life though. Not his brother's nor his brother's mate and unborn child.

Slashing, white hot pain seared his chest as the thought of Randal and Sophia.

So close.

Fuck, he'd come so close to saving them.

One day. Twenty-two fucking hours and twelve minutes.

The scientists had had the Coyote soldiers drag Randal and Sophia away exactly twenty-two hours and twelve minutes before the rescue of the Omega lab began.

Half an hour later, give or take a few minutes, the underground facility had exploded as Navarro and two of his men had fought to get to the couple.

He couldn't protect them, and God knew he'd tried.

He'd fought. He'd done everything he could, taken every chance he could have taken in his attempt to keep them from being discovered.

He'd failed.

What if he failed Mica? What if he was unable to save her when she needed him most, despite the promise he'd made to her. He'd never be able to survive it if he didn't manage to hold back just enough to ensure he didn't lose all his senses to her. Losing all his senses meant losing himself, and when he did that, he knew he may as well bare his soul to his enemies and allow them to begin shredding it then. Because that was exactly what they would do. The minute his enemies learned he had mated, then Mica would have a big red bulls-eye on her back.

Along with Merinus, and every other Breed mate, an inner voice reminded him. Their husbands protected them well, and still lived to find happiness. So far.

"Navarro, you still here man?" Gannon, one of Callan's commanders, asked with a laugh, drawing his attention back to the group rather than the woman whose gaze he had held.

He didn't flush. He had no idea if he should have been embarrassed, hell, he was still too damned off balance with the sense that Mica was sinking further inside him the longer their gazes remained locked.

"As I was saying," Jonas continued after his gaze flickered from where the back door closed softly as Mica reentered the house, back to the group. "I think we can flush out our last spy here. They're getting closer, getting braver each time they get closer to actually aiding Brandenmore in his escape."

"Do we have any idea who they are yet? Can we at least narrow it down to one of the guards?"

Jonas shook his head with a tight grimace. "There's no

way to narrow it down to even a Breed," he stated. "All we can say for certain? It's a Breed. Only a Breed would know how to slip past the codes, and only a Breed would have been able to detect that first camera we placed in the vent above the entrance to the cell hall."

Navarro crossed his arms over his chest as a frown pulled at his brow.

"Don't we have something to detect the jammers immediately, without alerting our spy to it?"

"That would make it easier, wouldn't it?" Jonas grunted. "But no. The advanced electronics should have canceled out the ability to jam it, but unfortunately, it seems they figured it out damned fast."

"This is your last chance to catch that damned spy, Jonas," Callan warned him, his tone commanding, filled with authority and anger. "It happens again and I'll take care of it myself."

Navarro slid a look to the pride leader, then to Jonas. He had no doubt Callan would find a way to ensure every Breed in Sanctuary understood the consequences of betraying the community. And he wouldn't go through Breed Law to do it.

"You can't do that, Callan." Jonas sighed.

"Of course he can." Navarro spoke up at that point as he turned his attention back to Jonas. "Volcanos aren't the only place on earth where bodies can be hid."

Jonas's lips tightened. There were few, very few, and most of them stood together at the moment, who knew that several of the Breed's enemies had become living sacrifices to a very active volcano.

"We can't afford Callan or Wolfe to be tied to any action outside Breed Law," Jonas growled. "Don't encourage him, Navarro. He's getting too damned close to becoming his father's son the way it is."

"Then I say let him alone," McCullum, the Panther

Breed commander said. "Let him get rid of the bastards as soon as possible. I for one would be a damned sight more comfortable in my own bed at night."

"A decision for another day," Navarro decided as he turned to Callan. "It's your home, your people, and no one could blame you. Just remember, you get caught, and we all pay for it." He turned and gave Jonas the same, hard look. "Now, if you'll excuse me, I have things to do today."

"Things like securing a mate?" McCullum spoke up. "Be careful, Navarro, you may end up becoming the only Breed to lose his mate through stupidity."

"Bastards need to keep your noses out of other Breed's business," he muttered as he cast the other man an icy look. "She's my mate, and nothing's going to change that. Not you, and sure as hell not Josiah."

It wasn't the first time he'd been given advice he didn't need. She was his, and son of a bitch if he wasn't sick of others believing differently.

As far as he knew there wasn't a single damned Breed who had faced a problem like this. He could have done without it himself.

Pulling the kitchen door open, he stalked into the kitchen, the scent of his mate immediately hitting his senses with the sweet, hot smell of her arousal. Lush, sexual, the scent of vanilla and spice and a hint of honey.

Damn, that hint of honey smelled good. It was his favorite damned sweet until he'd tasted her.

Following the wicked delicacy, he turned, strode through the doorway and then along the foyer to the curved staircase that led to the second story. She'd returned to their bedroom. Would she be waiting for him, knowing he would come for her the second he scented the sweet, hot juices that had gathered on her pussy?

Damn her, she better be waiting on him.

"Thanks, Josiah."

He came to a hard, shocked stop at the sound of her voice as he reached the top of the staircase, the sound of his mate's voice, a hint of laughter in it, affection filling it.

Hell no.

He moved along the hall silently as he watched his mate, who stood in front of the Breed's bedroom doorway, obviously talking to him.

"Come on, Mica, anything you need, sweetheart, you know that." She shook her head as another soft laugh both stroked his senses and offended them.

Her scent hadn't changed. She didn't smell of Josiah. He hadn't touched her, he hadn't kissed her, and the need that he knew was only for him still surrounded her.

As he stalked up the hallway, it wasn't Mica that realized he was there first; it was Josiah. Mica stepped back, surprise registering on her face as Josiah stepped out in front of her. With no shirt on. His chest, broad, though unlike most Breeds carrying a light sprinkling of dark chest hairs. His jeans rode low on his hips, the belt undone and Navarro knew without checking that he was aroused.

"She didn't do anything, Navarro."

Navarro didn't answer.

Approaching Josiah slowly, his gaze locked on the woman behind him, he came to a stop six feet in front of them, then held out his hand. "Mica." He spoke her name softly. "Let's go."

She moved to step from behind the other Breed when Josiah moved again, blocking her.

"Dammit, Josiah." In typical Mica fashion she gave him a hard push, surprising him long enough to skip around him before giving Navarro a wary look.

"You don't have to go with him, Mica," Josiah promised her as Navarro caught her hand and pulled her close to his side, his arm falling over her shoulders.

Damn, now that felt good. Too damned good.

Gripping her upper arm, he turned and moved back along the wing to the main hall, and from there to the suite they now shared.

He wasn't going to ask her what the hell she was doing there, no matter how desperately he wanted to ask. Nothing had been going on. Josiah was her friend, and Navarro knew her scents. She had no thought of betrayal, and he'd learned long before the rescues that nothing could change whatever a person decided they wanted the most. If she wanted Josiah, if his arms were the ones she wanted, then it would have been Josiah she would have mated.

That didn't mean he was going to let it go. He couldn't let it go.

He could feel the sudden hunger for her as it exploded through his system and sent a part of his control ricocheting through him before it was lost forever.

It was all he could do to maintain the wild, howling part of his psyche. That part of him that he didn't know, didn't understand, and hadn't even been aware he possessed until now.

He pulled her into their suite, closed and locked the door securely behind them.

He stared at her. Just watched her as he released her and she moved across the room before turning to face him.

"I'm not going to hurt you." He had no idea where those words came from, why he even thought she would need the promise until he watched her swallow tightly, watched as he began unbuttoning his white cotton shirt.

"I never imagined you would." She was breathing

heavy, her face flushed, her golden green eyes filled with trepidation.

"You're watching me as though you're expecting me to rip your throat out." He couldn't help the rough, rumbled sound of his own voice.

She shook her head, and he swore the soft brush of her hair through the air sent the smell of her arousal rushing through him again. He couldn't get the scent out of his head. He couldn't stop what it was doing to him.

His cock was thick, hard and fully engorged. There was none of the mating sensitivity that he could detect, but the hunger for her, the need for her taste, her touch, was beginning to pound through his system.

She swallowed tightly.

"If you don't want this, then say so now." He shrugged the shirt from his shoulders as her eyes widened.

He couldn't explain the hungers suddenly tearing through him any more than he could explain the dominance he could no longer keep a handle on.

She was his mate. That was all he knew, and he knew it for damned certain. She belonged to him. She had been born to belong to him, to be his mate, to touch him as no other woman ever had or ever could.

What more should matter?

Josiah didn't matter. Ely's fucking tests didn't matter. All that mattered was that before he left this room, she would never allow another man to set him up, even unconsciously. And he had no doubt in his mind that Josiah hadn't done just that. He was trying to prove to Navarro that he had a chance at Mica, when the opposite was true. He would never have a chance to touch her, she would always see to it. Especially once they finished with the need beginning to claw inside her.

He knew what was about to happen.

He could feel it. The need, the hunger, the pure iron-hard dominance raging through him was pulling a single white-hot need through his veins, burning through his senses.

He watched as she took a long, slow breath.

"Take off your shirt."

She hadn't told him to leave, she hadn't told him no, and he knew she was well aware of certain aspects of Wolf Breed mating.

He'd been pushed, and he'd handled it well.

For more than a week. He'd been pushed, he'd been chastised. And then, he'd stood still, silent, and allowed another Breed to threaten to take what he knew was his and his alone. And he hadn't killed him, simply because he knew Josiah was full of shit.

The other Breed wanted her, he'd always wanted her. From the moment she had landed her fist in his face Josiah had lusted for her.

But she belonged to Navarro.

And today, he was going to prove it.

"Undress, Amaya," he warned her. "Do it now. Because I'd hate to tear all those pretty clothes."

Because God as his witness, he didn't think he had the control left not to.

CHAPTER 16

She knew.

Mica swallowed tightly. She knew enough about mating heat and Wolf Breeds that she knew what had happened. She didn't know what had caused it. She had no idea how the loss of control had occurred, but as she stared across the room at him, she realized that she was seeing the primal genetics he possessed for the first time in all the years she had known him.

It should have frightened her.

She should have at least been wary.

Instead, she was doing just as he suggested, she was stripping her clothes off. Slowly.

She knew the creature facing her, and still, she was teasing him with the slow, lazy movements, with her gaze locked with his, with the scent of her arousal no doubt reaching out to him.

And as she did, she watched as he undressed as well.

Each article of clothing that dropped to the floor exposing the steel-hard, tense lines of muscle and darkly tanned flesh until finally, he wore nothing but his arousal as his fingers curved around the base of his cock and palmed the heavy flesh with a grimace of pleasure.

Thick, heavy, ridged with dark, throbbing veins and glistening at the tip with slick moisture. The sight of his fingers stroking the hard flesh, the heavy veins throbbing with hunger, had the breath trapping in her chest, a sensual weakness rushing through her.

Moisture rushed along the clenched muscles of her pussy as her womb felt as though a hard spasm ripped through it. Sexual hunger, sensual need and an erotic knowledge of what was to come had her feeling dazed, uncertain, and filled with weakening anticipation.

"Josiah is pushing his luck, Mica." His voice was low, the hint of a roughened growl layering it as he began to move toward her. "You're going to put a stop to this, aren't you, Amaya?"

Her lips parted, but not to speak. Oh, she wasn't about to make it that easy for him. Nothing she did, nothing she said, would change what was going to happen, and she didn't want it to. That didn't mean she was going to submit from the start. She had him this far, she wasn't about to let him off that easy.

"And why should I put a stop to it? I'm not doing anything wrong, Navarro. And I haven't seen Josiah do anything wrong." Lifting her hand, Mica allowed her fingers to trail down along the curve of the inside of her breast, the feel of her nails rasping against the sensitive flesh sending a shiver up her spine.

His eyes narrowed.

"Are you sure this is a game you want to play?" he asked softly as he came closer to her, his fingers moving from his cock as his hand lifted, his fingers following the same path hers had made.

The rasp of his calloused fingertips against her flesh, stroking so close to the tight, hard tip of her nipple had her breath catching in excitement.

"Are you sure it's one you want to play?" she asked. "Don't make demands you can't back up, Navarro."

She touched him.

She was dying to touch him.

With her fingertips alone she caressed down his chest, stopping just short of the straining length of his cock, feeling his abdomen clench beneath her touch, stomach and thighs tightening to iron-hard tension.

Hers.

He was hers.

Swallowing tightly, she fought to breathe as his fingers cupped her breast, thumb raking over the swollen, hardened tip of her nipple.

"Please," she whispered.

She needed. She needed so much more than he was giving her. A firmer touch. The heated, erotic pleasure and the burn of his cock working inside her.

And more.

So much more.

As she stood beneath his touch, feeling his fingertips rasping against her nipple, stroking a hunger and a need that clenched her womb and had her hips jerking forward.

The sensitive flesh of her pussy raked against his hard thigh, the swollen, slick bud of her clit. It pulsed. Throbbed.

Spreading her thighs, Mica breathed in roughly as the hard muscle of his upper leg pressed forward, the pressure against her clit sending a stroke of agonizing need racing through every cell of her body as one hard hand gripped her hip and jerked her forward on the heated flesh.

"Navarro." Weak, pulsing with hunger and dazed, oh God, she felt so dazed, so weak, but strong enough to grip his shoulders with desperate fingers and to clench her thighs around his to ride the incredible pleasure rushing through her. "Oh God, it's so good. So hot."

His head lowered, his lips brushing against her shoulder just before his teeth raked it sensually.

"It's going to get hot," he growled at her ear as he caught the lobe for just a second before releasing it with a quick lick and moving his lips to her neck.

"You know what you've done." His voice was now closer to a growl. "Don't you, Amaya?"

"I didn't do it." She breathed in roughly, her head falling back as a low, drawn-out moan escaped her lips and her hips rode his thigh harder, fighting for release, feeling it surge through her.

"You knew." He nipped the sensitive flesh of her neck, the pleasure burning through her womb and into her cunt.

Clenching. Slick, hot moisture easing along the walls of her vagina, creating an internal caress as Navarro's hard thigh created a friction against her clit. Her hips rolled. Her juices heated her cunt walls as she felt it easing past the swollen folds to heat the flesh of thigh.

His lips moved lower, his tongue licking along the base of her neck.

"I didn't know." She gasped.

He bent lower, his lips moving to the swollen mound below as one hand cupped her breast, lifting it to his lips.

His lips covered the engorged peak, sucked it and sent a maelstrom of brutal sensation surging through her. Her fingers sank into his hair, clenched. Arching into his hold, desperate to press the hardened flesh deeper into the hot cavern of his mouth, Mica was all but sobbing with the need for more.

She knew what was coming, but she hadn't known what to expect.

She actually felt the spicy heat of the mating hormone against her sensitive nipple. As he sucked the violently sensitive bud, a hint of the swollen glands raked against it.

She was dying for him.

His touch.

His hold.

"Kiss me." She needed his taste in her mouth, that hint of sweetened honey rushing through her. She was addicted to him, addicted to his taste, addicted to the intensity of the pleasure that would rage through her once the heat of the hormone hit her system.

And he didn't make her wait long.

His head lifted from her breast, one hand tangled in the long curls of her hair, and pulled her hair back as his lips covered hers with a fiery, deepening hunger. She felt his arm wrap around her hips as he lifted her.

She expected the bed.

She expected him to lay her down, but instead she found herself perched on the back of the couch that sat in the middle conversation area of the suite, her thighs spread, lifted, and his cock pressing against her.

A hard spurt of fluid jetted against the opening of her pussy, spreading fire inside and out as the engorged head of his cock began to stretch the tender opening. She felt it again, heated, numbing and sensitizing at once as Mica felt her pussy clenching tighter around the head of his cock as he began working it inside her.

His hips moved, shifting, rolling, pressing.

She was tighter than ever before, each spurt of mating fluid that splashed into the sensitive flesh tightening her cunt further, sending convulsive ripples through the clenching muscles milking him inside her.

Her juices were flowing, slick and hot, yet still, she was tight, clenching, milking his dick inside her as she arched into each rolling press of his hips.

Dazed, she looked down, the sight of his cock, so thick and engorged, spreading the folds of her pussy, the slickened flesh clinging to the darkly flushed shaft as he pressed farther inside.

"Harder." She could barely breathe, let alone speak.

Pleasure was a rush of flames spreading through every inch of her body. Heat suffused her, rushed through her until she was crying out with it.

"More," she moaned, arching closer. "Navarro, please."

It wasn't enough. Not enough sensation, not enough of the pleasure or pain she craved with every fiber of her being.

His hips jerked, thrust in deeper, and sent a wave of ecstatic pleasure burning through her.

"Say it," he growled. It was definitely a growl. A hard, chest deep rumble as he jerked against her, thrusting harder, pushing deeper into the agonizingly tight flesh as another spurt of mating fluid squirted inside her.

His cock throbbed with each pulsing ejaculation and still, she tightened, clenched, and cried out for more.

"Fuck. Too tight," he groaned, his back arching as her gaze lifted, watching as a rivulet of perspiration eased down the tight muscles of his chest.

Pulling back, then thrusting again, his hips straining as she arched and ground herself closer. She was shaking, shuddering with need. She couldn't get enough. He wasn't deep enough.

"Fuck this!"

Navarro jerked back, dragging the engorged shaft from the greedy flesh as she cried out and fought to get closer, to keep him from taking the pleasure from her.

"Come here."

Before she understood, his hands were pulling her to her feet and turning her, and he bent her longways over the back of the couch as he lifted one leg and guided it to the armrest at her side. Her knee dug into the padded cushion as his cock pressed against her again.

The fluid filled her, his engorged flesh began pushing inside her, stretching her with a pleasure and pain that had her crying out in desperation, pressing back, taking him, her pussy milking his flesh until with a final hard thrust, he buried his full length inside her.

She was crazed with pleasure. It was past ecstasy. It flew past rapture.

Each burning spurt of mating fluid ratcheted the sensation until the pleasure was vicious, raging through her until Mica arched, crying out weakly as she felt the first, explosive release as it ripped through her, lifted her to her tiptoes and had her shuddering in pure, white-hot rapture.

And she knew it wasn't over.

Before he came, Navarro pulled the swollen length of his cock from her pussy, and before she could assimilate to the change, he was rubbing the engorged head against the tender, previously untouched, virgin flesh of her anus.

Mica stilled as his hand gripped her hip and the rough, growling order to "still" rumbled behind her.

"You'll never let him touch you." He came over her as she felt the fluid spurt against her rear entrance.

Within seconds, the sensations began. The burn, the clenching, the need for not just pleasure, but for that brutal edge of pleasure and pain.

"You'll put a stop to it." His teeth raked her shoulder and she swore she felt just a hint of point in the canines he had once kept filed down. "Tell me, Mica. You'll put a stop to Josiah."

His voice was growling and rough, raspy.

His cock was rock hard and iron hot, spreading the tiny, untouched entrance as the mating fluid ejaculated inside her again, easing the muscles, allowing the thick, heavy length of his dick to begin penetrating her tender ass.

Laying along the back of the couch, her leg bent and propped on the couch arm. The perfect position for him. One hand clenched on one side of the rounded flesh of her rear and slowly parted it farther.

Mica felt the head of his dick pop past the tight ring of the nerve-laden ultratight entrance of her ass.

White-hot, blistering sensation raced up and down her spine. It tore through her senses. Mica jerked back, thrusting her hips into each thrust as he worked his cock inside her, his hips moving faster, the thick head spearing inside her as he pulled back to the thick ring of muscle, stretching it, burning it, thrusting inside again, working his cock inside her with each thrust as she began to cry out in agony, in ecstasy.

Her hips rolled on the heavy impalement, helping him work the engorged shaft deeper, thrusting inside her harder, faster until he'd buried every thick inch to the hilt and then stilled.

She could feel his cock throbbing in her ass, stretching her to the point that she wondered if she could survive it as she felt the mating fluid spurt inside her, deep in her anus, as the burning pleasure began to rise, to rush through her senses and tear the last vestiges of control from both of them.

As he pulled back, his cock sliding in the slick recess of the rear, his teeth gripped the curve of her shoulder as one hand slid beneath her, his fingers suddenly spearing into the hungry depths of her pussy.

Thick, throbbing, stretching her rear with a burning, vicious pleasure, Navarro began to thrust into her. Each impalement rocked the pleasure higher, sensations building, electrifying as his fingers followed suit, fucking her pussy with three hard fingers and driving her fast and hard to the edge of an orgasm that shook her to her soul.

She could hear herself crying out his name. Her nails clawed at the upholstery of the couch, and as she felt the release tearing through her pussy, up her spine, exploding at her clit and clenching her ass around the penetrating, shafting length of his cock, Navarro began to come.

She felt the first heavy, heated spurt of semen as the knot began to swell, to thicken. Each throbbing spurt of cum filled her rear as he jerked against her, the tiny thrusts moving the knot against tender tissue and sending sensations to rush through her again, to prolong her climax, to destroy her senses.

At the curve of her shoulder she felt his teeth pierce her flesh, just enough to break the skin, to leave a proper mating mark. His tongue lashed at the wound, the mating hormone burned it.

Sensation upon sensation.

Fire and ice and thunder and lightning. Mica was shuddering, shaking. Each breath was a gasping cry as the dark, brutal pleasure just simply consumed her.

She was crying, tears falling from her eyes as behind

her, locked inside her, Navarro growled and lifted his teeth from her shoulder.

"You *will* stay the hell away from him!" he snarled.

"Yes." She didn't have the strength to push him further. There was no further point he could be pushed to and there was nothing going on but a friend using whatever weapon he could find to force the recessed genes of the animal that had once been recessed.

It was no longer recessed.

How long it took for the swelling to ease, Mica couldn't say. She lost all sense of time. By the time he eased from her and picked her up in his arms, exhaustion was a heavy, lethargic contentment that left her boneless and sated as he carried her to their bed.

She was only barely aware of him moving away, then returning only moments later with a warm cloth, and if she had been conscious enough, she would have been shocked as she felt him gently clean the sweat and slickness of their pleasure from her body and between her thighs before gently drying her.

She was drifting into sleep as she felt him move into the bed beside her, before drawing her into his arms and pulling her against his chest. The warmth of his skin, the hard, heavy beat of his heart against her back, she drifted into sleep with an ease she hadn't known before.

"Sleep, Amaya," he whispered against her hair. "Sweet love, just let me hold you as you sleep."

◆   ◆   ◆

Navarro had never known a contentment or a sensual exhaustion as he did now. Holding Mica in his arms, feeling her slip deeper into sleep, he also felt that wild, uncontrollable sensation of heat and restlessness ease as well.

The Breed genetics, the animal side he'd never truly believed existed inside him. But it was there. Like a separate entity rising inside him when he'd seen his mate with another man, that man shirtless, teasing, laughing with her. He'd felt it, so sudden, so violently alive there had been no fighting against it. The animal had refused to allow anything but complete possession of his mate. Full possession. Full mating. Possessing his mate as only he could, in the only way that would ensure no other could ever take her from him.

She belonged to him. He'd known she belonged to him since she was sixteen years old and he'd stayed away from her as long as possible. He'd given her as much time as he could to be her own woman, before she became his mate.

Before she had to face Breed life in ways she had never faced it before.

Stroking his hand down the long, silken waves of her hair as it fell around him, stroked his chest and warmed him.

As much as he'd fantasized about having her in his bed, the true hunger that had raged through him had been for this. Holding her, warming her, and having her warm him.

He caressed her arm, the silken feel of it sinking into his palm, caressing it as a low, drowsy little moan slipped past her lips.

"Navarro," she whispered, clearly asleep and still reaching out to him, even in her sleep. "I love you, Navarro." Barely coherent, so thickly asleep Navarro had to strain to hear the words. And when he did, he felt his heart clench.

"I love you, Mica." He whispered the words in her hair, low, barely loud enough to hear himself as he closed his eyes and tightened his arms around her.

God he loved her.

He'd loved her for so many damned years that there were days he couldn't imagine not loving her. She had been the dream he'd had in those damned labs, and when he'd seen her in Haven she had become his greatest fantasy.

And he'd lived in hell ever since. Lived with a fear he'd refused to recognize as fear. If he lost her, if he failed to protect her, it would destroy him now. It would kill him.

Maybe, just maybe, he could have survived until tonight. Before she had awakened the sleeping animal that came awake with a surge of possessive fury.

And now, awake, prowling, though content at the moment, he could feel that wildness inside him. In the very depths of his heart. In the very depths of his being, that animal watched now, vigilant, determined to protect its mate.

In all the years he had fought, all the ways he'd wondered how to use the animal genetics he possessed, he'd never imagined it would happen like this. He'd believed his genetics were forever recessed, so weak that all they afforded him were the additional stronger senses and the training he'd been given in the labs.

He hadn't expected it to awaken, surge forward, and demand his mate with such possession.

Yet it had, and he couldn't regret it.

The sense of warmth that filled him, the sense of clear, vibrant life where before he'd felt shackled, always lacking in some way, was something he'd never imagined he could have with anyone, let alone a mate.

And she was definitely his mate.

His perfect fit.

The only woman he had ever loved.

◆　◆　◆

"We need to hurry, Dad." Cassie sat, composed and calm, as she waited at the heli-jet landing tower just outside the high, stone walls of the Wolf Breed community, Haven.

Dressed in jeans, boots, sweatshirt and heavy jacket, her body was warm, but everything inside her was cold as she stared at the cement wall across the waiting room as they waited for the heli-jet to land.

"It would be quicker to call Jonas, Cassie," he reminded her. It hadn't been the first time.

"You've already told Jonas there's a problem." She fought to hold back the tears that would have filled her eyes. She had to believe they would get there in time, it was that simple. That when they arrived, everything would be okay. That Mica would be safe and as happy and content as she was at this moment.

At this moment.

Cassie hadn't expected the contentment to come this soon. She had never ever believed Navarro would give in to what he felt so quickly. He was one of the most stubborn Breeds she had ever met. She had sensed that and he had moved so much faster than she had expected.

His animal had refused to allow that stubbornness. It had refused to allow him to hold back the love or the mating heat.

And now, the danger Cassie had sensed moving closer to Mica was building. She had to get there. She had to be there.

She should have never left her friend to face this alone, but she knew Mica. She knew that her friend would have never given in to what she felt for Navarro unless she was without her family, without the one friend she knew would never truly lie to her.

And Cassie had believed she would have enough warning to get to her in time.

She was wrong.

Oh God, she had been so wrong, and now Mica was going to pay the ultimate price for her lack of foresight.

She was cursed.

Cursed to see what she should never see, and cursed to live with the consequences.

But could she live with the consequences of not reaching her dearest friend on time? It wasn't possible.

"Mike and Serena are pulling in," her father said quietly. "Are you sure this is a good idea, Cassie?"

Cassie nodded. "But we need to tell Mike she's mated Navarro."

"Uh, Cass, sweetie," her mother said from beside her, "are you sure of that?"

Cassie breathed in deeply. "I'm certain, Mom. But I think Uncle Mike has suspected all along."

She knew he had. Like Cassie, Mike had watched Mica and Navarro dance around each other like prizefighters in a ring. They flirted, watched each other when the other wasn't looking, and if one was sensitive enough, then they could have caught the swirled air around the two like a gathering storm.

It was impossible to miss if one wanted to look for it, and Mike Toler adored his child. Mica was his baby. He watched the men that came around her. All of them. And he was as suspicious as hell.

Oh yes, he already suspected the truth, but it was a truth he needed to know before he was forced to see.

That is, if they reached Sanctuary before it was too late.

Her hands tightened where she held them politely in her lap. She was terrified and she admitted it. She could feel it; the darkness that had been hovering around Mica for so many months was finally coming to a head.

The danger, the men who had watched her, waited, certain they could use her for whatever their schemes were.

Cassie couldn't allow that to happen.

If she did nothing else in her life, then she had to save Mica. Mica and the beautiful little boy she was carrying, even now.

CHAPTER 17

Mica wasn't surprised that she didn't see Navarro when she awoke the next morning. But she did find his note. There were security matters to take care of and he would see her later when she came to the labs for the daily hormonal tests.

She had to smile as she stretched, feeling the pleasurable little aches in her muscles as contentment warmed every corner of her being. Only one small cloud darkened that contentment, the fact that Navarro was no doubt dealing with the dark evil being held in those labs. That had to be the security matter. Unless Jonas was hiding more monsters in the basement. Which wouldn't surprise her in the least.

In this case though, it was Brandenmore.

Mica shuddered at the memory as she followed one of the female Feline Breeds from her suite to the elevator later that morning to meet with Dr. Morrey. Today though, it wouldn't be the lack of hormones they discussed. She knew that today the whispers of Navarro beating mating heat would stop.

An anomaly, Ely had called it. That anomaly was well and truly gone, and she didn't expect it to ever show its ugly head again.

He was her mate, but even more importantly, she was his. Finally, that lost, empty place inside her was gone.

Now she just had to deal with today's tests, and hopefully, she would get out of the labs without having to deal with the stench of the decay Jonas was housing there.

Phillip Brandenmore. The pharmaceutical research giant that had been suspected of using Breeds for over fifty years in his research for many of his more lucrative drugs. A man who had been aligned with the Genetics Council from birth, taking over his father's position within it and funding it as well as using the Breeds as guinea pigs.

And now karma was a bitch. He may have what he had searched for most of his life, but he sure as hell wasn't enjoying it. He was a hell of a lot younger than he was supposed to be, and he was completely insane. His health was perfect, but his mind was slowly turning to mush.

And it was no more than he deserved, though, the thought of anyone suffering as she'd heard he suffered was a horrendous thought to her. Still, she knew he had been the cause of so many Breeds suffering. So many he had murdered in the name of science, destroyed for his own personal gain and used simply because he could use them.

The reports of his death had been no more than a lie Jonas Wyatt had perpetuated to allow him to keep the man in the cells beneath Sanctuary, but after what she had seen, she couldn't imagine anyone blaming him for it.

Brandenmore was a fruitcake. Even worse, he was a very dangerous fruitcake.

"Ely's been really busy this afternoon," said the Lioness that escorted her to the examination room, watching curiously as Mica took her seat on the gurney. "She's currently arguing with Jonas over security protocols." An almost shy smile tugged at the gamine-like features of the enforcer as she brushed back a stray strand of auburn hair from the braid it was confined in. "Sometimes even Dr. Ely wins."

"I have no doubt." Mica gave a small laugh of acknowledgment.

Ely was as stubborn as any Breed male, especially when it came to running her labs and her research.

"I have to leave then." The enforcer sighed. "I still have rounds to make and then I'll be back."

Mica gave a quick nod, then sat silently on the gurney as she waited. She saw several of the cameras on the walls above her, no doubt recording every breath she took and her temperature; they would be reading her thoughts if Jonas Wyatt could get the cameras to actually do it.

"Well, did Dr. Ely know you were coming?"

Mica swung around, terror racing through her at the sound of Brandenmore's rough voice penetrating the room and scraping across the senses.

She came off the gurney, nearly stumbling and falling to the floor before catching herself in a crouch instead.

She stared around the room, eyes wide, her heart racing in her chest as she fought against the overwhelming fear of facing him again.

Mica knew that the only reason she had survived her last encounter with him had been the Breeds surrounding them at the time. There were no Breeds now. There was just Mica and whatever weapon she might be able to find.

"I believe I might even be able to smell your fear," the

voice commented as a section of wall slid open across from her. "I like that scent, Mica. It smells especially good on you, little girl. Sweet and subtle."

Mica stared at the glass-enclosed cell in surprise. She had never seen where the Breeds kept their prisoners they were rumored to have. She had only known that they did indeed keep them. And now, she knew what their quarters looked like.

A twelve-by-twelve cell with white walls, a narrow bed, a vid- and halo-screen high on the wall and a partially enclosed shower on the other end.

Pretty swanky compared to the filthy cells and open toilets the Breeds were forced to use in most of the labs they were kept in. Few of them had had any conveniences outside of a mat or mattress to sleep on until they were old enough to put their training into use. Then, and only then, were they given decent sleeping areas or food in exchange for the services, or the killings, they were required to provide. And in the cases of those Brandenmore targeted, they had known nothing but the agony and horror of being nothing more than research projects.

Slowly, Mica eased up from the crouch and stared back at him in fascination. She knew for a damned fact he was more than eighty years old. But he looked no older than his early thirties, and if not for the evil glowing in his eyes, he wouldn't have been bad looking. But that evil was there. In his gaze, in his expression, in the very air around him as they stared at each other across the distance.

Phillip Brandenmore shook his head somberly. "I can't believe I had you in my grip and allowed you to live." He sighed in regret. "Your life is one of those that's considered to be one of importance among the Wolves. You do know there was a price on your head by the Breed's enemies, right?"

"So I've been told," Mica answered as she watched Brandenmore shove his hands into the pockets of the overly large pants he wore while his shirt seemed to hang on his well-muscled shoulders.

His smile was cunning and filled with sinister delight. "I helped put it there, you know. As the freak's favorite friend, you would be invaluable. What would she do to protect you?"

Mica knew the answer to that. Cassie would kill to save her, or she would die for her. The same as Mica would do for Cassie. There was no other option. They were too close to ever allow the other to be harmed if they could stop it.

Mica didn't tell Brandenmore that though, she just stared back at him silently, almost fascinated with the monster he had become and the fact that she was facing him.

"Excuse me for not dressing in my finest," he said, excusing himself drolly. "But then again, I guess this can be called my finest, can't it?" He leaned his shoulder against the glass, a dark brown eyebrow arching as he stared at her arrogantly. "Well, aren't you going to talk? Don't you think I get sick of listening to these pissant little Breeds? I'd like to talk to a human for once. Someone with more personality than a cat or a dog."

Mica wanted nothing more than to leave to escape the vile sense of evil he filled a room with. He was a bastard and he knew it. Hell, he reveled in it.

"I can't think of a single human or Breed that would want to discuss anything with you," she told him, fascinated by the reptilian air Brandenmore seemed to possess. There was no way to hide what he was now. Despite the charm, despite the good looks, that aura of evil still surrounded him, still acted as a warning so heavy, a premonition so painful, that humans and Breeds alike were affected.

"How little you know," he sneered, though he was clearly enjoying himself. "I knew several who would like to talk to you as well, my dear. About several matters. Your little mating anomalies as well as the fact that you're the best friend to one of the most unique Breeds living. Tell me, if I kill you, what happens to her?"

Mica could only shake her head. "You would die and Cassie would shed a few tears, nothing more. There's no way to hurt Cassie enough to destroy her. Her parents have done too good of a job in teaching her to protect herself and her heart."

Brandenmore merely grimaced, though his gaze was filled with amusement. "My my, you're not very important to anyone, are you, little girl?"

"Oh, I'm sure I am," Mica drawled, though she was just as certain that those few were only her parents.

It would destroy her parents, but there was no lover, no sister, no brother. She would quickly be forgotten.

"I'm obviously important to you," she stated. "Those were your men that attacked me in New York, wasn't it?"

"Of course," he admitted. "They would have traded your life for mine." He stared around the exam room, his face pinching into a look of distaste. "They're letting me die here." He turned back and glared at her. "With you, I could have had my freedom."

"You give me credit for having far more influence than I have," she said, mocking him. "Trust me, Brandenmore, they would have never traded my safety for your freedom. You could destroy them. Only a few of them would miss me."

"A mate?" His eyes widened as he laughed back at her.

"Give me credit for far more intelligence than that. Before you proved yourself unmateable, my men could have commanded any price they wished for you, from either the Breeds or the Genetics Council. But now"—he gave her a look of pity—"you don't have a human lover, and your Breed mate's genetics are rejecting you. Poor little freak. Don't you feel left out?"

"Actually, no, I'm mostly just feeling bored." And wondering when the hell Ely was going to show up. Brandenmore just freaked her out, and he scared the hell out of her. Having a conversation with him wasn't her idea of having a good time, but getting out of the exam room without help wasn't going to happen either.

The longer she had to stay here, the worse he was going to get. She could see it in his expression, in his very demeanor. As far as he was concerned, he had a captive audience.

Turning, she moved to the door and the intercom that she knew connected to the security room.

"Call them, and we can't share confidences." Brandenmore's confident, knowing drawl had her pausing before she activated the call button.

"And what confidences would we have to share?" she asked without turning, without looking at him.

"Well, we do have a bit of something in common," he stated. "I may know a few things about that commonality."

"And what would we have in common?"

They had Navarro in common. Brandenmore had been closely involved in the labs Navarro had come from. So closely involved that he had used many of the Breeds in those labs in his research projects.

"Your Breed. The mate who is not truly a mate," he said slyly. "Would you like to know why?"

She wanted to know. She was dying to know. But she

couldn't bear standing here to talk to him. The vile, corrupted monster he had become sickened her to the point that it would never matter how desperately she wanted to know more about Navarro, she would never accept that information from him.

Her hand lifted to the button.

"What if I told you he was created to never feel strongly, to never have the emotions that drive a human?"

She paused again.

"If you could have done that, then you wouldn't have stopped with just Navarro," she said knowingly without turning back to him.

"That was always the hope, with each genetic design," he told her. "To weed out emotion, to leave only logic, then to ensure it was only logical that they willingly give their loyalty to the Council and its membership."

Mica shook her head again and lifed her hand closer to the intercom.

"And if I told you he's already betrayed you?"

She shook her head as she swung around to stare at him once again. "Navarro hasn't been with anyone else."

"There are other ways to betray." He shrugged.

"I don't want to hear any more of this. You're a liar, Brandenmore. A vicious, evil animal with no morals or conscience. Don't expect me to believe a word out of your mouth."

"I am not the animal," he snarled back, suddenly erupting in fury. "I helped create that filthy creature you're fucking, you little whore. Do you think I'd actually create something that could ever have emotions? Ever have loyalty? Don't be such a stupid little bitch. He'll never completely mate you, because he can never love you."

Mica swung around and pressed the intercom button.

"Dr. Morrey?" There was a tone of surprise in the Breed that answered.

"This is Mica Toler. I was escorted here to see Dr. Morrey and she hasn't shown up yet, but Phillip Brandenmore has. Could you please ask the doctor to hurry or send someone to let me out of here?"

There was no answer.

Mica was ready to depress the button and call out again when the door suddenly slammed inward and several enforcers rushed into the room, followed by Jonas, Navarro and Callan.

Brandenmore was laughing as Jonas stalked across the room to the window dividing the cell from the exam room and slammed the heavy wide metal shutters across the partition before locking them.

The sound of the laughter was cut off, leaving Mica to stare at the men, amazed at the air of deadly violence swirling around them.

"How did you get down here?" It was Navarro that spoke first.

Stalking to her, he gripped her arm, staring down at her as though he didn't know whether to shake her or to fuck her.

"I walked," she retorted mockingly. "What did you expect?"

"This is the wrong time." His head lowered, his lips pulled back from his teeth, and she could have sworn she detected the faintest hint of a point returning to his canines. "Now answer me. How did you get down here?"

"As I said, I was escorted down here for an exam," she answered from between clenched teeth. "Dr. Morrey hasn't shown up yet though."

"Because you didn't have an appointment with her until this evening, with me," he snarled. "Who came for you?"

She stared up at him in surprise. "But, Navarro, the message was waiting for me in my room when I came out of the shower, and it was Ely's voice."

"I escorted her down here." The Lioness stepped from the doorway, her dark gaze lacking fear, but showing only resignation as Navarro's gaze swung to her.

"I too had a message left for me by Dr. Morrey that I was to escort Ms. Toler here for her tests and examination. At least, it sounded like Dr. Morrey." Her shoulders straightened as though preparing for a blow.

"Where is Ely?" Navarro growled as he turned back to Jonas.

"She's in Buffalo Gap until later this afternoon," Jonas stated, his gaze narrowed as he stared around the room. "But don't worry, I'll definitely find out how this happened."

"He did it." She nodded to Brandenmore's cell before turning her gaze back to Navarro. "Somehow, he did it."

"He doesn't have the means," Jonas answered before Navarro could.

"Bring a snake into your home and expect him to strike when you least expect it." Jerking away from Navarro she stared from him to Jonas with disbelieving mockery. "I'm ready to get the hell out of here now. And you can inform Ely I won't be returning this evening. Until my so-called mate actually begins experiencing this mating crap himself, then I see no reason to torture myself further. Later boys."

She turned and stalked from the lab before turning and heading back to the elevators, knowing someone would follow her. It wasn't as though they would allow her to actually roam the halls alone. God only knew who else they were keeping down there and intended to keep hidden.

First Jeffery Amburg. She hadn't seen him, but she knew

from Cassie that he was safely hidden in the labs and working for the Breeds now, rather than against them. Then Brandenmore. Who was next? The head of the Genetics Council himself?

She snorted at the thought.

"If you don't stop running from me, we're going to have words."

The sound of Navarro behind her had her heart rate tripling and her pussy creaming. The response was just enough to piss her the hell off.

Where was the fairness in it? It wasn't as though he was dying for the taste of her as well.

As soon as the thought passed through her mind she found herself pulled around, pressed into the steel wall, lifted until her legs automatically gripped his thighs, and his lips covered hers.

Ambrosia.

The subtle taste of honey filled her senses as his tongue pressed inside and stroked against hers.

Oh yeah, that was what she needed.

She needed this kiss, deep and drugging, filling her senses with the taste of wild sweet honey, and male heat. One hand wrapped into the strands of hair at the back of her head, tugging on them, caressing her scalp with heated little pulls as she begin to sink into the sensuous swirls of arousal that rose like a tidal wave inside her.

She wasn't alone anymore.

She wasn't aching, needy and hungry by herself at this moment.

She could feel the glands swollen at the sides of his tongue, just a bit larger than normal. The taste of honey that filled the kiss had changed, just a bit, as well. It was wilder. Just as a primal hunger filled his touch and his caresses.

Long moments later his head lifted, his eyes black, as black as the darkest night, as his lips lowered to hers for a kiss so gentle, so filled with possessiveness that she had to fight back more tears.

"I love you, Mica," he whispered back to her. "I love you as you'll never know."

As she would never know.

Mica felt her eyes fill with tears. "I always loved you, Navarro."

As he touched her cheek with his fingertips, his lashes lying at half-mast while he held her gaze, Mica felt the final, heated bursts of his come inside her.

His head lowered. "Only you could have freed me," he whispered against her ear. "You released what was hiding inside me, Mica, making me whole. Don't let that part of me sleep again. Don't let me lose you again."

She could barely breathe. She could barely believe she was hearing his request. That he was there, that he was holding her. That he was admitting, finally giving, his love to her, when she had all but lost hope.

"Ahh, how sweet."

The moment the heavy swelling had eased, the horrifying voice whispered through the silence of the room.

Dangerous. Heavy with menace. Rasping with animalistic fervor and cunning, Phillip Brandenmore stood just on the other side of a panel that had opened in the wall of the bedroom, revealing a hidden passageway that obviously led to the labs more than four stories beneath the ground.

"It's okay," Navarro mouthed. "Just follow me." Moving his lips silently as he eased from her, careful to keep the blanket over her, Navarro moved to her side, then slipped slowly from the bed.

Keeping his attention on Brandenmore, he dressed with no apparent hurry.

His fingers slipped over the activator located behind the small Wolf's head enforcer belt buckle he wore, sending a silent alarm out to the Breeds and activating the locator that would track them, no matter where they went.

"Is Ely still alive?" he asked the monster that had tortured the Breeds for so long as it watched him with curious disbelief.

"Unfortunately yes," Brandenmore said and sighed as though irritated, a frown creasing his dark forehead. "Strange, I couldn't kill her." His teeth snapped together as an odd, sickeningly mutated purr was heard vibrating in his throat. "And why are you dressing? Strange, Navarro, I didn't give you permission to dress."

Navarro let a growl rumble, dark and warning, a dominant alpha sound that affected Brandenmore immediately. The gun nearly dropped from his hand before he caught himself, shaking his head and pointing it toward Mica as he stared at Navarro.

"Stop, or I'll kill her."

Genetics could be a bitch. Navarro was the natural alpha, and Brandenmore's genetics were weak, submissive.

Navarro lowered the sound, knowing Brandenmore didn't have to hear it to be affected by it. It was natural law. He could and would do whatever it took to Mica to get what he wanted. But he wouldn't be able to strike against Navarro unless violently provoked.

"Put that gun down, Brandenmore. You don't want to die here today," he commanded.

It almost worked, but once again the crazed Brandenmore fought it back.

"I want the girl." Brandenmore waved the gun he carried at Mica as he let a smile cross his lips. "No need to dress, love. You'll just be undressing once I meet up with my friends. You'll be my gift to them."

Like hell.

Navarro wouldn't allow it to happen.

Briefly, barely felt against his lower stomach, the vibration of the answering call from the enforcers moving into place came from the buckle.

They knew he was with his mate. They would know by now that there was no chance of ever allowing her to mate with another Breed. She was his. She belonged to him. And he would be damned if he would ever allow Brandenmore to take her from him.

"Get up, Ms. Toler," the monster ordered, his voice brooding and deep, a gentle, pleasant sound from a creature of pure evil.

Navarro kept his eyes on the other man. Watching each move. Refusing to allow himself to be distracted even when Mica rose from the bed, dragging the sheet around her naked body and drawing Brandenmore's gaze.

At the same time Navarro sensed the men on the other side of the bedroom door, just to the right of where Brandenmore stood. There was always the chance the animal genetics he possessed now would allow him to sense the Breeds moving in on the other side of the door.

God, he prayed this worked. There was no way to warn them of his precise location, but their senses would have picked it up, just as they would have picked up Brandenmore's scent.

They were prepared.

As Brandenmore let his gaze focus entirely on the rich rise of the mounds of Mica's breasts above the sheet, Navarro moved.

Shock crossed the other man's face, because Navarro didn't jump for him.

He didn't move to take a prisoner, there was no time.

"Move!" Grabbing her wrist, Navarro jerked Mica to the floor as his hand moved to the side of the nightstand, jerked his weapon from the attached holster, rolled his body over Mica's and fired as the bedroom door was thrown open and Breed Enforcers rushed in.

Mica watched Brandenmore's body fall. A red stain bloomed across his chest as his eyes widened, first in shock, then surprisingly, in absolute horror.

His lips formed a desperate "No!" His hands reached out as though searching for something, someone to hold on to as he went to the floor, his gaze locked on hers, a pleading desperation filling them as he realized he wasn't escaping death.

She watched the evil cunning slowly fade from his eyes, the light of life dimming until it was gone.

It was over.

Brandenmore had killed so many. He had tortured Breeds as though they were of no worth. And now he was gone. He couldn't torture, he couldn't hurt anyone else.

Slowly, Navarro eased from her, lifted her to her feet and held her safely in his arms as he stared at the silent, icy facade of the director of the Bureau of Breed Affairs, Jonas Wyatt.

"I had no choice." Navarro knew the fears, the nightmares that would haunt Jonas now. And God help them all if his daughter suffered for this, because Navarro knew it would kill the other man.

Navarro couldn't help but believe Brandenmore no more knew what he had done to Amber than he knew what he had done to himself though. If he'd known, he would have traded the information, he would have given it to Ely for even the slightest chance it would save his own life.

No, he didn't know what he'd done. He had no idea the concoction he had taken himself. Navarro was beginning to wonder if it was something he had even created himself.

There was an evil that he could tell was slowly easing from the room, from the overall atmosphere of Sanctuary. As though Brandenmore's existence had somehow darkened the community and thrown a shadow over it.

"None of us did," Jonas answered as he gave the fallen Brandenmore a last look, one filled with loathing and burning rage. "None of us ever did."

As his head lifted, his nostrils flaring as he inhaled, a new scent suddenly caught his attention. At the same time, it caught everyone else's but Mica's.

Oh hell, they were all fucked now.

He reach for Mica, intending to get her into the bathroom until she could dress. To hide her until he could figure out how to handle this new threat.

"Mica!" Cassie burst into the room at a dead run, black curls flying around her, her blue eyes filled with tears, her face pale as she rushed for her friend.

Mica tightened her hands on the sheet, her gaze meeting her mate's as Cassie's arms enfolded her.

"Oh God, I didn't get here in time," she cried out desperately. "I didn't make it, Mica. I was supposed to be here before Brandenmore. What if Navarro hadn't been here?"

Cassie was clearly distraught, clearly upset. But it wasn't Cassie that worried either Mica or Navarro. It was the sight of Dash Sinclair and Mike Toler standing in the doorway.

Mike's gaze went from the dead Brandenmore to his daughter, his expression composed, calm. Thankfully, Navarro didn't seem to sense a building fury in him, or even an overwhelming anger.

The other man simply stared at his daughter as she kept a death grip on the sheet and the other Breeds began to file slowly out of the bedroom.

✦　　✦　　✦

Mica couldn't believe it.

She stared at Navarro, then her father, then back again, almost fascinated by the two men she loved most in the world and their silence. She didn't expect the silence to last for long.

From the corner of her eye she was aware of Jonas ordering two Breeds to get the body out of her room, which she appreciated, but the blood was still there, and the memory of the corrupt evil he had been wouldn't disappear so easily.

Her father still watched her silently.

"Mr. Toler." Navarro cleared his throat, clearly nervous as her father turned to him.

Taller by several inches, wider, but older and definitely not as powerful, still her father wasn't a comfortable man to have that fierce stare directed from.

"Yes, Mr. Blaine?" Her father had been around Breeds too long. He'd learned how to growl.

"Sir, I would like to request your permission to marry your daughter."

Mica's head swung around in shock as she stared back at Navarro in disbelief.

Wasn't he supposed to ask her first, or something?

Her father gave an irritated grunt. "Rather late for that, isn't it, son? Haven't you already mated her?"

"I have, sir." There wasn't even a breath of apology. "But I think we've both been aware that was coming for a while now."

Nope, no apology. But Mica was still shocked to the soles of her feet. Someone could have told her.

She glared at Cassie, who stood by her side now, a pleased little smile on her face, as though she had orchestrated it all. Mica wondered if she and Navarro would receive any of the credit for their own mating, or was everyone else simply going to steal the credit for them?

◆   ◆   ◆

"If everyone will excuse me, I think I'll get dressed." She all but glared at Cassie, as well as her father. "I'm sure Merinus won't mind a bit if you wait in the kitchen."

"Of course she won't." Her father shrugged. "But don't take all day." He turned and shot Navarro a hard look. "You'll be coming with us . . ."

"I don't think so, Daddy." Sweet as ever, her smile innocent, Mica stared back at her father as he glared over at her. "Navarro and I both will meet you later, if you don't mind. We have a few things to discuss."

"And a wedding date better be one of them," he shot back with an air of a father who had finally realized it was time to let his little girl go.

They would discuss it later, Mica knew, but for now, all he needed was—

"Daddy."

He turned to her slowly as he started going out the door and looked at her questioningly.

"I love you, Daddy. And thanks." She knew her smile was as teary eyed as she felt. "Thanks for coming for me."

He sniffed, rubbed at the side of his nose and then

rolled his shoulders as though settling a weight. "Love you too, baby girl," he finally grunted. "Don't you worry. I love you too."

As he left, Cassie followed, a wide grin on her lips as she too paused and looked back. "Hey, Mica, remember that contentment thing we were talking about and the secret I wouldn't tell you?"

"About what you scented?" Mica asked warningly. "Yeah?"

"I just wanted to know which Breed it was, that's all. Because I swore he had to have balls of steel to challenge Navarro for his mate."

Mica's eyes widened. "You knew!"

"Not all of it—"

"You knew!" Mica's voice rose incredulously as she repeated the exclamation.

"Of course I knew." Cassie laughed with a wink. "I know you, sweetie. Now, promise me you're going to name that gorgeous boy, and I might even forgive you for not telling me about the kiss."

And her friend escaped, rushing from the bedroom before Mica could rush after her. She turned to her mate then and smiled as his arms went around her.

Because there was no place she would rather be. And no place, she knew, that her mate would rather be, than right here, in each other's arms.

⋆ E P Í L O G U E ⋆

She was the life that kept his heart beating, she kept him breathing, she kept the dreams he'd never realized he was holding on to safe within the love she had never lost for him.

Weeks later, after more than one inquest into Brandenmore's death, and the investigation into the escape that had nearly been fatal for both Mica and Navarro, the last suspected spy at Sanctuary was weeded out.

There would always be spies, traitors. Neither Sanctuary nor Haven would ever be free of danger. But, finally, the last of the spies who had laid into the communications and security network of the compound had been disposed of and more information was coming in daily concerning the hidden files the Breeds had found within Brandenmore Research, once his death had facilitated their ability to get into the offices and begin searching.

The history of Phillip Brandenmore's evil had spanned eighty years, and more deaths than anyone could have guessed. And it wasn't just Breeds. He'd been an equal opportunity murderer.

Now, as spring was making its first appearance across the mountains of Colorado, Mica lay safe and secure in her mate's arms and simply let herself believe.

Her father was actually pleased, her mother proud as hell of her upcoming son-in-law. Strange how accepting her father could be if it meant the child he loved would have the best protection possible.

She'd never known that he'd rather see her mated with a Breed than married to a man he would always fear couldn't protect her.

"You're thinking too hard, Amaya," Navarro whispered against her hair as she lay draped over his chest. "No nightmares in my arms."

Her head lifted. "No nightmares ever," she agreed. "Just us."

"Just us, love. Always, just us."

Also from
#1 *New York Times* bestselling author

·LORA LEIGH·

Styx's Storm

A NOVEL OF THE BREEDS

When Storme Montague's father and brother are killed
by the Breeds, her father's research is also destroyed—
except for a crucial data chip that both the Council and
the Breeds would kill to possess. Betrayed to the Council, she is rescued by Styx, a Wolf Breed who is different
from most other Breeds she has ever known. Storme
has something he wants too—but it's not a data chip.

There's never been a woman who bad boy Styx
couldn't seduce. But can the charmer of the Wolf Breeds
charm the enemy?

M728T0610

From #1 *New York Times* Bestselling Author

LORA LEIGH

and National Bestselling Author

JACI BURTON

NAUTI AND WILD

**Two all-new novellas of the games men and women
play between chrome and hot leather.**

Lora Leigh revisits her sultry Southern landscape
with a story of a good girl gone bad. But she's not
the only one going down that road . . .

Jaci Burton writes the story of a hot biker hired to
keep an eye on the reckless daughter of a Nevada
senator. She's hooked up with a rival biker gang—
a dangerous move that makes the wild beauty
more vulnerable than she imagined . . .

penguin.com

M698T0510